SONS OF HEAVEN

SONS OF HEAVEN

BAD TIMES BOOK FIVE

CHUCK DIXON

DISRUPTIVE IMAGINATION

LMBPN Publishing
PMB 196, 2540 South Maryland Pkwy
Las Vegas, NV 89109

First US edition, June 2020
Version 1.01, February 2021
eBook ISBN: 978-1-64202-850-8
Print ISBN: 978-1-64202-851-5

1

NANKING, 1864

The Heavenly King was hungry.

It was a sensation he was not accustomed to experiencing. Not for many years, in any case. A stirring within his belly, a grumbling complaint as his physical needs made themselves known.

With the help of a coterie of his wives, he dressed in layers of rainbow silk and donned a robe trimmed in hems of pearls and silver. He stepped into the dusty path of one of the many courtyards that encircled his palace. He squinted into the sunlight filtering down from a sky hazed with dark smoke. From over the high walls of his palace came the rumble of distant cannon and the patter of musket fire. It was unheeded by all as these sounds were commonplace after months of siege.

The Heavenly King was followed by scribes, who wrote down his every utterance in three different languages. His wives, who doted upon his every whim, followed behind. There were valets who saw to it that his raiment was flawless, and a trio of pretty young boys, who carried carafes of chilled water should he feel thirst.

It was hunger that vexed him now, and he announced that he

1

would eat. His food preparers were sent for. A score of servants arrived, crawling toward him across the courtyard on hands and knees, foreheads on the dirt. Their hands were empty of offerings. "I would have my afternoon meal. Only I sense that the assigned hour of its serving has passed," the Heavenly King pronounced to the backs of the men prostrated before him. The scribes dutifully wrote down these words as he spoke them.

One of the kitchen servants crawled forward to raise his head but not his eyes.

"Your meal was to consist of curried sparrows in honeyed rice, O Excellent One," the servant stammered.

"And how does this explain the absence of my meal?" the Heavenly King said in an ethereal voice, free of rancor or suspicion. The passive tone did nothing to quell the servant's fear. The man was aquiver from ankle to wrist.

"We cannot find any sparrows, Excellent One. They have either flown from the city or been trapped and consumed." The servant banged his head on the dirt in abject apology.

The Heavenly King pondered this. His entourage stood breathless. The hands of his scribes were poised, quills ready to record his next words.

"The Israelites," he said in a faraway voice.

The scribes hurriedly wrote down those words. None followed as the Heavenly King stood frozen in mid-gesture, lips pursed to continue. His eyes shifted focus into the infinite, seeking deeper truths hidden from the eyes of mere mortals. After long moments, he spoke again.

"Lost in the desert and starving, the Israelites called out to God, My Father. They asked Him for his aid. They prayed for Him to show them the way to game or grain or fruit. Days and days, and many more days passed, and My Father did not answer them. The Israelites feared that He had abandoned his chosen people, and they might perish there in the wilderness under His uncaring eye." His entourage, feeling very much like the ancient

Israelites, stood in the baking sun and waited while the Heavenly King gathered breath.

"And, one day, God cast manna upon them and told them to partake of it. It fell from heaven like rain. The Israelites picked it from the ground and ate it. And it was good. It was sweet and satisfying and filled their souls with My Father's love, even as it filled their bellies. From God's love came abundance."

All stood, or knelt, waiting for further remarks from the Heavenly King. Some prayed silently. Most prayed that their lord would reach a conclusion to his lecture sooner rather than later. His proclamations routinely went on for hours and hours. And though he showed no sign of the slightest discomfort, his entourage was broiling in the afternoon sun, sweat soaking their fine silks, and their heads growing light in the heat.

"My father offers us manna in our time of need. He strews it upon the ground in all directions. We need only pluck it up and end our hunger."

The Heavenly King gestured grandly, his manicured and powdered hands taking in the broad courtyard. All turned to follow his gesture, but all they saw was a walled enclosure of hard dirt. Once it had held a magnificent garden with flowers and fruit trees, koi ponds, and all manner of colorful birds. The deprivations suffered by the city had reached even here, in the inner sanctum of the most divine Heavenly King. The trees were long ago cut down for firewood, the fruit consumed, the flowering plants ripped up for fodder, the colorful songbirds trapped and eaten. The fountains were drained, and the glorious silver and gold koi consumed. What was once a sumptuous refuge was now dust, dotted here and there with clumps of weeds.

"Do you see it? All about us? Manna from My Father," the Heavenly King announced with a beatific smile.

All looked about them and saw nothing that looked anything like it might be a gift from God.

The Heavenly King touched the arm of the kowtowing kitchen servant and lifted the terrified man to his feet.

"See the offering of My Father? It lays awaiting you. There is no need to be hungry. God is great, and God is kind and has not abandoned His children. We are as the Israelites before us, blessed and chosen, anointed by His love and showered with His abundance."

The entourage looked about, their distress growing. The fear was plain in their eyes, fear of displeasing the Earthly issue of God the Father Himself.

The Heavenly King laughed, a tinkling, feminine titter. He was amused rather than angered. The childlike ignorance of his closest followers charmed him.

"Here. Here on the ground at your feet, manna from heaven." He chuckled as he lowered himself to his knees. To the astonishment of all those about him, he plucked a clump of weeds from the dust and began eating the leaves.

The Heavenly King, the second son of God, brother to Jesus Christ, their savior and unquestioned master on Earth and in Heaven, was on his belly munching pea-weed, as contented as a kid goat.

SHANGHAI

He was determined to walk from the car on his own.

In the end, Dr. Morris Tauber surrendered to his keepers. They grabbed him by either arm and walked/dragged him along the pier. His feet skipped, sneakered toes scraping over the asphalt surface. The drugs they had given him reduced the pain in his joints and limbs to a muted ache. The cold rain drizzling down brought him around from his stupor just a bit. He could see they were walking under the enormous legs of a cargo crane. He saw lights set high above on moored ships and grain towers. The harsh glow twinkled and blossomed against the wet lenses of his glasses seated crookedly on his face, a firmament of shifting red and yellow illuminations.

They marched him to where a cargo container ship loomed high over them. The words across the bow struck a chord in him.

Ocean Raj.

His home away from home for... how long had it been?

A group of men stood in a pool of wavering light at the foot of a gangway. Two of them stepped forward to meet Morris and his escort.

"He looks like shit," said a familiar voice. Jimmy Smalls? The US Army Ranger and Pima Indian.

"Mo, you hear me? Give us a sign, brother." Lee Hammond. Another Ranger.

"Caroline," Morris croaked. His own voice sounded miles away.

"Back off, asshole," Jimbo said.

Morris felt his axis shift as he was pulled back and forth, then he was finally in the hands of the two men he knew. His friends.

"Caroline's fine. She's away from here. Safe with the baby." Jimbo's voice was close to his ear as they half-carried him up the gangway.

"Dwayne's with them. Rick Renzi and N'itha too," Hammond said.

"Who's Neeta?" Morris said through lips that felt like balloons.

Then he was washed away on a current of sputtering lights that swept him spinning down a deep dark hole.

They had him up walking on the open deck the next day, or maybe it was the day after that. Lee Hammond and Jimmy Smalls walked with him. The cold salt air felt good on his face. What didn't feel good was the presence of strangers on board. Everywhere they walked, they were under the eyes of glowering men in dark clothes. Men like the ones who took him and held him beat him and drugged him.

"So, we're all working for Jason Taan now?" Morris said with a bitter tone.

"For now," Lee said.

"I really got us in a corner," Morris said.

"Could happen to anyone," Jimbo said.

He still felt like a child who'd walked into a trap without

considering the consequences. The team had traveled back to prehistoric America and unconsciously left behind an artifact: a clear boot print. The story made the news as a clickbait kind of story. A college student had a petrified bird print that, overnight, was altered when Bat Jaffe, the former Israeli Defense Force soldier, stepped in the mud of a pond bank one hundred millennia before. The print was echoed in the artifact, a frozen relic of a chronal anomaly.

Morris went to meet the kid to offer him a big payday in exchange for the slab of calcified stone. Other interested parties got there before him. Jason Taan, a Taiwanese billionaire with a keen interest in time travel. He abducted Morris Tauber and held him for ransom. The ransom? The use of the Tauber Tube to reach back in time for purposes unknown.

Lee Hammond walked Morris to the sheltered aft deck of the *Raj*. Morris leaned on the ice-rimed rail and looked out over the gray world of Shanghai harbor. They were moored at the end of a long pier, well away from other container ships off-loading at ports all along the shoreline. Through the gloom across the water, he could see men and machines moving under lights so bright the wharves looked like movie sets.

"What does Taan want? I mean other than to use the Tube to make himself richer?" Morris said.

"All we know is we're heading back to Shanghai in 1865," Lee said. "We have a general outline of what's expected of us, but Taan is withholding what the final mission objective will be. We'll be back in The Then a minimum of thirty days. We have the needed gear in the works."

"We just need you to crank up the Tube one more time," Jimbo said. "Taan put pressure on Quebat and Parviz to work the Tube, but they dummied up."

Quebat and Parviz were two Iranian ex-patriates and apostates on the run from the mullahs in Tehran for two reasons. One, they'd stolen an experimental mini-reactor. Two, they were gay. In Iran, there really is no going home again.

"You already know that I have all kinds of problems with everything you just told me," Morris said. "But I'm letting that go for now. Where's Caroline?"

"Better you don't know anything other than she's safe. Little Stevie, too. We got them off the *Raj* early to take your sister out of play. That gave us a bargaining chip," Lee said.

Morris tilted his head at the ex-Army Ranger.

"It was the only way of getting your ass back safe. Without a Tauber, there's no Tauber Tube," Lee said.

"They need me to open the field and monitor the mission. I get that. Thanks."

"No problem, brother," Jimbo said and laid a hand on Morris' shoulder.

There it was again.

"What's with the 'brother' stuff ?" Morris said.

"You've been through the shit, Mo. Blooded. You're one of us now." Jimbo grinned. Lee nodded assent.

"Yeah. And you can *have* the shit," Morris said, overcome with the sudden desire to lie down.

DOWN ON THE BAJA

"I could get used to this," Dwayne Roenbach said, lying back on the warm sand. He squinted at the sun setting over the Pacific in a spectacular bronze sky. A solitary figure splashed in the creamy surf spreading across a beach of sand the color and consistency of sugar. A naked female skipped through the rollers tumbling against her ankles.

"Are you talking about my company or the view?" Caroline Tauber said from a lounge chair under a grass umbrella, their son asleep in her arms.

Little Stephen was crawling now and babbling something close to speech. Dwayne had missed much of his son's life. Time travel multiplied absence. He was back in The Then for just under a month, but more time than that had passed in The Now. He'd missed all of his son's infancy, not meeting Stephen until the child was six months old. The op that returned him and the team to prehistoric Nevada was about two weeks in the bush. He came back to a son three months older.

"You mean the sunset?" he said.

"You know what I mean," she said. The warm ocean breeze

carried to them the gleeful laughter of the girl playing in the waves.

"I mean being here with you and Stephen, silly. Spending time together. Real time, at the same time," he said, turning on an elbow to smile at her.

"Really? I thought you'd be bored out of your skull by now."

"I think I may have had enough of that life," he said.

Caroline looked at his near-naked form and saw signs of the 'that life' under his deep tan. White ridges of scar tissue from old wounds. Fading purple bruises surrounded by yellowish auroras of flesh around more recent injuries. His arms and legs were criss-crossed by strips of scabs. He was still healing from a week-long excursion to prehistoric California. He'd only told her the broad strokes of what happened there. He'd been put out of the action early after an encounter with a sabretooth tiger, a concussion and broken ribs. The rest of the team continued a long trek over rough ground to free Richard Renzi from the same proto-human canni-bals who'd once held her captive. They returned with Rick and an aboriginal girl they'd found Renzi shacked up with back in The Then, the same girl who was now skipping through the foam, giggling like a child, one hundred millennia from her own time.

"You don't wish you were with the others?" Caroline said.

"Lee can lead the team. He's more than capable. We'd only butt heads anyway. Someone had to make sure you and Rick got away safe," Dwayne said.

"Part of me wishes you were with them. A very selfish part of me."

"I know, honey. You're worried about your brother. But he'll be back on the *Raj* by now. They'll do what this lunatic wants and, one way or the other, it'll all be over."

"One way or the other?"

"I should say Lee will make it go his way. He'll get the whole team out of this. Mo included. Tight spots are his thing."

"And then what?" she said and shifted the sleeping baby in her arms.

"Let's just think about the next few weeks. We have to be here for Rick. We may as well enjoy it." Dwayne rose from the sand to join her on the broad chaise under the cabana. He hugged her to him, fingertips resting gently on the wispy mop of hair atop the baby's head.

"It is nice here," she said and nestled her head against his chest. It was a sleepy and secluded beach on the coast of Baja a couple hours' drive north of Cabo. The beach was private, part of the property of the private medical clinic that Lee found for them through one of his many contacts. Mexico was full of clinics like this one, half surgical and recovery center, half resort. Very secretive, with a list of patients from the world of politics and celebrity. Caroline was sure it was a famous pop star she saw lounging by the pool, nose, and chin encased in bandages, on their first day at the clinic. Lee Hammond told them this place was renowned in the medical underground for treating the injuries of professional athletes who needed to keep any off-season surgeries on the down-low.

Rick Renzi was here for some extensive orthopedic surgeries to his leg. He had suffered a severe fracture just below the knee, and it had set all wrong since Rick was one hundred thousand years from an emergency room at the time it broke. The surgeons re-broke the leg and set it properly with a set of rods and pins. Rick would be in traction in an ankle-to-hip cast for the next couple of months. His limp would be reduced and, with corrective shoes, eliminated. The pain he'd been suffering for the past five years would be reduced to a manageable level.

Until then, they had nothing to do but read, swim, make love, watch their baby grow, and enjoy the Baja weather.

"I'm hungry," Dwayne said.

"So's the baby," Caroline said, sitting up as Stephen wriggled against her. "And we need to put some weight back on you, soldier."

"Thought you liked me lean," Dwayne patted his flat stomach.

"But not skinny. Get N'itha back here. I want to try the lobster at Cerritos. Everyone says it's killer."

He took the burbling baby from her and stood, cradling the diapered butt of his son in the crook of his arm. Stephen clung to his chest hairs, warm and drooling. Dwayne put two fingers in his mouth and let out a piercing whistle. Down at the water's edge, N'itha raised her head then started back toward the cabana at a run.

"And for God's sake, hand me her robe," Caroline said.

Dwayne swung his son up to take a seat behind his neck, much to Stephen's delight. They both watched Caroline trot down the sand to meet N'itha, holding a robe spread in her hands.

"Yeah. I could get used to this, son," Dwayne said.

Caroline's sleep was disturbed by a dream. A figure of a man spoke to her from clouds of fog. It was a world of swirling dark. The man reached out a hand. His lips moved, but no sound came out. His eyes were emphatic, blazing with passion.

It was Samuel Renzi, the son of Rick Renzi. He was born two years before, but Caroline knew Samuel as an adult, a time traveler who visited from the future to offer them guidance. Samuel had saved her life a number of times but he was still a mystery to her. In this dream, he appeared to be older, hair graying and features drawn. His eyes were on her, hand reaching, calling a soundless warning from a place of shadows.

She awoke with a start beside Dwayne, dripping with sweat. Caroline raised herself from sodden sheets to see Samuel Renzi standing at the foot of their bed. As in her dream, he was beseeching her, mouth forming words in mute pantomime. His figure was translucent and shimmering. It appeared obscured, as through a clouded lens.

"Dwayne," she whispered, hand to his arm, eyes locked on the specter reaching for her.

"I see him too," Dwayne said, already awake beside her.

4

MEETING WITH THE ENEMY

J ason Taan visited the *Ocean Raj* the following day. He parked a Sixties vintage Aston Martin at the foot of the gangplank. He was free of his usual company of security muscle. He didn't need it. The security contingent on the *Raj* and on the quayside was at platoon level.

He wore an open Burberry raincoat since the morning air was damp with a cold mist. Under the coat, golfing togs were visible. Light khakis and a navy blue polo. *Just stopping in to visit you chaps before I hit the links.*

Taan held the door for an elderly Asian man in a rumpled parka. Together they climbed the gangplank and came on board.

He took over the chartroom and made it his presentation room. Hot coffee, tea, and an assortment of Danishes were served. All had been delivered earlier by caterers. The Tauber team was called to attend, and took seats about the table. Only Morris, Lee, Chaz, Jimbo, Boats, and Bathsheba showed. Parviz and Quebat, who maintained the mini-nuclear reactor below decks, were essential personnel but not tactical to this mission. And Byrus, the Macedonian pit fighter brought back from the time of the Romans, was in his quarters enjoying his newest passion, Netflix.

"I first must express my disappointment that Caroline Tauber is not among us. I hope she is well," Taan said, idly stirring a spoon in a damask-patterned cup of hot oolong.

The question was for Morris. He sat opposite Taan without responding.

"I would have thought that her participation might be vital to the success of this endeavor." Taan's mouth curled in his professional smile. His eyes remained cold.

"I can operate the Tube without her," Morris said, struggling to keep his voice level. This was the first time he'd been in the same room with Jason Taan since Taan ordered him away into the hands of rough men who held him in a cell lit with painfully bright lights every hour of the day. Those days were marked by beatings delivered with skill so as to cause pain but no lasting physical damage.

"We don't want to hold up your tee time, Mr. Taan. What's this about?" Lee said, locking Taan's eyes with his.

"How rude of me," Taan said with a more open smile. He turned to the elderly man, slurping tea from a cup held in both hands. "This is Dr. Wesley Fong of the University of Macau. He will be spending the next week on board with you. Dr. Fong is the world's leading historical expert on the period you will be visiting."

"Thanks. But we can Google what we need," Chaz said.

Dr. Fong raised his eyebrows at that. He looked deeply appalled. Taan's smile broadened.

"Dr. Fong has certain proprietary research tools that were obtained at great expense. You can take my word that his expertise is crucial to accomplishing the set goals of this mission," Taan said, a hand to the elderly man's arm.

"Your word," Jimbo said.

"When have I not kept my word? Though the circumstances

that bring us together have been regrettable, and my methods have sometimes been brutal in your eyes, I have never lied or misled you. I need your device and guidance and participation in this effort. For this, you will be released from my employ with a generous reward upon the successful conclusion of our endeavor."

"Well, this 'endeavor' isn't going to come to a successful conclusion or even a successful start given the current conditions," Morris said, an edge in his voice.

"You have concerns, Dr. Tauber?" Taan said.

"You can't expect us to open an insertion field here," Morris said. "We have no idea what the ground or water was like on this site one hundred and fifty years ago. We need to be on open water. My guess would be that this mooring was dredged in more recent times. It might be a mud bank or even higher ground back in the time you want the team to be sent to."

"Do you have a suggestion for us, Dr. Tauber?" Taan was displeased, and his outer layer of cool élan was growing brittle.

"There are deeper anchorages in the Yangtze estuary. The *Raj* could be moored in the west channel off Changxingxiang Island." Morris stood and sorted through charts of Shanghai harbor to stab a finger at a spot midway between the China coast and a long island in the center of the broad mouth of the Yangtze.

"And how would we explain your presence there, Dr. Tauber?" Taan said.

"That's your problem. You're the only billionaire fixer in the room," Morris said, retaking his seat.

"Make up some bullshit about studying tides or currents," Lee put in.

"It can be done, Mr. Hammond," Taan said. "All it takes is some bullshit, as you say. And enough money placed in the right hands."

"I have some other logistical requirements," Morris broke in.

"All will be met once I have examined your needs and approve them, Dr. Tauber," Taan said. "Now, as Mr. Hammond suggested, I am due to meet a party on the links. I leave you with Dr. Fong. Make him welcome and pay special heed to his instruction. I will see my way back to the dock."

With that, Jason Taan stood from the table and made his way out the hatch into the rain.

Wesley Fong produced a laptop from beside him and opened it on the chart table.

"Will this cabin be okay to use as a classroom?" Dr. Fong asked in fluent English with a Southern California accent.

5

GOD'S OTHER SON

I t started as a lecture but turned into an open forum intel briefing. Dr. Fong was well prepared with a PowerPoint presentation projected on a screen mounted to the bulkhead of the chartroom. "The Taiping Rebellion was begun by a man named Hong Xiuquan in 1850," Fong told the Rangers, SEAL, and IDF vets seated around the long chart table.

"He was a low-born Chinese, and had a mental breakdown upon failing tests to become a civil servant. His breakdown took the form of visions in which he believed he was taken to Heaven to meet God. There, he was told that he was the younger brother of Jesus Christ. What's most amazing is that he was able to build an entire theology with himself at the center and get millions of followers to believe in it. The ruling Manchu emperor in Peking did not realize the danger until the Taipings had taken several cities and put hundreds of thousands to the sword. The Europeans in Shanghai, Macau, and Hong Kong were complacent as they mistakenly believed that the followers of Hong Xiuquan were true Christians when actually they were zealots following a charismatic madman and his twisted version of a religion. His ravings led directly to the bloodiest civil war in history."

"Worse than the American Civil War?" Lee asked.

"Yes. The Taiping war left between twenty and thirty million dead. Your Civil War resulted in a little over six hundred thousand fatalities," Fong said.

Bat asked, "What part of the war are we dropping in on?"

"For our purposes, it is the final days of the war you'll be visiting. The summer of 1865. The last stronghold of the Taipings was at Nanking. You will be arriving when that city is in the last stages of a long siege by the Imperial Manchu army and mercenaries hired by the emperor and mandarins."

"European mercenaries? Americans? Can we expect to fit in?" Lee said.

"There was a merc army formed by an American. I read about it," Jimbo said, holding up a Kindle. "And there's Brits and French along, too. We should be able to blend so long as our ordnance and uniforms match the period."

"He's right. Frederic Ward was a Yankee adventurer who led the Ever Victorious Army made up of other Americans, Europeans, and Filipinos," Dr. Fong said, taking up the story. "He was killed in battle before the time you'll be experiencing. Robert 'Chinese' Gordon, a British officer, will be in command in 1865. You should blend in with his forces easily enough."

"What's the order of battle? How many troops are deployed in this siege?" Chaz asked.

"Hundreds of thousands on either side," Fong said. "Maybe as many as a million men under arms. The Taipings themselves within the walls. The emperor's army is outside with artillery, cavalry, infantry, and sappers. They also have a slave army to build earthworks, trenches, and mines. You'll see Mongol and Tartar cavalry, Sikh lancers, and endless bannermen, musketeers, jingal men, and swordsmen."

"Cool," Jimbo said and then grinned when he realized he'd said it aloud.

"What are the city's defenders like?" Lee said.

"They are a formidable army. Well trained and disciplined with fifteen years of war behind them. They will be weary and starving after long months of siege but don't expect them to be demoralized. They are fanatics and will fight for every inch of the city."

"And we're expected to go downrange into that with a smile on our faces? Why're we deploying into the shittiest situation? Why not before or after?" Boats spoke up for the first time to say what was on all their minds.

Fong took a sip of coffee before answering.

"We have a historical record of the siege written by a scribe of a Taiping general known as the Shield King, one of the many kings within the Taiping hierarchy. He places the object you're being sent to find in a very specific place within the walls of Nanking and during a very specific period of time. We know where the object is and when it will be there. Before and after that, the object's whereabouts are unknown."

"Taan's spending a buttload of cash on this operation. What's this object we're talking about? What makes it worth all this?" Lee said. The others nodded.

"That information is not necessary at this point. I am told you have a lot of prep work to do in the meantime. Mr. Taan asked me to withhold the nature of the object you'll be retrieving until closer to the start of your mission," Dr. Fong said with a shrug.

"We're like mushrooms," Boats said with a smirk.

"Excuse me?" Fong said, looking to the others for clarification.

"Kept in the dark and fed shit," Chaz said.

"Well," Fong said, "I can provide you a clearer picture of the fall of Nanking along with a timetable of the battles and you gentlemen, and lady, can weigh your options for success. I'm no tactician. I can only offer you as much historical data as I can.

And I'm not lying when I say that this the most complete, most diligent collection of research on the places, personalities, conditions, and events in question that you will find anywhere."

"Let's let the doc finish his presentation. He has the intel we need, and we need to listen," Lee said to the table.

Dr. Fong returned to his lecture and was pleased to see each of his students were rapt with attention, and most were taking notes. He thought that this was the most attentive class he'd ever spoken to. Of course, his usual students only thought of grades and transcripts and course requirements. None of his classes relied on his tutelage to determine their chances of living or dying.

After several hours, they agreed to take a break. Bat hung back as the others hurried out of the hatch into the fresh salt air. Wesley Fong was closing his laptop at the head of the table.

"Is this period of history your main area of study?" Bat asked.

"I read and teach on a broader area of study of China and European influence in the early Nineteenth Century. The Opium Wars up to the fall of the Taipings," he said, visibly pleased to have the attention of an attractive young woman.

"And Jason Taan found you how?"

"I wrote some papers based on journals written at the time of the Taipings. Hong Xiuquan, the Heavenly King, and his officials produced mountains of texts, proclamations, and detailed inventories of treasures they looted on their march down from the north. Mr. Taan took an interest and funded my research."

"Funded? You're on his payroll?"

"It's more than that. These texts are not easy to come by. A lot of them are locked away in stacks or in private collections. To find the prize that Taan is looking for, he spent millions of dollars and a great deal of influence so that I could read and collate thousands of documents written by the Taipings."

"It all seems so dry, right? Just reading lists and regulations and red tape from a century and a half ago?" Bat said.

"I find it fascinating," Fong said with a smile. "It's like peering into the past, capturing a moment in time revealed by the minutia of a long-ago day."

"Then you must envy us, Doctor. We're going back to see, to experience, a time you can only read about," she said.

His smile broadened, and he shook his head with vigor.

"Oh, no. I wouldn't go there for all the money in the world. You will be traveling back to hell on earth, my dear."

Chaz put on cross-trainers and went for his evening run. Twenty laps around the deck. He needed it after that afternoon's lecture. A lot to take in.

Boats joined him on his third lap. The pair usually found themselves jogging in tandem or joined by others. There was little to do on board but wait for the day the mission dropped. The daily runs were a welcome part of the routine.

"Sounds like we're inserting into a world of shit, brother," Boats said, trotting easily beside Chaz.

"It's a fucked up deployment, that's for sure. But it's not our fight. We just need to get the goods and get gone."

"You make it sound easy."

"It'll all work out the way it's supposed to, or it won't. Most likely, it won't. But it's all in the Big Man's hands in the end."

Boats said nothing to that but for a grunt of assent.

"Got me thinking, though. We might have an edge in this," Chaz said as they rounded the broad curve of the *Raj's* aft deck.

"Yeah?"

"This Hong Shoo-juan dude said he's Jesus' brother. He's a lying motherfucker. We've probably been close enough to Jesus to touch him, you know. In real-time," Chaz said.

"So?"

"That's got to count for something, right? I figure the Big Man owes us one," Chaz said and kicked up his speed to sprint down the long starboard rail with the SEAL huffing after.

6

VISITING HOURS

"That's the last thing I need," Caroline Tauber said, her hand covering her coffee cup when Dwayne made to pour from the steaming carafe.

"Still shook up from last night?" he said and poured a mug for himself before sitting down at the table on the veranda of their rented house.

"You're not? What was that?" she said, trying to spoon cereal into Stephen's mouth. Their son was seated by her in a highchair. He seemed to be enjoying having breakfast on his face more than in his mouth this morning.

"A projection. Like I said last night. Samuel's come to us that way before as a hologram projection."

"It was like an old television set. Like when they would get stuck between channels or a plane flew over."

"So, they have glitches where Samuel comes from. He'll make contact again when conditions are better," Dwayne said.

"I don't know. I had the feeling something was deliberately interfering with him transmitting himself." She looked past Dwayne to see green trees, white sand, and a turquoise ocean spreading out beyond.

"He was trying to talk to you. He was looking at you, not me. You make anything out?"

"He was warning us. Why else appear to us?"

"Warn us of what? We're away from the team, away from the Tube. Off the grid. No one knows we're here."

"I don't know," she said and looked to the giggling baby, cheeks smeared with goop, beaming back at her with eyes crinkled in simple amusement.

"All we can do is keep our eyes open," Dwayne said.

N'itha bounced out onto the veranda, a flower-patterned dress swirling about her legs, beaded bracelets jangling on her wrists. Her shock of black hair was held back by a strip of red cloth that looked suspiciously as if it may have been cut from the bedsheets in her room.

"We go see Ricky?" she said, face aglow with anticipation. She plucked a mango from atop a pile of fruit in a bowl in the middle of the table.

"Sure, right after breakfast," Dwayne said.

"Hurry, please. Ricky is missing me. I am missing him," N'itha said around a mouthful of fruit, juice running down her chin. She took a banana from the bowl as well.

"Okay, get your sandals, and I'll take you over now. Soon as I've had my coffee," Dwayne said.

"Fucking A," she squealed, took an apple from the bowl, and raced back inside.

"I wish I had half her energy. I'm not even thirty, and she makes me feel like an old lady," Caroline said with a shake of her head.

"Must be that caveman diet she's on." Dwayne grinned.

Both were surprised at how well N'itha was adjusting to a world a hundred thousand years in her future. She arrived on board the *Raj* out of the manifestation field, too consumed with Rick Renzi's condition to pay attention to the world around her. In the days coming down to the sea off Baja, she explored the container ship, eyes wide with wonder. But nothing she saw seemed to scare her. Not being on a ship that was ten times the size of her home village back in prehistoric Nevada. Not the wonders of electricity or the strange clothes and customs. Even her first sight of a commercial jet flying high above ahead of a white contrail streak was greeted with childlike glee.

N'itha accepted that this was the world of her beloved Rick Renzi. No matter how alien it was to her, she would learn to live here with him. Since her people back in The Then were annihilated, she had no home in any place or any time. This would be her world too, beside her mate.

"Call if you need anything, okay?" Dwayne said, sweeping a burner cell and key ring for the rental off the table.

"Sure," Caroline said, looking far out at the sunlight glittering silver off the Pacific but seeing the pleading face of Samuel speaking across the gulf of time in words she could not hear.

———

At the clinic, Dwayne let Rick know that their situation might not be as secure as they thought.

"What the hell does that mean?" Rick asked from his bed, where he was propped up with N'itha seated beside him, her fingers idly caressing his arm. Rick's leg was raised at the ankle and knee inside a heavy cast. A pin went through his knee, with cables attached to the pulley rig. His foot rested in a cloth loop. A morphine drip was slung up by him, the line run into the back of his left hand.

"Maybe this Taan asshole. Maybe Sir Nigel. I don't know. We might need to relocate," Dwayne said.

"Well, give me time to get my sneakers on, and I'll be right behind you," Ricky scoffed, gesturing to the traction rig he was entrapped in.

"It might be nothing. But I need you to keep your eyes open."

"Check it out, bro. I'm tied up here in this one room for the next sixty days. What the hell am I going to see from here but Mexican soap operas?" Rick's hand swept the room. It looked more like a hotel room than a hospital room, with a view of the sea, big screen tv, and kitchenette.

"I'm doing my best here. Just keep an edge on, Ricky."

"Yeah, yeah. Who am I to bitch? You reentered hell to save my sorry ass."

"You'd have done it for me."

"As far as you know," Rick said, a grin spreading across his face.

"Fuck you," Dwayne said, grinning also.

"So, where'd you get word we might be compromised?"

Dwayne hadn't told Rick about his son. Neither that a son had been born to him nor that Samuel, as a grown man, had helped the Rangers out of one corner after another. Not that Rick's son led them to rescue his father from the primordial past. He'd made a promise to Lynn, Renzi's estranged wife, never to tell Rick that they had a third child. That promise didn't mean as much to Dwayne as the reluctance to tell Rick that he had a son who existed across multiple timelines. News like that could fuck with a man's mind.

"A feeling. Radar. Whatever."

"Okay. Can't ignore that. You hear from Lee and the rest?" Rick said, a hand cupping one of N'itha's ass-cheeks. She giggled. Even racked up and drugged, Renzi was still Renzi.

"We agreed to no contact. Better that way. This Taan has a global reach," Dwayne said.

"Can they trust him?"

"No. But you know Lee, he'll rework the scenario in his favor, eventually."

"You don't need to stick around if you have somewhere else to be," Rick said, smiling lazily. N'itha pressed against him, her mouth nuzzling his neck.

"I get the hint," Dwayne said and left the room. A high squeal followed by joint laughter trailed him down the hall to the nurse's station.

7

ORDNANCE

The guns arrived.

The crates were marked as engine parts. The invoices and customs forms claimed they were out of a tool-and-die plant in Taiwan. The plant was a steel fabrication factory owned by Jason Taan through a few shell corporations.

The team was anxious to get at the weapons. They had the crates pried open in minutes. The deck of the *Raj* was littered with strips of bubble wrap. The chemical tang of packing grease and fresh gun oil filled the air. The ship's crew stopped work to watch. The *Raj* was down to a skeleton crew of Boats' loyal Ethiopians led by his first mate Geteye. Their minders, Taan's security force, stood at a distance on an upper deck and pretended disinterest.

Morris had a very keen special concern in seeing the weapons even though firearms weren't really his thing. He stood in the blazing sun, watching the load come aboard, and Lee Hammond and the others descending on it.

"Chronal integrity. You considered that, right?" he said to the seven men and one woman unpacking the crates on the main deck of the *Raj* like kids under a Christmas tree.

"Every step of the way, Mo," Chaz said. He stripped the greased paper from a rifle with a wooden stock and held it out for Morris to inspect. It appeared to have three barrels and a brass action and buttplate.

"I suppose it looks in period," Morris said, though he had no idea.

"Check it out," Chaz said and worked a lever under the rifle's action. "It's based on a military version of a Henry rifle with some modifications. It has a longer barrel, full military stock, and this is the best feature."

Chaz held the rifle up to Morris and worked a brass toggle set before the trigger guard of the lever.

"See the two magazine tubes? This little switch changes the feed from one barrel to the other. Two tubes loading fifteen rounds each for a total capacity of thirty rounds of .44 ammo. That is some badass shit." Chaz beamed.

"And none of this is anachronistic in 1864?" Morris said, his skepticism growing in parity with Chaz' enthusiasm.

"All of this technology already exists in the period. The Henry was around seven years at the time we're jumping to," Lee Hammond said, looking at the rifle in his hand with deep appreciation. "We just added magazine capacity to it. The mechanism to switch between tubes is based on any double-barreled weapon of the period. We just moved the device to the feed tubes."

"At first glance, it looks like any rifle carried by armies at the same time. We even added a bayonet lug to the end of it," Bat Jaffe said, working the action of one of the rifles. She was as pleased as the others.

Jimbo put in, "The Imperial Chinese army at the time was in the field with early bolt action rifles. Trust me, that's way more revolutionary to the period than these babies."

"But the markings. They're Chinese?" Morris said, taking a rifle in his own hands. At first touch, a film of grease coated the palms of his hands.

"The Chinese have been knocking stuff off since Marco Polo's time," Chaz said. "Any decent forge could have made these. We marked them as coming out of the Hing-Fat factory, Shanghai 1861. Patent pending in the US and Switzerland."

"We'll bring them all back or make sure they're destroyed on site," Lee said, a hand to Morris' shoulder. "Even if we left one behind and it was found, it's just a one-off oddity. Probably go for millions at an auction, but no real questions raised and no connection back to us."

"And the revolvers?" Morris asked.

Boats was standing on the deck with a long-barreled revolver in each fist.

"Old-school Remingtons in reinforced frames. They're customized to take the same cartridges as the rifles. We had them fitted with gutta-percha handles for a better grip," Boats said and twirled the pistols in his hands in imitation of a Western gunfighter. One of them went flying from his finger to skitter over the deck. Morris had to leap aside to dodge the spinning handgun.

"Sorry." The big former SEAL shrugged with a sloppy grin. "Here's my baby," Jimbo said in a mix of awe and delight. He lifted a long rifle from a wooden crate and lovingly peeled away the paper cover. It was four feet in length with a curved butt plate and long brass scope mounted atop it. Steel fittings in a burled walnut stock.

"And that is..." Morris said.

"A Whitworth. English-made. Well, not this one. This one was worked up by one of Taan's fabricators," Jimbo said and examined the breech. "It's modified to be a breech-loader and take a .50 caliber Minié bullet. Effective range is over one thousand yards. This is our overwatch weapon."

"And I can trust you that none of this is so anachronistic, so out of place or advanced, as to cause some kind of disastrous change in the temporal environment?" Morris said.

"We researched all this up the yin-yang, Mo," Chaz said. "We know ordnance, all right? We took your guidelines seriously. These weapons give us an edge but are still within the guidelines."

"I hope so. Because this is the closest insertion to our time we've ever taken. You won't have the luxury of a couple thousand years' buffer. Leave a modern weapon back in the sand of Judea or on a beach in Phoenicia, and time will turn it to a layer of rust. And no one in that time possesses the technology to reproduce it," Morris said. "But that same weapon carelessly left behind in 1865 could change the nature of warfare. You guys may know guns, but I know my science and my history."

"None of these weapons are going to turn the tide for anyone, brother," Lee said, hand raised in a mock Scout oath.

"And I plan on bringing this son of a bitch back with me," Chaz said, gripping his faux-Henry in his fists with a childlike gleam in his eyes.

Byrus was excited at first, sharing the others' enthusiasm as they unpacked crates and displayed the contents on the deck. But the firearms didn't interest him. Like a faithful dog, he squatted back on his heels and watched his friends celebrating their new weapons.

"Bruce, I think this one's for you." Jimbo waved him over.

Byrus approached to see that his former master and good friend had laid out an array of edged weapons on the deck. Long bladed knives, Bowie-style, tempered steel blades with brass bolsters, tangs and butts, and polished wood handles with finger grooves. There were slim bayonets in leather scabbards. Nasty things, eighteen inches long with beveled triangular blades. Chaz snapped one into place at the end of one of the rifles and tested its range and heft. Jimbo was taking the bubble wrap off a longer blade. He held it out to Byrus, who goggled at it in awe.

It was close to the design of a gladius, the sword of the Roman army and a weapon that was a familiar tool to the hand of the

Macedonian. Familiar as well as deadly. An eighteen-inch flat blade tapering down to two razor-sharp beveled edges. The point ended in a spade shape. The handle was dark wood set in a heavy brass tang ending with a rounded pommel that was a blunt trauma weapon as dangerous as the blade. It came with a leather sheath lined with an envelope of oiled steel for easy draw.

Byrus slid the blade from the scabbard and held it balanced on his palm, only his thumb on the center of the tang holding it in place. He gave it a few practice swings. The blade sang through the air. A broad grin split his face.

"It is good. Bitchin' good blade," Byrus said. His English was improving but sprinkled with terms he learned from hours of watching what he called "the story box." He stuck his open hand out to Jimbo.

"My gift to you, bro," Jimbo said, taking the hand in his.

"You now give me two swords. I am grateful, and in your debt," Byrus said, pumping Jimbo's arm.

Jimmy Smalls had gifted Byrus with a wooden sword upon their return from ancient Judea. The wooden sword was a symbol that the Macedonian was freed from the bondage of slavery that he had known all this life. He no longer had to treat Jimbo as a master. They were equals now. But rather than break his indentured service to Jimbo, the gift of his freedom only deepened his debt to the Pima Indian, who had become his closest friend in this strange world of the far future.

"That is an anachronism," Morris said, pointing at the gladius in Byrus' fist.

"If anything, it's a reverse anachronism," Jimbo said. That gave Morris pause.

"There's all kinds of knives in that period, Mo. Everyone had one. They were as individual as a signature, custom knife makers in every town. So, one guy wanted something heftier," Jimbo explained.

"It will still draw attention."

Jimbo shrugged. "Well, you can take it away from him then."

Morris looked at the little man, admiring the gleaming blade of his new prize.

"I suppose it will pass. You guys know best, right?" Morris said.

8

FOUL SHOTS

I n the days that followed, Morris had his hands too full of his own logistical challenges to be concerned with anomalies and paradoxes. He worked with shipwright engineers from Dex-Tan Marine, a shipbuilding firm owned by Jason Taan with dry docks and yards in Shanghai, Taichung, and Panama. He made rough designs for a kind of floating boat barn that would rest on pontoons and be anchored mid-channel in the mouth of the Yangtze. The *Raj* would be concealed within the giant buoyant box. Taan shared Morris' concerns about security and provided the financing and personnel to see the shelter built.

"You are an engineer, Dr. Tauber. But not a structural engineer," Li Chen, a structural engineer informed him.

"Excuse me, but I'm more informed of my requirements than you are," Morris insisted to the trio of dour men standing with him at a table in the galley. Schematics were unfolded on a table. The three men peered at the drawings with supreme disapproval when they were not doing calculations on their tablets.

"It is too heavy, Dr. Tauber. Too unwieldy. It will not float," Li Chen said. He was the only one of the trio who spoke English.

"By your assertions, the boat we're currently standing on is too heavy to float."

Li Chen resisted the urge to correct the doctor that it was a ship they were standing on, not a 'boat.'

"It is your choice of materials, Dr. Tauber. A carbon steel frame is not needed. Aluminum would do. Or a similar alloy. Much lighter. More buoyant."

"The carbon steel arches are important for reasons that are need-to-know for the time being. I'm sure Mr. Taan has impressed on you the secretive nature of this endeavor," Morris said.

Li Chen's frown deepened. He turned to the other two men. All three men engaged in a muttered exchange, trailing off each utterance in the whine peculiar to the Cantonese dialect. Li turned back to Morris. The other two bent to their tablets, hands moving over the screens like agitated spiders.

"We can do the walls and roof in fiberglass to lighten the total load. We also suggest angling or curving the roof to allow rain to run off. The supports and arches of the superstructure could be tapered to prevent the entire structure from being top-heavy."

"That all sounds promising," Morris said.

"Only if the computer models work, Dr. Tauber," Li Chen said and smiled for the first time.

"Make them work, Mr. Chen. I know what your boss is like when he doesn't get his way," Morris said, touching a hand to a tender spot on his arm where his shirt hid a bruise still livid after two weeks.

Confined aboard the *Raj* while the work on the boat barn was progressing, the crew was getting restless. Lee, Bat, and Chaz decided that something needed to be done before they all went mental. They approached the leader of the security team, their guards, to contact Jason Taan and ask about some kind of parole.

Binh was the security team leader, a man with a hard face and harder heart. A by-the-book asshole who projected anger that probably covered a mortal fear of his boss. Binh pretended not to understand what the crew was talking about.

"Let a couple of us ashore. Just a few at a time. Dinner and movie. A walk in the park," Lee said to the unsmiling man standing on the weather deck before the bridge.

"No one leaves the ship," Binh said. "You can send guards with us," Bat said.

Binh stood silent, not even recognizing that she had spoken.

He would only look at Lee.

"It's not like we're going to run off. You're holding our friends," Lee said again.

"No one leaves the ship," Binh said again, voice flat.

"Jesus, what a prick," Bat said and walked away, flinging her hands up.

"Look, Binh, these guys have watched all the movies on board. Ten times. We've read all the books, played all the games. And the water around here is too fucked up to catch any fish in," Chaz said, stepping up.

"You want more movies?" Binh said.

"You're not really listening to us, Binh. We're bored, and there's no fun, only one woman on board, and she's taken. You digging me, Binh?" Chaz stepped up within inches of the smaller man, looming close to stare Binh down, speaking low.

"I will call the office and share your concerns," Binh said but did not move from where he stood, boots braced on the deck.

The next day a pole, hoop, and net were delivered along with a box filled with basketballs. This would be their new distraction. They bolted the pole down to an open area of the main deck and played three-on-three in the afternoon sun and under the lights. It wasn't shore leave, but it was something. They worked up a sweat and an appetite anyway.

Further distraction was provided when the pre-fab sections

of the boat barn were delivered to the pier. A crew of workers arrived on a bus along with a rolling crane and began assembling the structure in a dry berth opposite the *Raj*. Air hammers whined, and sparks from welding arcs blew like runaway stars on the wind. The work went on in shifts, night and day.

Jimbo taught Byrus how to dribble and free-throw. The little man picked it up quickly and made up in speed what he lacked in height. He'd never be able to jump high enough but developed a killer overhand shot. The two were playing one-on-one on the dark deck under a pool of light from an overhead lamp that illuminated the half court they'd marked out with paint. Crewmen smoked and watched from the rails, making remarks and applauding points made.

Two of their guards stepped into the rim of light. Jimbo caught a rebound and stood dribbling in place.

"Problem?" Jimbo said to the pair. One was about Byrus' height but with thick arms and wrestler's shoulders. The other was just shy of six feet with a horse face and sad eyes.

"We play too?" Horse Face said.

"Why not?" Jimbo shrugged. He turned to Byrus who said nothing.

The two guards stripped off their jackets and shirts and neatly folded them. They set their holstered handguns atop the stacks, well off the court and out of easy reach.

"Twenty-one okay?" Jimbo said. Horse Face nodded followed by the wrestler, who Jimbo suspected spoke no English.

The guards had game, and soon all four men were bathed in sweat in a tight match under the lights. Most of the crew was watching now. Boats and Chaz stood leaning on the rail of the observation deck, calling encouragement and sharing criticism. They were joined by Lee and Bat, who brought a bucket of iced beers with them. Even Dr. Fong came to the port of his cabin, drawn by the noise.

Byrus played guard to Jimbo's center. The smaller man kept

pace with the Pima, always to Jimbo's side, covering the blind spot left by the eye lost two thousand years before on a hillside in Judea. Byrus blocked the two security men, dashing like a terrier close by Jimbo's side all the way to the net again and again.

Jimbo slammed his twenty-first shot down through the hoop, beating the guards who only reached eighteen after a hard-fought game.

"Again," Horse Face said and gestured for the ball.

"Yeah, okay," Jimbo said, winded but game.

The second game wasn't friendly. The loss stung the two guards, and they played for keeps this time. Jimbo was fouled each time he jumped. Shoulder checks and jabbing elbows. The two guards weren't concerned with niceties and rules. If that's how they wanted to play it, Jimbo decided, then he was willing to take them downtown the hard way. He grew up playing b-ball reservation style and had dirty tricks of his own. Byrus picked up on the shifting tone of play and brought some pit-fighter moves to his game.

They were tied at sixteen apiece when Byrus came out of a jump with his sandaled foot driving down on Horse Face's instep. The man howled and swung at Byrus, catching the smaller man by surprise and sending him to the deck. Jimbo was across the half-court in a second, firing a rebound into the wrestler's face that sent the man staggering back. Then he was in Horse Face's grill, both men with fists clenched and elbows cocked.

Binh appeared, marching into the light, barking a blistering string of Cantonese that didn't need translation. He shoved Horse Face away and kicked at the wrestler. He was reaming them both fresh new assholes while they put back on their shirts, jackets, and weapons. He continued the harangue as he followed them aft where the dressing down continued for the better part of an hour, Binh's high voice echoing over the harbor.

It was Boats who came up with a name for the two guards. The Bruise Brothers.

9

THE WORM IN THE BOTTLE

"So, this is the prize in the piñata," Chaz said in a sour tone. "Looks like something from a gay garage sale," Lee said.

The team was studying the image on the big screen in the chartroom. The computer model was as accurate as it could be based on descriptions from texts at the time. Dr. Fong said that a detailed description was recorded in meticulous detail in a hand-written inventory of the palace of the East King.

"There are a lot of lesser kings among the Taiping. Think of them like vice presidents of a corporation," Dr. Fong said.

On the screen was a fully rendered image of a white tubular shape with a slight curve to it. Its surface was engraved with row after row of Chinese characters inlaid with jade. It was capped either end with matching devices in gold fashioned on one end in a swan drifting across a pond with wings spread, on the other was a frog squatting atop a lily pad. Both had eyes made of some kind of red gems.

"The reliquary is approximately two and a half feet in length and roughly six inches in diameter," Fong said, holding his hands apart in approximation. "The barrel is prehistoric mammoth ivory, preserved in peat in the northern tundra and recovered by

Mongols who carried it to the markets in the south where it was fashioned by artisans into the object you see here."

The team knew all about mammoths.

"A reliquary? It's a container," Bat said, standing close to the screen to study the image.

"What's in it?" Lee said.

"That is need-to-know. But you can assume that Jason Taan believes it's worth all this trouble and expense," Fong said.

"His expense. Our trouble," Chaz groused.

Fong touched a key on his laptop, and the image on the screen changed to a detailed schematic of a series of buildings enclosed within concentric walls.

"This is the palace of the East King in Nanking," Fong said, stepping to the screen and touching a finger to a long building set within the walls.

"The prize is there?" Bat said.

"In a holding room somewhere in the northern wing. Here."

"And what's the situation there?" Jimbo said.

"Uncertain. The city fell to Imperial forces on July 19th, 1865. That is the last recorded sighting of the reliquary found in the diaries of a clerk for General Sang of the Emperor's army. After that night, it vanishes into the mists of history."

"That's the timetable then. A ticking clock," Lee said, frown deepening.

"It's a clusterfuck. We've all read this bullshit after-action report. It's a meat grinder." Chaz held up a hundred-page report written and printed up for them by Dr. Fong.

"Makes Fallujah look like Lilith Fair," Jimbo added. "One million-plus troops fighting by medieval rules of engagement. 'Clusterfuck' doesn't cover it."

"You will have to enter the city with the invading forces once they've made a breach in the walls," Fong said, changing the image on the screen to an interactive three-dimensional model of the city of Nanking of a century and a half ago. It was a formidable fortress of towers, walls, moats, and earthworks. Inside, it was a labyrinth of closely packed buildings with winding lanes leading off broad avenues arrayed like the spokes of a wheel.

"It is as accurate as it can be based on historical records and the findings of archeologists," Fong said with an apologetic tone.

"So, we go charging in, a pack of round-eyes, under heavy fire against determined defenders, with an invading force hot to steal anything that's not nailed down, killing anything that doesn't kill them first and raping anything that moves," Jimbo said, riffling pages of the report.

"But with an advantage the pillagers do not have," Fong said, adjusting his glasses.

"What's that, doc?" Chaz said.

"You know what you are looking for and where the reliquary is. You should be able to reach it first." Fong shrugged.

"We can't keep calling it 'the reliquary.' That word sucks. Tell us what it is, doc," Lee said, stepping close to put a hand on Wesley Fong's shoulder.

"It is referred to in the inventory as the Chronicle of the Khan," Fong said in a quiet voice.

"The Khan? There were lots of Khans," Lee said.

"Which Khan are we talking about?" Bat said, leaning on the table, eyes fixed on the elderly man.

Fong's face flushed.

"Hot shit," Jimbo said, a broad smile creasing his face.

Bat lay spent in the shaft of moonlight coming in through the port, her head on Lee Hammond's chest. Cool air from a fan dried the sweat from her naked back. The damp sheets beneath them were suddenly chilled. She snuggled closer. He drew her tight with an arm about her waist.

"Chaz is right," he said after a while.

And that's the end of the afterglow, she thought and made to move away. His hand pressed her back against him.

"About what?" she said, fingers playing with the hair on his stomach, feeling raised furrows of scar tissue atop the muscles there.

"This is a clusterfuck."

"It's looking that way."

"The intel is unreliable. We're on our own. The plan is based on horseshit and hearsay."

"Ever been on an op that wasn't?" She felt him shrug under her.

"We need an exit strategy," he said.

"From Nanking back to the exfiltration point? That's the part I'm least worried about," she said, voice becoming drowsy.

"I mean from this whole fucked-up situation. We get this thing for Taan and bring it back. What does he need us for?"

"Not a damn thing. We need an exit strategy for our exit strategy."

"Exactly. We'll be away from him and his hired goons, out of reach back in The Then. That's our leg-up on him, that's the variable. That's where we make our move."

"What move?" she said and raised her head to look into his eyes, her chin on his sternum.

"That's what we need to think of," he said, eyes on hers.

"Well, for right now you need to think of your current tactical circumstance," she said, smile lazy and eyebrow arched.

"Which is?"

"Which is, the only way out of this room is to get past me. You can advance or retreat, Ranger, your choice." Bat levered herself up to slide a leg over to come to rest atop him.

"Retreat, hell," he said and reached up to take her hips in his hands.

10

GEEKS

"**B**ecause I'm a physicist *and* an engineer, that's why!" Dr. Morris Tauber was banging a fist on the chart table and shouting, red-faced, at Li Chen and his two constant companions. They stood regarding his tantrum like unblinking sphinxes.

"I am a *doctor* of engineering. Your wiring diagrams make no sense," Li Chen insisted, finger stabbing the sheets spread on the table.

"That's because you don't understand how my device operates, and I'm not about to explain it to you," Morris said, taking deep breaths. "Just wire it the way I showed you."

Li conferred with his comrades in rapid-fire Cantonese. They shook their heads with vigor, glanced at Morris' reddening face and narrowed eyes. They slowly nodded their reluctant consent.

"Good. Have it done by this time tomorrow," Morris said and folded the thick sheaf of wiring schematics and shoved them into Li Chen's hands.

The men retreated through the hatch. Morris followed a few moments behind to step up to the navigation deck. He observed with satisfaction the joists of carbon alloy bolted in place high above the ship's deck. Crews were working with cranes to secure

47

the fiberglass sheets to the walls and angled roof. By the end of the week, the *Raj* would be fully covered and concealed within the floating boathouse built to his specifications.

His stomach rumbled, reminding him that he hadn't eaten since breakfast. Yesterday. He stepped into the galley to nuke a frozen pizza and wolfed three slices washed down with a Diet Coke. He snatched a bag of rice chips to eat on the way down to his lair beneath the foredeck. Whatever else he could say about his host Jason Taan, he couldn't complain that they weren't well-fed. They couldn't leave the *Raj,* but they could send guards for takeout from any one of hundreds of great restaurants in Shanghai.

He made his way forward, skirting the basketball court where Lee and Bat were challenging Jimbo and Byrus to a game under the eye of guards seated in lawn chairs under an awning. Parviz and Quebat were resting in sun chairs, stripped to swim trunks and gleaming with oil. Iced buckets of beer were by their sides.

Morris let them be. The pair of nuclear technicians wouldn't be needed until the days running up to insertion. They spent eight hours a day fussing over their mini-reactor. The pair was professional and diligent and, like everyone else on the *Raj,* bored to agitation. Morris was the only one who felt like time was passing too quickly. The design and construction of the massive boat shed took up a lot of his day as did the modifications to the Tube chamber and work on new algorithms and computer models. Add to that all of the delays and arguments with the Chinese engineers and construction crew, and he had little time to be bored.

The smell of hot metal filled the below decks passageway that led forward to the Tube. Geteye was leading a work team of welders from the *Raj's* crew. They had greatly expanded the enclosure constructed of Conex container panels which formed the Tauber Tube's manifestation chamber. It was now a five thousand square foot chamber with a forty-foot ceiling. The crew reinforced it with steel beams as well as building a broader approach platform into the Tube itself. From the outside, it still looked like the hold was filled with stacks of steel cargo containers.

The work was near completion, but the chamber containing his and his sister's field projector looked like a cyclone had been through it. Scaffolds and ladders, stacks of steel beams, all kinds of tools, tanks, hoses, and debris. But Morris knew well the speed and efficiency with which Geteye and his crew worked. He was confident they'd finish ahead of the Chinese contractors. In one corner of the chamber, Boats, the giant red-bearded former Navy SEAL was finishing work on a wooden boat. It was a recreation of a nineteenth-century longboat that had been fabricated at a furniture plant in Vietnam from old blueprints. The plant was owned by a subsidiary of Tee-Han Home Furnishings, a company wholly owned by one or another arm of Jason Taan's financial empire. Boats was applying a fresh coat of paint to the hull with a thick brush.

"Is that your paint I'm smelling?" Morris shouted to be heard over the construction noise.

"Yeah. Second coat. It's got lead in it. Fucking Chinese, right?" Boats said, lowering his face mask to reveal a broad grin.

"That's toxic, isn't it?"

"Chronal integrity, brother!" the SEAL said, grin growing broader.

Morris covered his mouth with his hand and hurried back toward the command console set at the front of the room. He pulled the plastic tarp from a terminal box and set to work on the complex rewiring job ahead of him.

Caroline had given Morris a wealth of advanced books and papers and equations that came from the mysterious Samuel Renzi. They were works certainly from the future and, as she hinted, possibly from an alternate future from the one that lay ahead of them. In any case, the work was an eye-opener for

Morris, and he devoured it all. Particularly a slim little volume called *Mica Prima* by Kosimo Trivenchy. He wasn't certain, but it seemed like some of Trivenchy's ideas were based on Morris' own, though there was no direct mention of the Tauber Tube.

Thinking about how his work might have influenced scientific advancement in a parallel timeline was too much all at once for Morris to deal with properly. In any event, Morris was able to use the calculations and theorems to streamline the Tube's operation and increase energy efficiency. He could think bigger now, see beyond his own thinking to expand the functions of the Tube both literally and figuratively. Other than supervising the work of others, Morris' main task was assembling a larger Tube channel along the configurations described in the *Mica Prima* and by his sister who had actually seen a much larger scale manifestation chamber during a brief sojourn into an alternate future.

The Tube's arches were much higher and wider now. A hundred feet in circumference with clearance for a forty-foot wide approach platform. The chamber containing it nearly filled the entire forward hold of the *Raj* and the hollow tower of container shelves above. The control console was moved farther aft, separated now from the main Tube chamber by a wall of tempered glass. They learned from past experience that the team might be returning in an urgent rush with God alone knew what in close pursuit—like the mass of man-eating primates that invaded the first Tube chamber back in Nevada. The control room needed to be protected.

Morris spent late into the evening working on the complex array of cables for the massive jolt of electricity needed to power the Tube, punch a hole through time, and maintain the tenuous opening for the minimum thirty minutes needed for the team to safely travel through the manifestation field.

He was absolutely certain this new, rebooted Tube would work as designed once completed. After all, it was the same Tube he and his sister had constructed in their desert laboratory back in Nevada, only bigger. What concerned him more were the thick bundles of wiring that would run out to the support arches of the new boatshed going up over the *Raj*.

Though he made an issue of their ignorance, Morris Tauber was very, very grateful that Li Chen and his team were *only* engineers and *not* physicists.

11

INCOGNITO

"Do we have to wear the hats?" Chaz asked, frowning in deep disapproval at the butternut-brown cap in his hand.

"It's called a *kepi*," Jimbo said, fitting his to his head after working a curve into the leather bill.

"We going to Nanking or Gettysburg?" Bat said, admiring herself in a hand mirror, her own cap worn at a jaunty angle.

"Same period. We'll be dropping back close to the same date two years after Gettysburg. These are standard issue army combat wear for the period. North and South. The French and Brits wear similar tops," Jimbo told the team gathered in the galley to try on the uniforms that arrived on board that morning.

Brown tunics and trousers with brass buttons and epaulets and high choker collars secured by eye-hooks. They were all roughly sized for each team member down to the underwear, socks, and boots. Everyone on the team, except for Byrus who had never worn so much clothing in his life, was used to adjusting military issue clothing. But the bitching went on anyway.

"Heavy," Boats said, testing his ease of movement in the uniform.

"Check this out," Chaz said, "These things are lined." He held his tunic up to show the others a white linen lining inside.

"They made it that way, so the Yankees could turn it inside out to surrender," Lee said.

"Just be glad we didn't have them made in serge wool. We had these done up in cotton because we'll be deploying in the summer heat," Jimbo said, pulling Byrus' tunic closed to show him how the buttons worked. The Macedonian shifted his feet like a kid being fitted for school clothes.

"Won't they look too new?" Bat said. She was admiring herself in the uniform, pinching in the sides of the tunic to judge how much, or how little, tailoring was needed.

"We can run them through the dishwasher in the galley to fade them a little, tarnish the buttons," Boats said. "Take some sandpaper to the seams."

"There's a box here of patches and brass," Chaz said, rooting through the bottom of a cardboard carton.

"How are we ranking ourselves?" Jimbo said.

"I'll take the captain's bars if nobody minds," Lee said, taking the double bars to pin to his collar.

"And the sergeant chevrons are mine," Chaz said. "The black man takes a lot of shit back when we're going. I might take less if I'm a top kick."

"How are we planning to explain ourselves? White guys, a black, an Indian," Jimbo said.

"A midget," Chaz said, glancing at Byrus.

"And a Jew who's also a girl," Bat put in.

"You'll need to man up for this op, honey," Lee said with a sly smile.

"I'm going *yentl*?" she said perplexed. The reference was lost on the others.

"You either go as a boy or go as a camp follower," Jimbo said.

"Is there something wrong with being a camp follower?" she said.

"Females tagging along after armies were usually prostitutes," Jimbo said.

"Okay, *yentl* it is." Bat shrugged. The others looked blankly at her.

"None of you have ever seen a Streisand movie?" She smirked.

She decided to leave the tunic as it was, to allow it to fit a little baggy, the better to hide her breasts.

"You're going to need to cut your hair short," Lee said, touching the mane of black curls that reached her shoulders.

The door of the galley swung inward, and security chief Binh entered followed by the Bruise Brothers, who sneered sullenly at the costumed men and woman.

Binh waved a hand at the Bruise Brothers.

"They go with you," Binh barked to the room at large. "Go with us where?" Lee said, stepping up to the chief. "Where you go. Nanking. On mission."

"The hell they do," Lee said, moving closer, voice lowering.

"There's two extra uniforms here," Jimbo said, holding up a pair of spare tunics.

"Boss Taan's order. You will follow. They speak for you. They fight with you," Binh said, glaring at Lee Hammond whose hands fisted in reply. An immovable object and an unstoppable force.

"You mean they'll fuck us," Lee said through his teeth.

Binh blinked at that. Then his eyes went black with suppressed rage.

"Master Taan says they go with you. That is all. It is done," Binh said, biting off each word.

"You said they'll speak for us. Can they speak *to* us, chief?" Jimbo said, stepping forward.

"I speak good enough English," the horse-faced one of the pair said.

Lee let out a breath and studied the man. "What are your names?" he said.

"I am Shan," Horse Face said and jerked his head at his shorter partner. "He is Wei."

"We're stuck with them," Jimbo said to Lee.

"You going to fuck us?" Lee said to Shan.

"We will not fuck you. We are good soldiers. You will see," Shan said.

"For shit sure we'll see," Lee said and stepped back from Binh.

The room took its first breath in what felt like minutes.

"Try these on," Chaz said and spun a pair of kepis to their new team members.

12

DEPLOYMENT

A monsoon rain fell on the Szechuan coast under a moonless night sky.

The armored limousine arrived at a boat pier along the western bank of the Yangtze. The SUVs, in front and behind the long black stretch, belched out men in black raincoats who spread out to establish a perimeter. The limo unloaded a passenger concealed under a trio of umbrellas held by a phalanx of more men in black coats. They provided cover for the passenger all the way down to a dock where a launch was waiting.

After a harrowing ten-minute journey over storm-tossed waters, Jason Taan arrived under the sheltering roof of the lofty boathouse that housed the *Ocean Raj*. He gripped the rail and looked up the rust-streaked hull of the slab-sided ship with an expression of disdain.

He sighed. "I built a palace to house a pig."

"Sir?" said the armed man closest to him on the heaving deck. Taan ignored the question and watched the launch reach the pier at the foot of the ship's gangway. He batted away an offered hand

and stepped from the swaying deck of the launch to the swaying surface of the dock without mishap.

His patience was wearing thin. He heard nothing but requests, complaints, and excuses from Dr. Tauber. The latest was a delay until weather conditions were right to operate the miraculous machine hidden in the bowels of this scabrous scow.

Taan was weary of the American explaining that delays in the present time did not represent a delay in their arrival in 1865.

"The past has already passed," Tauber would remind him, as though speaking to a backward child. "It will be there no matter how long preparations take here."

Tauber swore that the collateral effects of powering up the Tauber Tube would draw attention unless they activated it under conditions that would conceal an electrical flash that he promised would be seen in the city. The waiting was necessary unless Taan wanted more attention from the government in Beijing than even his wealth could paper over.

Tonight would certainly seem to fit his proscribed conditions. Visibility was limited to the hand before one's face in the driving rain. And anvil lightning flashed in the belly of the cloud cover from horizon to horizon. Even now the roof above the top of the *Ocean Raj's* superstructure rattled under the assault of a long peal of rolling thunder.

He climbed the gangway to find Binh Ho waiting at the top to escort him below decks. He looked up to see that a section of the boathouse roof above the rear of the ship was left open. The rain came down in torrents through the opening to lash the aft deck. He could see men moving on the raised bow deck.

"I'm glad you could make it," Morris Tauber said without a trace of sincerity as Taan entered the control cabin with his mob of glowering bodyguards.

"I like to see what I am paying for," Taan said, shrugging from his drenched coat with the help of Binh.

"We'll be opening the manifestation field as soon as the team is ready," Morris said and went back to his array of monitors and keyboards. One monitor showed an interactive computer graphic of the Tube. Another showed an animated Venn diagram with floating circles intersecting and retreating in an indiscernible pattern.

A third was filled with racing columns of numbers, letters, and symbols scrolling and changing with dizzying speed.

Past the control array and through a Plexiglas window wall, Taan could see the Tube itself. It looked simple enough, too simple to perform the extraordinary tasks promised. A ramp led to a platform with rollers installed in its floor. This led into the center of a row of concentric rings of black steel. These rings were covered in a thick rime of white ice that dripped clumps of frost. The frigid air was creating a mist of fog that clung to the floor around the base of the Tube. There was a humming sensation coursing through the deck that he could feel through the soles of his feet. Taan was reminded that there was a mini-nuclear reactor operating in a shielded chamber somewhere nearby.

At the foot of the ramp before the Tube was the anomalous sight of eight figures dressed as though for a costume party or, more accurately, movie extras. They were loading wooden boxes into the bottom of an open wooden boat perhaps fifteen feet in length. Across the bow of the boat, Taan could see the word *Pennock* painted in neat lettering.

"Pennock? What does that mean?" Taan asked.

"According to your Dr. Fong, the USS *Pennock*, a Yankee clipper, was anchored in Shanghai during our operational period," Morris answered without taking his fingers from a keyboard or eyes from the screen of rapidly scrolling numbers.

"Isn't there a chance our expedition might run into crewmembers of the same ship?" Taan asked.

"They only need the longboat to get to shore. They'll scuttle it once they reach port."

"Then how will they get back to here?"

"These guys? Trust me, they'll find a way. We always work it out," Morris said, turning to Taan with a smile.

Taan pierced him with a cold stare.

A voice came from a speaker above them. "Mo, you ready to wind this thing up?"

"I'll give you the 'go' sign in ten," Morris answered. He then touched the keyboard and spoke again.

"Geteye? Your guys ready?"

"We are inflating now, doctor," a voice in African-accented English responded.

"Thanks. Get back to me when it's fully deployed." Morris touched another key.

"You have my jolt ready, boys?"

"Powered up and running hot." This time a Persian accent. "Wait for my word."

Taan knew from Morris' explanations that a balloon was climbing into the night sky through that open hatch in the boathouse roof. A balloon with a magnesium/carbon alloy skin and reinforced cable leading down to the *Raj* and, ultimately, through transformers, into the Tube before him. If he understood correctly, the mini-nuke provided a multi-megawatt charge to the balloon that resulted in a multi-gigawatt explosion of energy as the balloon gathered electromagnetic energy from the surrounding air. The massive static charge powered the Tube and provided the terrific electrical force needed to punch a hole in the time continuum.

How it worked from there was beyond the understanding of Jason Taan. He prided himself on possessing a fine mind capable of making simultaneous complex calculations. But that was with strictly fiscal matters, material things like money, profits, and trends. What the Taubers accomplished with their purely theoretical imaginings seemed to him to be, frankly, magical.

Morris received and acknowledged transmissions through

the speakers of a bud in his right ear. He turned to Taan, an eyebrow raised.

Taan felt a charge in the air, a frisson of electricity that chilled rather than warmed. Through every surface came a rapid, insistent pounding that felt as if it might shake the ship apart down to the last rivet and weld. It ended as abruptly as it began. Through the reinforced glass of the window wall, he could see the haze of fog growing thicker, rising to envelop the whole Tube array in a cloud of white.

As one, the eight figures shoved the longboat up the ramp and down the platform to disappear into the shroud of condensing air. The mist climbed the walls and filled the large chamber beyond. He watched fingers of ice grow on the far side of the panes of glass as the air in the room beyond fell to arctic temperatures.

"Are they..." Taan halted, uncertain of how to phrase what he wanted to know.

"Gone into the past," Morris said with a mixed tone of awe and gratification.

13

CAST ADRIFT

G ray dawn light cut through the chill mist as the longboat drifted, stern turning starboard, on a mild current. The air was thick and hot with a cloying musty smell coming off the water.

Boats gripped the tiller to bring the bow facing the flow. The rest of the crew was recovering from the crushing effects of travel through the manifestation field. The rush of nausea, swimming vision, and all-over body aches were what they'd learned to anticipate, so they were not overwhelmed.

Not so for the Bruise Brothers. The pair of keepers lay across the thwarts on their hands and knees, heaving up the steaming remains of a fish and noodle dinner the others had seen them wolf down just an hour before. The team knew better than to travel through the Tube on a full stomach. For the next ten minutes, their unwanted chaperones would be out of commission.

Lee and Jimbo stripped Shan of his weapons, boots, belt, and tunic. Chaz and Byrus did the same for Wei. The pair slowly regained their senses to find they were stripped to their underwear with two rifles trained on them.

"What is this?" Shan said, eyes on the wavering barrel before his eyes.

"This is where we say bye-bye," Jimbo said and motioned with the rifle at the brown water drifting past under the billowing white mist.

"You want us to drown?" Shan said, making to rise.

"We want you to *swim*, asshole. The field stays open thirty minutes or more. You've only lost five. Plenty of time to swim back to the *Raj*," Lee said, holding the other rifle on them. Bat and Chaz were working oars to keep the longboat in place.

Sounding like an angry dog, Wei barked out a string of Cantonese until Shan translated Lee's words for him. Wei's eyes went wide, tinged with fear.

"Clock's ticking, guys. Make your choice. Go home to hot food and cold beer or take your chances in Manchu China," Jimbo said and nodded to the water.

"In your undies," Boats added.

The pair slipped over the side and into the muddy stream. Shan lowered himself in, one hand remaining on the gunwale to fix them all with a murderous expression before immersing himself. They swam and, with the aid of the river current, were out of sight in the icy fog within seconds.

"Think they'll make it?" Chaz said.

"Do I give a shit?" Lee said and sat on a thwart to take an oar.

A mist rode atop the swirling current of the river to join the artificial bank of fog created as a byproduct of the manifestation field. The team rowed the longboat toward the western bank of the Yangtze, glowing with lantern light in the gloom.

There was no telling where the port began and the river ended. The entire harbor was filled with boats bobbing in the water. Junks, barks, barges, and smacks with sails down and masts swinging in time with one another on the ebb and flow created by the retreating tide. Beyond them, closer to the mainland, taller masts and smokestacks were visible. The black edifice of coastal fortifications stood about the harbor rim, crenelated stone walls with stout towers, wide bases, and sloping walls at the intervals.

The team rowed in among a wide mixture of boats anchored in the open water or moored to narrow wooden docks that snaked out from either arm of the encircling waterfront. It was a maze of wooden craft noisy with activity. A funk of smoke, garlic, and frying fat hung over the water. Voices could be heard calling as well as the sounds of livestock. Pigs squealed, chickens squawked, and geese honked to add their own part to the cacophony.

Bat stood at the prow of the longboat to guide them along a serpentine path between the closely moored vessels looming either side. The shore was invisible, so she aimed them toward the taller masts that she could only presume were docked along the wharf front.

"Take this next right," Bat called back.

"That's starboard, darling," Boats said from the tiller.

"You want me to learn ship talk or find a way out of here? This right here. Turn now," she said.

"Damn place looks like a floating trailer park," Chaz grumped at an oar. A woman dumped a bucket of stinking ooze into the water close enough to his left, or port, to splash him.

They saw figures moving on the decks, but none came to the rails to take a look at them. It was just another boatload of round-eye barbarians to them. They found a path through the archipelago of boats and out onto open water. They could see the port of Shanghai now. Rows of wooden sailing ships, steamships, and mixes of the two rested along stone piers, merchant and military craft side-by-side. Flags flew from the tops of masts, British, French, Imperial Russia, Spain, and others, some of them unfamiliar. The Stars and Stripes fluttered lazily in the warming air of the morning atop the yardarm of a steam warship.

Boats steered them along the towering wall of one of the piers, massive stone pilings green with algae. They glided, oars inboard, between the pier and a big stern-wheeler riverboat moored there. The longboat came alongside a set of steps ending in a slime-covered shelf. Bat tied the bowline secure through an ancient ring of rust-crusted iron. Boats did the same at the stern. Without a word to one another, they unloaded the wooden cases containing their rifles, gear, and ammunition. They formed a chain up the slime-slippery steps and handed each crate up until they were all stowed up on the pier. All climbed the steps, leaving Boats to secure the oars in place before pulling out the cocks in the floor of the longboat. It filled quickly and settled into the brown water until only the very tops of the oarlocks were visible in the eddying muck. Then it vanished below into the opaque water in a cascade of bubbles.

The pier was a madhouse of men unloading the sternwheeler on one side and a sailing ship on the other. Chinese men, nearly naked but for loincloths, worked like ants hauling bales and rolling barrels while others created orderly stacks all along the quayside. Orders were shouted in pidgin Chinese by European handlers.

No one noticed their arrival or paid the slightest attention to eight Yankees making their way landward carrying four large wooden crates by rope handles between them.

14

SHANGHAI

B athsheba Jaffe fought down the sensation that all eyes were on her.

Her dumpy tunic and baggy trousers, belted at the waist with an ammo belt and holster, served to hide her figure. Her hair was cropped above her ears, sprigs of black curls hidden by the white neckcloth that hung from the back of her kepi. She wore no make-up and had smeared a bit of dirt on her cheeks and chin for good measure.

Still, she had the feeling that somehow everyone around her *knew*.

She stayed close by Lee Hammond while they cut between the rows of sweating laborers until they'd wended their way to the foot of a broad embarcadero, which bustled with carts and wagons and countless pedestrians moving along with purpose. The embarcadero was lined with three-story buildings built in long rows. They all had signs hung from them in a babel of Asian and Occidental languages.

Bat watched young boys who were shinnying up lantern poles to snuff the lights atop them as the sun rose to light the harbor. Merchants called from carts, some banging pots and pans together to draw attention to their wares. One stood upon a box and swung live chickens over his head, held by the legs, and bawled his pitch to an uncaring crowd. A trio of drunken English sailors, supporting one another with arms about their shoulders, sang a shanty as they stumbled past. A quartet of men trotted through the mass carrying a fat man seated in an open sedan chair while a servant banging a gong ran ahead of the chair to clear a path. The carriers and the gong player were dressed in matching liveries of white silk trimmed in black and conical hats tied down around their chins. The passenger was an Anglo in a naval uniform of some kind, and he cursed the bearers between pulls from a flask. Other sedan chairs moved more sedately. These were covered boxes with silk drapes and gilt frames.

The team found themselves getting attention for the first time. Beggars thronged about them, open hands or wooden bowls held out. They were mostly children, and some had shocking afflictions. Missing limbs, missing eyes, scars from wounds, and the ravages of sores. Their clothes were filthy rags, their feet bare and black with ground-in dirt. They surrounded the team, preventing the newcomers from making any forward progress. Bat recoiled from them.

"Should I give them something?" she said.

"And attract *more* of them?" Lee said, trying to wade through the clutching, chattering mass. The Rangers had seen their share of desperate poverty in some of the shittiest corners of the world but never anything like this. The mob about them was growing, now joined by adult beggars perhaps sensing a soft touch in these brown-clad *laowai*, foreigners. The chicken merchant was here, shouting and waving his hens to create a snowfall of white feathers over the crush.

The crowd parted when a man taller than the rest pushed his way into the mass swinging a wooden club over his head. When the beggars failed to yield, he laid about with blows to shoulders and arms. A way opened to the team.

"*Hai! Hai! Duidelijk een pad, rotzakken!*" the man shouted before resorting to sing-song pidgin Cantonese, all the while with the clay pipe clenched between his teeth. He wore a white shirt and suspenders with a braided nautical cap slanted on his head. He had thick shoulders and arms and a ponderous gut hanging over his belt. The beggars and merchants scattered, howling curses as they retreated to a safe distance.

"English, *ja?*" the man said, grinning as he stepped up to Lee.

His breath was rancid with liquor and tobacco.

"Americans," Lee said.

"Yankees. Is good, *ja?*" The man eyed the team and their burden of wooden crates.

"Yeah, it's great," Lee said and made to shoulder by until the man stepped in his way, smile fixed on his face.

"You looking for something, *ja?* You are needing something, *ja?*"

"We're looking for pack horses. Mules," Jimbo said.

The man broke into a laugh that made his paunch wobble and face redden.

"He say something funny?" Lee growled, growing tired of this exchange and the Dutchman's attitude.

"*Nee! Het is grappig!*" The man snorted and wiped his nose with the back of his arm. "Only the army has horses. There is not a horse, mule, or donkey for sale in all of Szechuan Province."

"We need to carry this cargo inland to Nanking. How does stuff get freighted around here?" Lee said.

"All is carried by coolies. Plenty coolies. *Goedkoper*, cheaper than horses. A few pence a day, *ja*." The Dutchman nodded with enthusiasm.

"So, where do we find all of these coolies?" Lee said.

The team followed the Dutchman across the crowded embarcadero. The big man menaced approaching beggars and merchants with the wooden club to clear the way. They stopped to allow a double column of soldiers march by. They were

English redcoats with rifles at their shoulders and sweating under heavy packs. A whiskered non-com strode before them calling cadence and swinging a riding crop.

As they tramped by, a few glanced from under the bill of their white kepis at the mixed company of Yankees. The Dutchman brought them to the front of a long warehouse building where a crowd of Chinese crouched in the shade of an awning. They shifted and glanced upward at the newcomers. The Dutchman rattled off a string of pidgin at them. One of them, a chubby-faced man in faded red pants and a filthy blouse belted with a strip of black cloth, asked a question.

"You pay how much?" the Dutchman asked Lee.

"What's the going price? What do they usually work for?" Lee said.

"A ha'pence a week. That's five copper wen," the Dutchman said.

The chubby-face man stood and looked at Lee.

"Where you go, sir? Where carry cargo?" he said in a high, reedy voice.

"Nanking," Lee said. Chubby's face fell into a frown of deep disapproval. The crouching coolies muttered among themselves.

"Twenty wen a day then," Lee said. Less than twenty-five cents.

Chubby's eyes widened. All the men under the awning leaped to their feet.

"A day? *Stront!*" the Dutchman hollered. "I thought you meant by the week! *Verdomme!*"

"I know good men, strong men! Better than these!" Chubby insisted, stepping closer.

"We need eight men. Eight!" Lee said, holding up eight fingers. "Pick 'em out, Jimmy."

"Look at their teeth, *ja*? The puggy, *ja*?" the Dutchman said and curled Chubby's lip back with a thumb. Chubby put up with the indignity to reveal a double row of mustard-colored teeth.

"Puggy?" Jimbo said.

"The opium, *ja*? Makes them stupid with smoke," the Dutchman said, releasing Chubby's lip to point at the others with the point of his club.

Jimbo chose eight of the healthiest, picking the men based mainly on the condition of their teeth just as he would with horses. Almost two-thirds of the men had teeth black from the tar of smoked opium. Their eyes were dead as marbles and their skin like paper. One of the men he chose was Chubby, who told them his name was Ya Wu. The team took to calling him Yahoo, and he did not protest. Though he was insistent that he knew much better bearers than the low-born rubbish they had chosen.

"Let me bring them to you. They are strong men. Good men," Yahoo said as the others took up the load of the four heavy crates.

"We're on a timetable here, pal," Jimbo said, pointing to his wrist and realizing instantly that his words and gesture were a hundred years out of step.

"Just move your ass," Lee growled, and his tone got his meaning across. Yahoo took up a rope handle and the team, with their new employees, started away along the wharf.

"*Neem me niet kwalijk, gelieve, ja?*" The Dutchman said and held out an open palm in the universal language of "where's mine?" Lee dug in a pouch on his belt and dropped a pair of silver coins into the waiting hand. They were fakes minted by yet another Taan-owned outfit. Circular coins with a square hole in the center and bearing the mint marks of the Imperial Bank of China. The Dutchman's eyes gleamed wetly at them.

"*Veilig reizen, yankee vrienden,*" the Dutchman said, nodding and touching the tip of his club to his hat before turning to trot away to the nearest beer hall.

"So, which way do we go now?" Bat said.

"Damned if I know." Lee shrugged. "West, right?"

15

MUTE WITNESS

Yahoo served as a guide as well as a self-appointed head bearer. He chattered endlessly in pidgin English to no one in particular, informing them that he learned good English at school before it was burnt to the ground, and soldiers butchered his teachers. Who these soldiers were, he did not say.

"Teachers all killed. Fine teachers. Christian men of God. All dead now in war that never ends," he said as part of his unrequested oral biography. He began gulping in a high giggle and pointing to a merchant selling caged monkeys from a stall.

"This guy's either an idiot or pretending to be," Jimbo said to Byrus, who was also fascinated with stacks of bamboo cages filled with shrieking monkeys.

They moved through crowded marketplaces and across broad open squares, heading for a road that would follow the west bank of the river and take them to Nanking.

Inside the city, the military presence was more in evidence. There were sailors and soldiers from a dozen nations either on leave or on guard. French sailors in white uniforms, blue waistcoats, and canvas gaiters, and disc-shaped black caps on their heads. More redcoats marched in tea-stained pith helmets and belts and gear white with fresh pipe clay. Sikh cavalry in crimson turbans looked dour, their lances, long blades gleaming, couched in their arms. On one side of a square was a palatial building flying the American flag. Soldiers in Union blue jackets and white trousers stood at the ready by a pair of Gatling guns set either side of the entry steps of what was probably a consulate.

The Euro troops were vastly outnumbered by Chinese imperial troops. The soldiers of the Manchu emperor were even more varied than the western troops. Men waving huge banners covered in dragons, storks, clouds, and tigers, ran before trotting troops holding long bolt action rifles at shoulder arms. Men in crimson garb decorated with the character of the Qing Dynasty stood at every intersection and gateway.

Tartar horsemen with curved bows and packed quivers of long arrows on their saddles went past them in columns. They wore fur-lined caps even in the stifling heat. Each had a curved sword in his sash, and a long-barreled musket slung over his back. Their officer, riding in the front, wore a steel helmet trimmed in white ermine, and a cowl of glimmering chain mail. Their silk banner was the size of a queen-sized bedsheet and bore a stylized rearing horse stamping on a twisting serpent.

In their mile-long walk through the heart of the city, the team saw more soldiers in one place than they'd seen in all the years of their own service and deployments.

"You believe this shit?" Boats said in awe when the Tartar cavalry galloped past over the cobbles.

"Hell yeah," Jimbo said with a boyish leer. These trips to the past had turned him into something of a history nut. He was loving the spectacle.

"We might be in over our heads this time," Bat said, wary eyes on a clutch of white-clad spearmen glowering at them from a doorway.

"I hear you, lady. I been on six deployments, and I'm feeling like I've never been to war before," Chaz said.

Their little column made to a broad gate in the walls that surrounded the city. They joined a queue of carts, bearers, sedan chairs, and pedestrians awaiting passage through the gate. The way was cleared occasionally for military traffic. The largest group consisted of British troops in red jackets and plaid trousers. They were led by a pair of bagpipers and a flagman carrying a furled Union Jack.

Anyone coming into the city was being hassled by imperial troops in white pajamas and blue vests. Merchants had their wares scattered on the ground. Bundles were unraveled, and baskets tipped open. One man squealed in complaint and got the butt end of a spear in the teeth in answer. Others, especially women, were rudely searched. The only ones to escape the rough treatment were the occupants of lushly decorated sedan litters or those who dropped coins into the hands of the sentries.

To the team's relief, those exiting Shanghai were not subject to those kinds of searches and abuse. They were waved through by sullen soldiers barking for them to move along quickly. The sentries would not meet the eyes of the barbarians.

Once through the gate, the team passed through rows of trenches and earthworks that were unmanned, in ill repair, and many were filled with stagnant water. Dragonflies hummed over the weed-choked surface of the stinking pools.

"Shanghai's been threatened with a siege over and over for the past twenty years," Jimbo said, interrupting Yahoo's continuous commentary. "First by the Imperials threatening to throw the Europeans out over the opium trade. Then by the Taipings who kept promising to take the city but never succeeded."

"So, where's the war?" Chaz said, walking alongside Jimbo.

"It's winding down now. The Taipings are holding a few towns but Nanking's their capital. Most of the fighting is around the city. That's where the last of the Heavenly King's troops are," Jimbo said.

"Is this Hong Shoo-juan there?" Chaz asked.

"He's been dead for a few months by now," Jimbo said. "Dead from a stomach ailment."

"So, he's explaining himself to Jesus." Chaz smiled

Aboard *L'Arrogante*, the French gunboat anchored in the still water at a bend in the river, Mssr. Quentin Ratal, photographer of *Le petit Parisien*, stood atop the sloped roof of the ironclad and aimed his camera shoreward. A group of what appeared to be American soldiers were in conversation at the crest of the muddy banks, their entourage of coolies resting while the group shared their thoughts with one another. It seemed a likely subject for a photo with the forest of young trees on the slope behind to frame the grouping. In any case, he was bored and anxious to take a photograph of almost any subject.

He slid the plate home in the camera, set the tripod steady, draped the black curtain over his sweating head, centered the group of Yankees in the front site of his viewfinder, and whipped the cover from the lens, counting silently to ten before replacing it. He removed the smothering cover cloth and was pleased to see that the group was still relatively stationary. They would be small figures in the overall composition, but it would make for a fine photograph. Enough to justify his meager stipend from the *Parisien*.

Ratal removed the camera from the base of the tripod to take it below decks where he could remove it in his cramped cabin-come-darkroom. The collection of soldiers and bearers broke up their *tête-à-tête* to continue their long march upstream.

Jimbo caught Yahoo glaring at them, his face dark with rage, as he stumbled along carrying the crate of rifles with the help of another coolie. Yahoo saw that Jimbo was studying him. Within seconds, his face melted back into its usual bland smile.

Lee was walking drag with Bat. He turned to look back at the walls of the city. They showed signs of age and wear from either the ravages of warfare or time. The black barrels of cannon were visible along the battlements. Banners hung limp in the still, humid air. From the top of one of the towers, he was surprised to see a kite flying high in the sky, a waggling golden dragon with the morning sun sparkling off its painted scales.

The road took them through the earthworks and became a causeway crossing between vast flooded fields of paddies separated by earthen dikes. They spread to the horizon in either direction.

Countless men and women worked in the knee-deep water harvesting rice stalks, and baskets slung over their backs. They wore broad conical hats and worked with curved sickles. Young kids played along the dikes, throwing stones at ducks or chasing one another. Older children worked on the banks, beating the grain from the stalks creating mounds that gleamed white on the dirt. Some kind of bosses, in yellow robes and pillbox hats, rode on the backs of donkeys, calling out orders or just berating the workers for the hell of it.

The causeway forked left and right after a few miles and Yahoo led the team onto the smaller path to the right which led down through dogwood trees to the river. The Yangtze was wide and brown with boats moving along in either direction at center stream. Junks plowed west against the current, passed by steamships, paddles churning the water to yellowish foam. There were two-man fishing smacks anchored off the bank with men working nets and poles. Close into shore upriver a shallow-draft ironclad sat at anchor away from the current at the center of the river's span.

It flew the French tri-color from a stern mast. There was movement on the deck, and they could see shirtless sailors seated along the upper deck above the gun ports. Some had fishing lines in the water. The trail off the main causeway joined what looked like a towpath at the crest of the bank. Yahoo nodded and grinned and pointed, assuring them that this was the best way west, the best way to Nanking.

"We have a three-hundred-mile hump ahead of us to reach Nanking by the eighteenth of July," Lee said, surveying the path. It was occupied mostly by foot traffic. Wheeled conveyances and military traffic were up on the main road, a less direct route, and one filled with opportunities to be stopped by officials and asked unanswerable questions.

"Does anyone have an idea of today's date?" Jimbo asked.

"There's no calling home to ask," Lee said.

"I'll bet my left nut none of these bearers even know the year," Chaz said, eyeing the coolies seated now atop the crates resting by the road.

"Hold on." Bat fished inside her tunic to pull out a sheaf of yellowing paper. She held up a tattered copy of the *Hong Kong Daily Express*. The headlines concerned the visit of Giuseppe Garibaldi to London. The date on the masthead read 3 June 1865.

"I bought it off a stand in the first square we passed through. The vendor said it came across on a steamer sometime last week," she said.

"So, today could be as late as the thirteenth. We have more than a month to reach Nanking," Jimbo said, taking the paper and scanning the columns, fascinated.

"A month in this shithole?" Boats griped.

"Mo missed by over thirty days," Chaz said, reading the boxes on the back of the paper in Jimbo's hand. Ads for patented stomach bitters, cures for cathartic constipation, eyeglasses, and hair ointments.

"Don't bitch. We're on the right side of our target date," Lee said.

"A long way on the right side, bro. This place is crawling, right? One of us is going to come down with something," Boats said, swatting at a swarm of mosquitos that had taken an interest in him.

"We've had every shot in the book, sailor," Lee said. In preparation for their op back to a place rife with disease, they'd all had shots for malaria, yellow fever, rabies, typhoid, cholera, three kinds of meningitis, an alphabet of hepatitis, encephalitis, and tetanus boosters.

"Just keep your dick buttoned up and away from the local honeys and you'll come back fine, Boats." Chaz grinned.

"I still say there's shit flying around here that's not in the medical books, okay?" Boats said, crushing a bug that had landed on his neck, leaving a splotch of insect guts and his own blood.

"We still need to average twenty miles a day if we want to get into our target area with some wiggle room," Bat offered.

"And these boots are already killing my feet," Chaz said with a wince.

"Bitch, bitch, bitch," Jimbo said. "Do what Bruce did."

Byrus was seated on the bank, yanking off his socks. His boots hung about his neck on a length of cording.

"If I had his callused-ass feet, I just might," Chaz groused.

With a grunted command from Lee, echoed by Yahoo, the coolies lifted the crates and formed a column to follow the winding river pathway.

16

UNDER THE ALL-SEEING EYE

In the great and seemingly limitless pantheon of Hindu gods and saints, there is Visvamitra.

Gifted with special powers of sight, Visvamitra is a seer whose vision is not limited by the confines of time and space. His predictions of future events are unfailingly accurate as if the veil of time does not exist for him.

How apropos that Sir Neal Harnesh named his vast, world-spanning search engine for this demi-god of infallible prophecy. The power program of Sir Neal, hidden as a Trojan horse within the hard drives of millions of computers across the world, could see the past and present with the same degree of exactitude as the mythic figure born of the god Brahma.

In addition to continually scanning Sir Neal's vast collection of handwritten documents, manuscripts, letters, and journals, the program also searched for any changes in the online archives of thousands and thousands of print publications across the past eight centuries. The slightest anomalous change would be noted while Visvamitra churned through terabytes of data an hour, twenty-four hours a day, completing a search/review of every archive on the planet every seventy-two hours.

That is how Sir Neal became aware of the substitution, over one hundred and fifty years after the day, of a photo of performing jugglers in an October 1865 edition of *Le petit Parisien* with another image.

A photograph of American soldiers standing at rest in the shade of a grove of dogwoods on the bank of the Yangtze River on or about the fifteenth of June the same year.

"No more! No more!" N'itha shouted, stabbing at the remote control.

"Give me that!" Rick Renzi said from the hospital bed, taking the remote from her hands and tabbing the power button to turn off the John Wayne movie, dubbed in Spanish, playing on the tv.

"Good. It's good now," N'itha said and returned to cutting slices from a tequila basted chicken on the rolling tray by Ricky's bed. She was feeding him like a baby, and he was allowing himself to be spoiled.

N'itha did not care for television of any kind. Unlike Byrus, who had become a movie addict since his arrival in The Now. She found the images and sounds confusing and irritating. Recorded music did not have the same effect, and she had taken to Shakira in a big way. Caroline Tauber suggested that perhaps N'itha, being from a primitive Neolithic culture whose story-telling had not advanced past songs and spoken stories, didn't have the cultural basis to make sense of the shifting images on the screen. Byrus, on the other hand, had been exposed to some representational art and heard more complex stories as part of his mythology. It was a working theory—Caroline admitted that she could be all wrong. In any case, she was sure there was a doctoral thesis in there for some anthropologist. *If* their immigrants from the distant past were ever allowed to speak to an academic.

"Some of the potatoes, baby," Ricky said, and N'itha scooped up a forkful of twice-baked potatoes in garlic cheese sauce and stuck it in her own mouth, giggling.

"Funny. That's my lunch, and you're eating it," he said with an exaggerated pout.

She lunged forward to lean over him and lock her lips on his to share the mouthful.

"Okay, now I don't know if I want lunch or want you," he said, grabbing for her. She leaped out of reach with a pleased squeal. His raised leg rocked in the traction harness, sending a shock of pain up his thigh.

"Shit!" he said, wincing.

"My Ricky!" N'itha said, alarmed, and climbed onto the bed to cover his face with kisses.

The door opened, and a pair of men entered the room. A man in a doctor's white coat, the other in surgical scrubs. The guy in scrubs had weightlifter muscles that strained the sleeves of his shirt.

"Señor Markham?" the doctor said. Renzi had been admitted to the hospital under the name Robert Graham Markham. The orderly stepped around the foot of the bed to Ricky's other side.

"Yeah. I haven't seen you before, Doctor... Ruiz," Ricky said, squinting at the name embroidered on the breast of the lab coat. He pushed N'itha away. She looked displeased, sniffing as she backed away.

"Could you leave the room, please?" the doctor said to her. She came up against the rolling tray and her hand went out to steady it.

The orderly was kicking the brakes off the wheels on the bed and raising the side panels.

"Am I going somewhere?" Ricky said.

"Radiology. Your osteopath wants a look at how your knee is progressing," the doctor said.

N'itha remained where she was, eyes fixed on the doctor, nose wrinkling.

"Will Dr. Ortiz be there?" Ricky asked.

"Yes. He will be there," the doctor said as the orderly began rolling the bed from the place.

"My osteo is Dr. Soto. A woman," Ricky said, pulling a stubby handgun from under his pillow.

He fired two rounds through the orderly's skull, dropping the big man to the floor in a shower of blood and bone fragments.

With a howl of fury, N'itha launched herself at the "doctor's" back, a steak knife in her fist.

Ricky trained the .38 on the doctor, but N'itha was already on the man's back, legs locked about his waist, her hand rising and falling to stab the man in the side of the throat over and over. Her teeth clamped hard on his ear, blood gushing over her face.

They crashed to the floor together, the man in the white coat slipping in a lake of his own blood.

N'itha stabbed until the spray of blood from his wounds died away, and he lay still on the tiles. She was crimson with blood, still seething with rage.

"How did *you* know?" Ricky said to her, breathless.

"I did not like his smell," she said, the wrath melting from her face to flash him a bloody smile.

17

THE SWITCH

The team camped in a copse of mulberries at a bend where the Yangtze turned sharply west. They opened their crate of rations and shared salt pork and dried peas and carrots with the bearers. All were cooked in what Yahoo called "most excellent" rice.

Water was going to be a problem. The slow-moving river was rust-colored with mud. It was certainly loaded with all kinds of parasites that there was no protection from. The Chinese drank their fill straight from the bank. Jimbo filtered a bucket of the stuff through a double layer of cheesecloth, and the water that entered their collection bottle was still tawny. They filtered it a second time before boiling it over their campfire. They dropped a chlor-floc tablet and a squirt of iodine into each quart. It was a concession, and one they all agreed on. An anomaly worth the risk.

"You know we're all coming back with intestinal worms. No lie," Boats said, stuffing rice and pork in his mouth with his fingers.

"Like in Tikrit. One kebab and I'm shitting worms all the way back to the Green Zone," Chaz said, scraping a bowl with a pair of chopsticks.

"As much as I'm enjoying this conversation, I think I'll take a look at the view," Bat said, carrying her bowl from the fire to sit on a grassy ledge. Dusk was falling over the river. Lee followed and took a seat by her, a mug of hot tea for both of them.

"War is hell, but your mileage may vary," he said as he settled in.

"I don't have the same experiences you guys have. My time in uniform was different," she said.

"We were far away from home. Far away and for too long."

"I think that's the difference, Lee. I was *at* home. My second home anyway. I was in streets I was familiar with, shooting people who looked just like me."

"Regrets?"

"Not a one. They took a wrong turn in the desert a long time ago. Doesn't give them the right to blow up schools and hospitals and pizzerias," she said.

They sat quietly for a while, sipping tea and watching the lantern lights of boats crawling past on the surface of the river, golden under the light of the setting sun. From one of the boats, an armored gunboat came the tones of an accordion playing a sad song for the crew.

"It's pretty here. Once you get some distance from the misery," Bat said as the ironclad drifted south, the music fading away in the distance.

Lee snorted. "This is the worst shithole I've ever been deployed in. Neanderthal Nevada was better than this. Iraq was better than this."

"Jimmy seems to be enjoying it." She laughed.

"Jimbo is turning into a history nerd. It's killing that Indian that he couldn't bring a camera. He'd be taking pictures every couple steps."

"I admit the place smells. The river is like a toilet. And I think they put garlic on their garlic."

"And other stinks. Smell that? Take a good whiff." Bat filled her nose.

"Sweet. Like caramelized sugar and... oranges..." she said. "Black tar opium," Lee said and nodded to where their bearers sat about their own fire. Smoke drifted from their faces. They spoke in low languid tones to one another.

"So, we hired junkies."

"Beginner junkies, at least. Jimmy says they all still have their teeth. He told me the whole damned country's nothing but addicts. The Brits fought their way up the rivers, fighting the emperor's army the whole way just to keep the market open."

"That's horrible," she said.

"Same in Afghanistan. They smoked that shit like Marlboros. The stuff our coolies are smoking probably came from the same valleys me and Jimmy and Chaz humped chasing Taliban."

"It's always about war, isn't it? It's how we measure man's progress and mark history."

"It's a business, honey. Our business. And business is always good." He set his mug aside to lay back on the soft grass to listen to the wind through the leaves above.

They took four two-hour watches through the night. Two guns to a watch while the others rested and slept.

There were bandits roaming the surrounding country, taking advantage of the general chaos that war always brings with it. Lots of refugees on the roads carrying all their worldly goods, ripe for robbery. With the Taipings facing the end there would also be renegade units and deserters prowling around. And the relationship between western troops and the Imperials was uneasy at best. They could just as likely get jumped by their presumptive allies. This was not the time and place for relaxing their guard.

Their position was on high ground with the river to one side and open grassland behind. They opened the rifle and ammunition crates, so they were each armed with a long gun in addition to their revolvers. They wore belts and bandoliers holding a hundred rounds of ammo each. There were an additional five thousand rounds packed in the crates along with the two repeating rifles and revolvers that had been meant for Wei and Shan.

A white mist rose off the river, and they could hear the blasts of steam horns echoing out of the fog below. They ate the leftovers from the night before, downed some coffee, and rucked up for the next leg of the hike to the west.

"Hey, is it me or do our carriers look different?" Chaz said, standing to watch Yahoo gesturing and squawking at the coolies to get the crates packed and on the road.

"You want me to say they all look alike?" Jimbo said.

"I mean it, they're not the same guys. Except for Yahoo." Jimbo stepped closer and saw that his friend was right. He recalled one man from yesterday, taller than the rest, his long queue of bound hair secured with a strip of yellow cloth. He was not among the men lifting the crates now. There was another one, always smiling, who had a dark port wine stain down one side of his face and neck. He wasn't here either.

"I think you're right, bro," Jimbo said, stepping back.

"And look, they all have the same black sash now," Chaz said, pointing.

Yahoo noticed the attention of the two Rangers and approached them, grinning and bowing.

"Good morning, gentlemen," he said, head bobbing.

"What the fuck, Yahoo? Where's the guys from yesterday?" Chaz said.

Yahoo blinked at them in a pantomime of complete incomprehension.

"You switched on us. When the hell did you do that? These are different men," Jimbo said.

"Not. The. Same. Asshole," Chaz growled.

"They are much better," Yahoo assured them with hands clutched together before him. "Trusted men. My cousins. All good and excellent men. Much better. Most excellent."

Chaz jacked a round into his rifle and held it to Yahoo's belly. The man's chubby face grew pale and his eyes stared at the weapon in the big black man's hands.

"Your contract is up, fucker. You and your cousins move your asses down the river and don't let any of us see you again," Chaz said in a deeply dangerous tone that crossed all language barriers to leave no room to mistake his meaning.

Bowing and cooing, Yahoo backed away to where the coolies stood watching with blank faces. He yelled a stream of curses at them, stopping to pick up handfuls of dirt to throw at them. The others dropped the crates to the ground and fled down the slope to the river path with Yahoo chasing after, kicking and shrieking.

"Now we have to carry this shit ourselves." Chaz sighed. They turned toward the team to share the good news.

"Better than a knife in the back," Jimbo said.

When told of the change in personnel, Boats said, "I know sure as shit I didn't fall asleep on sentry last night. How the hell did they make the switch?"

"I have a better question," Lee said. "What happened to the guys they replaced?"

They learned the fate of the missing coolies when they reached the pathway along the river's edge. Seven corpses floated in the murky water, bobbing in an eddy swirling around partly submerged deadfall. Jimbo saw a length of braided hair coiling and uncoiling like a serpent in the sluggish current. The hair was bound at the end with a strip of bright yellow cloth.

BAJA JOYRIDE

The Toyota moved slowly on the pitted surface of a winding two-lane. The headlights were shut off, leaving Dwayne only the light of a full moon in a cloudless desert night. He picked his way around cavernous potholes and areas where the crushed gravel roadway had been washed away. The light of the moon turned everything silver and black all around them. The desert appeared to shimmer like the surface of a vast sea dotted with islands of rocky spires and towers of cirio cactus.

"We would pick the longest, narrowest peninsula in the world to hide on," Dwayne groused.

"Shh," Caroline hushed him from the passenger seat, speaking low so as not to awaken the baby in her arms or N'itha sleeping in the back seat, cradling Rick Renzi in her arms. Nothing was going to wake up Renzi, zoned out on the painkillers they gave him to allow Dwayne to shoulder-carry him to the SUV.

"We can go east or north. Three options," Dwayne said, quieter this time.

"East or north is two options," Caroline said.

"Option three is finding a place to hide and wait them out."

"Is waiting really an option? Time doesn't mean anything to these guys."

"We're sure that's who this is? They could have been someone Ricky pissed off. We've all wanted to kill him sometimes. *You've* met him." Dwayne eased the Toyota onto the loose sand to skirt a crater in the road.

"Samuel's warning?" Caroline said, head cocked and eyebrow arched.

"The guys who went after Ricky were local talent, not hitmen from the future. They weren't wearing those freaky bracelets."

The two men killed by Ricky and N'itha didn't wear the wristlet of seamless black steel that they'd seen on Samuel Renzi as well as other men who came to kill or abduct them across the centuries. The wristlets were transmitters that could be used to open rifts in time, personal control devices that activated advanced versions of the Tauber Tube situated in the future of a parallel timeline.

The pair lying dead on the floor of Ricky's hospital room were *sicarios*, hired gunmen. Dwayne found tattoos affiliating them with the Zetas cartel. He'd searched them while N'itha used a knife to cut Ricky's traction cables free.

"Sir Neal didn't see the need to send his own men." Caroline shrugged. "He'll send them now. They have a time and place for Ricky, and, by now, they know you, and I are here, too. And we're stuck here, in this time and only space to move in."

"And no way to contact Lee or the guys. And nothing they could do about it if we could. How'd Harnesh do this? How'd he zero in on us?"

"We may never know. Samuel told us they have massive search programs seeking anomalies in the timeline. They're alerted to any change. Then they draw lines right to us."

"Something the guys did on the current op?"

"Could be."

"Does that mean they're in trouble back in The Then? We

need to get to your brother somehow. Let him know to give them a heads up," Dwayne said.

"They won't have a transmitter this trip. Too much risk going back to a time that near to our own. That kind of tech would alter things irreparably if it was left behind or taken from them," Caroline said.

"Shit," he said, banging a fist on the steering wheel.

"The best we can do is stay off the grid and hope Samuel contacts us again," she said.

"Who wants to go camping?" Dwayne asked with a wry smile.

The Toyota moved on toward the mountains in the distance, a black smudge on the horizon like the shoreline along a sea of silver sand.

19

THE EVER VICTORIOUS ARMY

Their column, smaller now with the loss of the bearers, continued west along the river path. They'd consolidated the load into two crates. Each walked with a rifle slung ready and bandoliers of ammo across their chests as well as shoulder bags of gear. Byrus walked free, carrying the two extra rifles and their canteens. Bat took point, eyeing the banks above, the river edge below, and the foot traffic approaching from downrange.

"They killed those guys for their shit jobs?" Chaz said, sweating under the shared burden of one the wooden crates containing ammunition. He'd stripped off his tunic. His long underwear shirt was sodden.

"We've seen men killed for less," Jimbo said, following behind, a hand in the other rope handle.

"It's more than that. Where did Yahoo's cousins turn up from all of a sudden?" Lee said, trailing behind with a crate he carried with Boats.

"You think he's a spy? For whom?" Jimbo said.

"Or a thief. Who knows? A reminder that we don't have any friends here," Lee said.

"We need to find some pack animals," Chaz said, grunting as he shifted the load to his other arm.

"Or a boat or raft or something I can pilot," Boats called. Punts and smacks moved on the current close to either shore. Center current was taken up by a big side-wheeler belching black smoke from twin stacks, creating a rippling wake that swayed the reeds along the bank.

"Shut up and hump the load," Lee said.

A half day's march ahead, the river widened and turned north in a hooked bend. On the opposite bank, inside of the curve of the river's turn, squatted a fortress. Gun ports along stone walls atop sloping earthworks covered in grass. The guns were trained on the river and could cover any ships trying to round the bend from either direction. There was a pair of towers with tiled pagoda roofs and a gateway of the same design. A Union Jack flew from the peak of one of the towers. From the other, a yellow banner with a Chinese dragon snapping at a red sun.

"That's an imperial fort. But it doesn't appear to be in the hands of the Manchus right now," Jimbo said, lowering the Whitworth rifle. He'd been studying the fortress through the scope, weak as it was.

"I see the Brit flag. What's the other one?" Lee had an eye to a telescope of his own.

"The Manchu banner. That would be the Ever Victorious Army posted there. Mercenaries working for the emperor. Started by an American named Ward. The Chinese called him the White Devil," Jimbo said.

"We need to watch our step if he's in command now. Last thing we need is to be questioned by a 'fellow" Yankee," Lee said.

"He's been dead for a year or so by now. The EVA is under Charles Gordon at this point, an English mercenary adventurer who's going to go on from here to become a big deal in the Victorian era," Jimbo said.

"Yeah? Well, let's try not to become part of that legend, all right?"

"There's bound to be a marketplace near the fort. Maybe we can pick up some help with the crates."

"So long as it walks on four legs." Lee collapsed his telescope to step back to the others taking a meal break along the side of the path. They chewed jerky and cold rice, and Jimbo purified some more water for the canteens before they set out again.

A mile down the trail, they came up on a squat stone building by the roadway at the apex of the river bend. Bat stood on the shoulder of the path to allow the others to catch up.

"Looks like a checkpoint to me," Bat said, without pointing at the soldiers in buff-colored uniforms with red cuffs and shoulder boards, leaning on rifles by the stone building.

"We go around?" Chaz said.

"No. They've seen us," Lee said.

"They're probably collecting a toll," Jimbo said.

"Then we pay it and move on," Lee said, picking up the rope handle and lifting his end of a crate.

The men at the checkpoint regarded the approaching column with casual interest. They were barely as tall as their Enfield rifles. Buff tunics and pants with soft-soled shoes. They wore brown turbans and were clean-shaven. Each was armed with a broad-bladed cane knife that hung from their belts in a wicker scabbard bound in wire. The knives were a nasty cross between an ax and a short-bladed machete.

"They're Ever Victorious Army," Jimbo said as they neared. "They don't look Chinese," Chaz said.

"They're not. Filipinos. The EVA is a kind of foreign legion," Jimbo said.

The checkpoint created a bottleneck on the road, slowing the passage of pedestrians. The soldiers seemed content to watch the passing parade, allowing traffic to move past them without remark. Carts and sedan chairs crept past. Two silk-dressed women under parasols and behind fans kept up a tittering exchange from a pair of open litter chairs. A tiny boy, near-naked, led an enormous bullock by a ring through its nose.

The team picked up the pace, confident they were going to make it through without being challenged.

An officer in a powder blue uniform and clay-white belt and matching pillbox hat strapped on a shaven skull stepped from the shadows within the sentry building. He stood with hands at hips and examined the approaching soldiers through pince-nez specs perched on his nose.

He stepped into the roadway and spoke to Bat who was still on point.

"Who are you? What army? What peoples are you?" he demanded in accented English.

Bat turned with a helpless look on her face to the others.

"Who commands here? You will speak!" the officer thundered.

He was shorter than Bat, who stood five foot six in bare feet.

"I'm the officer here," Lee said, setting down his end of the crate to step between Bat and the officious pipsqueak with the crimson face.

"What army? I do not know this uniform. You are captain?" The officer, outraged, reached out a hand to touch the bars pinned to Lee's collar.

Lee grabbed his wrist with a snake-fast move. The officer's eyes widened, his mouth twisted, and his lips turned white with rage.

The lounging troops didn't need an order. They came alive to stand with rifles braced and bayonets pointed. There were a dozen on either side of the path with more trotting from within the sentry house. The officer's expression of rage turned to a contemptuous smile as he pulled his wrist from Lee's grasp.

"You will surrender your arms and come with us," the officer said, voice cool now.

"But we have urgent business upriver in Nanking," Jimbo said, dropping his load to hold his hands with palms open.

"I suppose that may be true. And you may continue your journey when the Pasha is satisfied," the officer said and waved a hand. Some of the soldiers broke from the wicket of blades to take the offered rifles and gun belts from their captives.

Carrying the crates, the team was led off the pathway at bayonet point down to a wooden bridge that crossed the river to the fort on the opposite bank.

"Who's this pasha we have to see?" Chaz asked.

"Pasha Gordon, I think. If I'm right, we're about to meet an actual legend," Jimbo said, though he didn't sound thrilled about it. The bridge ended on the opposite bank at another checkpoint with firing positions either side. They were constructed from stacked gabions, wicker baskets loaded with dirt and rocks. Jimbo saw rifles and lance points poking from atop the ramparts as well as the business end of a Gatling gun. The officer in powder blue was speaking to a big bluff character, two heads taller than him, a guy in mutton chops and a cork helmet wrapped in white linen. He wore a powder blue tunic like the smaller man, except his had sleeves and front, heavily embroidered in ropes of gold braid. In one enormous hand, he held an incongruous china teacup decorated with blue and pink flowers. A silver tea set rested atop a rolling cart manned by a perpetually grinning coolie who looked about a thousand years old.

"Oo this then ye bring me, corp'ral?" the larger man said, tipping back his helmet with a thumb revealing sky blue eyes in a brick-red face.

"They cannot say, sergeant! The Pasha orders all foreigners to be questioned. These *kano* have no answers," the Filipino corporal said, head bobbing.

"I see. I see. Bring the lot of them along sharp then," the large man said, waving the entourage on with one hand as he lifted the steaming brew to his lips with dainty precision.

At bayonet point, they were forced into a trot under the bridge gate, through a gap in a curtain wall and under the arched opening of the fortified gateway into the main fort. Open ports in the face of the gate bristled with the mouths of cannon. Inside the encircling walls was a wide-open courtyard lined along the edges with stables, tents, barracks, farrier sheds, and gun ramps.

In the center of the square was a wooden gallows that showed signs of recent construction. Eight forms, bound at the wrists and ankles, hung unmoving from the long top board. As the team was escorted by the feet of the hanged men, Jimbo glanced upward at them.

About the waist of each was cinched a sash of black cloth. And at the end of the row, a swollen tongue pressing against his teeth was a familiar face.

Yahoo.

20

STANDING AT THE DRUM

The team stood in the scalding afternoon sun at attention before a grand tent the size of a house. It was constructed of red silk hemmed with tassels of gold. Their weapons and crates of ammo and goods were stacked at the opening of the tent. The little corporal had disappeared inside the tent and emerged moments after a muted conversation with someone within. He yipped an order and marched his little troop of sentries away, leaving the team under the watchful gaze of other soldiers dressed in blue uniforms also trimmed in red cuffs and collars. These were westerners in kepis and neck scarves. They stood at ease, rifles cradled as they eyed the rank of prisoners warily. More troops watched from the ramparts, a bit of diversion from their usual afternoon posting.

"Who're we waiting for?" Boats said from the corner of his mouth.

Jimbo started to answer but was interrupted by a roaring voice. "Quiet in the ranks, youse!" bawled a squat man with three chevrons on his forearm. A distinctly American voice even though separated from the prisoners by a century. The man arched an eyebrow and spat a stream of tobacco in their direction.

They stood silent, sweat beading and skin burning while biting flies found every inch of exposed flesh. The soldiers guarding them kept to the shade of the tent's broad canopy and drank dippers filled with water from a bucket set there for them by a coolie.

After an age, a prim-looking officer in a black brocaded tunic and peaked cap emerged from the tent. The soldiers straightened and brought their rifles to port. He pursed his lips a moment at the sweating row of strangers before stepping up to Lee Hammond.

"You are the officer in command of these men?" the officer said in a clipped accent meant to be English but concealing a bit of a brogue.

"I am," Lee answered.

"General Gordon will see you now." The officer turned on a heel to lead Lee into the tent.

"Not until my men are allowed to get out of the sun and drink some water," Lee said, remaining at attention.

"What the devil—?" the officer said, turning back to raise an eyebrow.

"My men and I haven't broken any laws. We don't deserve this punishment. Innocent until proven guilty, right?" Lee said, eyes leveled on the other man's shocked expression.

"You're mad, you are," the officer said, outraged, the Belfast creeping into his tone.

"Our operation is being interfered with, and we're being held prisoner with no charges brought against us. You'll treat my unit with more respect, or your precious general can go to hell," Lee said, eyes fixed over the officer's head.

The officer's face turned red with rage. The soldiers in the shade of the tent fly looked at one another from the corner of their eyes. "And I'll be bringing my sergeant with me," Lee added and glanced at Jimmy Smalls standing rigid beside him.

The officer made a few noises from between pressed lips but waved them forward. Lee stepped to the tent with Jimbo on his heels.

"Give them water," the officer hissed as he strode after the pair of prisoners followed by four soldiers holding rifles ready.

A soldier came forward with a dripping ladle, holding it out to Boats, who curled a lip at it.

"No thanks, bro. I'd rather have my own water, okay?" the SEAL said, nodding toward the pile of canteens in the dirt by the crates.

The air was musty but cooler within the tent. It had a high ceiling and was vented at the peak to provide a draught. Mirrors were cleverly arranged to reflect sunlight into the interior, giving the area at the center of the tent the effect of being a theater stage revealing two figures, one standing and one seated.

A tall man stood by a campaign desk in a jacket of yellow silk girdled with an indigo sash under a belt of polished black leather from which hung a curved dagger and a revolver in a flapped holster. The man was bareheaded, with chestnut hair brushed back to a shine. A trimmed mustache on his upper lip emphasized his youth. He gave the appearance of a college student dressed for a school play. Only his eyes betrayed the man within, a seasoned warrior who'd seen his share of horrors. He held a thin volume of prayers bound in limp leather in one hand.

The second man was a Chinese of indeterminate age. He was dressed in layers of painted and embroidered silk robes that covered him from neck to ankles. His head was shaved, but his eyebrows were thick and pronounced. Long mustaches drooped from the corners of his lips. On two fingers, he wore long nail covers of silver that ended in cruel-looking points. He had a book open on his knees and seemed more interested in the words on its pages than in the strangers being ushered in at rifle point. Though upside down from his perspective, Jimbo could see the words of the book were in English.

"The prisoners' ranking officer and his second, sir," the Irish officer said, saluting smartly.

"Thank you, Haverty. Your men will stand by to escort this pair away," the Englishman in the yellow jacket said, closing his missal and setting it atop the campaign table.

"Sir!" Haverty barked and saluted once more before stepping back to join the guards behind Lee and Jimbo.

"You are Americans," the Englishman said in mild rebuke. "We are, sir," Lee said, giving this officer his due. For now. "We've had our share of troubles with Americans," Charles Gordon said. "Hard to determine where your loyalties lie, what with your own country at war with itself."

The seated man said something in sibilant Chinese, and Gordon nodded before going on.

"Prince Kung wishes to know if you were acquainted with the late Frederic Ward," Gordon said. "The Chinese cannot fathom the world beyond China's borders. They reckon it a small place where each man knows the other."

"We never met the guy, sir," Lee said. He heard Jimbo swallow hard beside him.

"Just as well. Though Ward was a man of courage and certainly possessed of a martial spirit, he was quite mad. It was a job of work to continue what he started here. A deuced job of work." Gordon sniffed before turning to the prince to offer a translation of Lee's reply. The Prince lifted his head from the book to give the pair of strangers a brief glance of bland interest.

"What is your purpose here? My officer tells me you are making way to Nanking. To what end?" Gordon demanded. All pretense at civility was over now. This was an interrogation.

"We were hired by a merchant back in Kowloon, sir," Lee said, stating the cover story they all memorized. "He has some goods, bolts of silk, in a warehouse in Nanking. He's paying us to confiscate it."

"His name?" Gordon said, raising an eyebrow.

"Hing Fat, sir. A silk merchant in Mulberry Street. He has holdings all over Szechuan province, sir."

"And is he aware that Nanking is currently invested with a half-million rebels likely to object to you visiting his silk warehouse?"

"He is, sir. But he's also aware that Nanking is about to fall to the Imperial army. He's paying us to get inside and secure his warehouse against looters."

"Six of you," Gordon sniffed. "Yes, sir."

"And you're quite certain that Nanking is about to fall?"

"For us, it's already in the history books, sir," Lee said. He heard Jimbo gulp again.

"Well, those unfortunates dangling out there told a different story, captain," Gordon said, his tone darkening.

"Sir?" Lee said, voice level, eyes focused over Gordon's shoulder as the man stepped closer.

"They were Taiping spies. They bear the mark of the Heavenly King on their backs, and they told us that, until this morning, they were coolies for you, helping you find your way to Nanking through our piquet," Gordon said, voice rumbling.

"Sir..." Lee began.

"Trust me, captain, I have cause to believe the word of those wretches over anything you might declare to be the truth." Gordon turned from the two Rangers.

"You're calling me a liar?" Lee left off the required "sir" this time. Gordon stiffened, composed himself and went on speaking in a professorial tone edged with menace.

"The Chinese excel in many areas of endeavor. But no more so than their attention to minute detail. You will find nowhere else in the world, a place where nearly every exchange, transaction, and agreement is so thoroughly documented as here in the land of the Celestials. If what you are promising me is the truth indeed, you would have already presented me with a packet of papers including your contract with the Hong Kong merchant, travel vouchers, and signed warrants from both the English in the colony and the mandarins of Szechuan." He concluded, one corner of his mouth turned upward, satisfied at his unassailable logic.

Lee began to protest, but Gordon held up a hand and turned his head to listen to the prince who was speaking softly, eyes still on the pages of his book.

"Prince Kung would see you flayed alive or perhaps quartered," Gordon said after bowing to the prince. "I assured him I would not even consider doing either to Christian men. So, you will hang with your fellow spies in the morning. Time to set your affairs in order for the sake of your eternal souls."

Lee took a step forward. Jimbo grabbed his arm. From the shadows of the tent behind Prince Kung stepped two Mongol swordsmen, curved swords raised. The muscles of their bare chests and arms tensed for the swing.

"See them to the cells, Lieutenant Haverty." Gordon sniffed.

The officer in the black jacket barked. Jimbo and Lee were prodded with bayonets back toward the white light beyond the tent opening. Jimbo looked back to see Gordon standing with his back to them, hands clasped behind him and the prince with head lowered, his attention absorbed in the adventures of Tom Sawyer.

21

DOWN ON THE BAJA

The camp looked like any other bunch of gringo tourists living rough on the Baja. A tarp stretched from the open hatch of an SUV. Camp chairs and a folding playpen in the shade. Plastic coolers and tubs, sleeping bags, and mosquito netting. A campfire of red embers surrounded by stones, a coffee pot bubbling at its edge.

The Toyota was backed into a sandy niche in some rocks well up a jeep trail. It offered shelter from the desert wind and protection from the afternoon sun. The camp was nearly invisible from the trail in a copse of paloverde and boojum trees.

They loaded up on canned and dried food at a market on their way through Migriño before hooking east into the San Felipe. The coolers were loaded with ice to keep eggs and milk good for a week. They had bags of cloth diapers and their luggage packed with changes of clothes. They were off the grid in a remote place with the protective camouflage of a family on an adventure vacation. It all looked like something out of an SUV ad except for the endless bitching of a guy in a leg cast.

Dwayne had unbolted the rear bench seat from the Sequoia to make a couch for Rick. He rigged up makeshift traction as best he could, using tent cording suspended from the lowest branch of a tree. They had a month's worth of oxycodone to manage Ricky's pain, and more importantly, his mood. At least to the extent that pharmaceuticals could blunt Renzi's abrasive manner.

"How long do we have to sit on our asses in this shithole, bro?" he barked at Dwayne, who was helping Caroline change the baby's diaper.

"You have to sit on your ass until that leg heals anyway. What do you care?" Dwayne said, folding the soiled cloth and stuffing it in a plastic bag with others.

"This is one fucked up escape strategy. We're going to sit here and let these assholes find us again?" Ricky said.

"We keep our heads down, and they can't locate us. It's about low profile, not doing anything that lets them get a fix on us," Dwayne said.

"It's Mexico. We have money. We could be in a five star under any name we pick with room service. But you want to play Eagle Scout," Ricky said.

"Look, Ricky, Dwayne is doing the best he can," Caroline said from where she knelt in the shade under the tarp, struggling to fasten the diaper on a ticklish Stephen. "We go to a hotel, or anywhere where there are people, and we risk exposure. We're not even sure how they're tracking us. So, we stay here and figure our next move."

"Motherfuckers from the future. What did we do to get them this pissed?" Ricky snorted.

"We stole Sir Neal's nuclear reactor and the time travel technology that he financed," Caroline said, lifting Stephen, wriggling, and grasping, to her.

"And we know a lot of shit he'd rather not have known," Dwayne added, snaking a beer from the cooler and cracking the top. "What would happen if we went public? Imagine that shitstorm. Some billionaire asshole trying to change the present by visiting the past, alternate universes. Imagine that."

Rick nodded. "We'd have more than this Harnesh dickhead wanting to kill us. That's real deep conspiracy shit there. We'd have the CIA looking to whack us over that."

"You're catching on," Dwayne said and took a long draw of Rolling Rock.

"How about one for me," Ricky said, holding out a hand. "Oxy and beer? I don't think that's a good mix," Caroline said. She was sitting the baby on the blanket and offering him a bowl of Cheerios.

"If it'll shut him up, I'm saying 'hells, yeah,'" Dwayne said and tossed a can from the cooler.

"Like having a brew is going to kill me after all the shit I've been through." Ricky easily snagged the can from the air.

There was a rustling in the brush. Dwayne turned, a hand to the Colt auto tucked in the waistband at his back under an aloha shirt. Ricky drew his .38 from behind his pillow. Caroline's free hand moved to the butt end of a shotgun lying under a baby blanket by her side.

N'itha stepped into the camp with a pheasant swinging from either hand. She'd returned to nature, to the familiar, on this getaway. Her only concession to civilization was a pair of cut-off jeans. Other than that, she was naked. She smiled at the others before crouching by the fire and began pulling feathers from the carcasses.

"How did you do that?" Caroline asked. N'itha looked at her, puzzled.

"How did you kill those birds? You don't have a weapon," Caroline said.

N'itha shrugged and picked up a golf-ball sized pebble from the ground by the fire. She held it up for Caroline to see.

"That's my baby," Ricky said with a dreamy smile, his beer raised to her.

22

THE CELLS

They were broken up to be shoved into separate cells. The cell Lee Hammond and Chaz shared was a forty-foot square cellar set in one of the fort's thick walls. A windowless box with a packed dirt floor. A heavy wooden door crossed with iron bands stood flush in the wall at one end. The only source of light or air was through a barred slot set in the door at eye level. The interior was stifling. The body heat of the two men turned the enclosed space into an oven.

From somewhere outside, the sound of men singing in chorus reached them.

"I know that hymn," Chaz said. "'Children of the Heavenly King.'"

"Nice to know we'll be lynched by God-fearing men," Lee said. There was no thorough search of their clothes or persons before they were shoved into the cell. Lee was grateful for that. Bat Jaffe's gender was still a secret. For now.

Because they weren't competently frisked, they each had clasp knife still concealed on them. Chaz had his in a sheath inside his boot, Lee had one strapped to his leg with surgical tape. In addition, Lee had a cutting wire hidden inside the leather of his belt.

No conversation was needed between the two men. When the door to their cell reopened, they'd fight. Hopeless as it was, they wouldn't walk to the gallows easily. They knew the others would have blades and other weapons squirreled away and would be preparing in the same way.

"You know what's weird about this?" Chaz said, seated along the wall watching Lee pace the four steps from one end of the cell to the other.

"I can't think of one damned thing that isn't weird about any of this," Lee said.

"This is our first one of these missions where we ran into people who speak English," Chaz said.

"If you call it that," Lee said. "That big guy outside of the fort? I needed subtitles."

"What was that? A Scot?"

"That asshole Gordon sure liked to hear himself talk," Lee said, leaning on the cell door, head canted to see what he could see through the barred slot. The corridor they were in ended in a dead-end of a T-intersection. He could just see a pair of guards moping where the two corridors met.

"Think they'll feed us?" Chaz said. "Or let us go to the latrine?" Lee said.

"This *is* the latrine," Chaz said and nodded toward the crusted wooden bucket in the corner of the room.

"I think we both know the next time these guys come for us, it'll be for the walk to that hanging bar," Lee said.

Lee was feeling the wall around the doorway with the tips of fingers. His nails explored the gaps between the stones. The surface of the mortar was brittle and broke into powder with a little pressure. Under that, it was spongy, gone soft from years of moisture creeping in to be trapped. He dug further with the blade of his clasp knife until the mortar was cleared away.

"We can loosen these stones," he said to his brother Ranger, voice low.

Lee and Chaz worked their blades into the spaces between the stones that framed the cell door. Within an hour, they had loosened a few. Another thirty minutes and they removed two stones to reveal another row of stones keyed in behind them.

"This is going to take a while," Chaz said, bathed in sweat from the effort.

"We have till morning," Lee grunted under the weight of a stone he was prying from its place.

They took either side of the doorway, working as quietly as they could, scraping away ancient mortar and prying hundred-pound stones from place to stack them in the center of the cell. The men had stripped off their shirts. Their fingers bled.

Gray light was coming through the bars of the view slot as they removed the last interior stone from around the doorway. They broke a blade doing the silent work of disassembling the wall. It took both of them to drop the massive lintel from atop the door frame to the floor without making a sound above their groans of exertion. The door and frame now sat braced in only the section of stone that fronted the cell on the corridor. Chaz tested the frame with a shove and a tug. It moved in place, a stream of dust rained down from atop the frame.

"On three," Lee whispered. They braced for the rush.

As one, the two Rangers crashed their shoulders against the stout wooden door. Their weight tore the door and frame from the opening, and men and door tumbled to the floor of the corridor.

They rushed to the right and down to the corridor's end where they overcame the pair of soldiers dozing at their sentry post. The soldiers, a pair of Chinese in red turbans, were clubbed unconscious before they knew what was happening to them. Lee snatched up one rifle, Chaz the other. Chaz helped himself to a curved sword hanging from the sash of one of the soldiers. Lee grabbed a ring of keys resting on a niche by an oil lamp.

They opened the second cell along the wall to find Boats and

Jimbo standing crouched and ready for a fight. Jimbo held a clasp knife in one fist. Boats had a straight razor open and held ready to strike. They relaxed when they saw their friends.

Lee moved to the third door and worked the keys in the lock to thrust the door open.

The cell was empty.

23

RUM AND THE LASH

"Damn it, Bat!" Lee seethed.

The center of the floor of the empty cell was covered in a heap of loose dirt. In a rear corner was a dark hole just large enough to admit Bat Jaffe and the diminutive Macedonian.

"Where the fuck?" Boats said.

"We found Bruce in a mine, remember? The guy digs like a mole," Jimbo said.

"No way in hell any of us are fitting in that rat hole," Chaz said.

"Bat! You hear me?" Lee called, lying on the floor, his face at the opening of the tunnel. His voice echoed in a room somewhere beyond.

"They're gone, bro," Chaz said.

Lee leaped to his feet and raced from the cell with the others following. At the T intersection, they hooked right to go deeper into the interior of the fortress, the floor sloping down into shadows thrown by the light of guttering lanterns. Jimbo took a lantern off the wall and turned the dial to lengthen the wick to throw more light. He shouldered past Lee to lead the way down.

The ceiling dropped lower, forcing them to stoop as they progressed.

"I don't know how the army does it. This is the opposite of an exit strategy," Boats said, bringing up the rear.

The corridor ended in a damp, musty chamber, the walls stacked with wooden kegs. There was a sweet vinegar smell in the air. Something puddled around a stopped drain in the floor. Boats touched fingers to a leaking tap and touched it to his tongue.

"Rum," he told the others.

The men turned to a scraping sound on the cobbled floor.

Bat Jaffe and Byrus, black with dirt, stepped into the lantern light.

"Looks like you guys found the easy way out," she said, white teeth gleaming from a filthy face.

Boats struck the head of a rum barrel with the butt of his rifle until it broke. The sweet liquor rushed through the break to make a river on the floor.

"What the fuck, sailor?" Chaz said, stepping back as the lake of spirits grew toward them.

"We're all together. Now we need a distraction," he said, grinning.

The fire woke the entire camp. Gongs rang. Horns and bugles sounded. Voices bawled. Deep in the belly of one of the fort's walls, an inferno was building. Men were roused from their sentry posts and bunks to form bucket lines. Spurring them to action was the knowledge that it was their own rum rations being consumed in the flames of a furnace. Smoke rose from the ramparts where the heat sought an escape. The opening to the cells and stores was sucking wind to feed the blaze.

There were some Welshmen among the troops who knew a thing or two about fires such as this one. They'd fought their share in the coalfields of Clee Hills and Flint. They directed the others to shovel dirt over the entrance to starve the fire's source of air. Hundreds of soldiers and coolies set to work with shovels, buckets, and bare hands to build a berm over the entrances to the cellars. A killing heat filled the air before the openings. A thick pall of choking smoke filled the fort like a bowl. A sergeant shrieking orders in two languages collected men in a line stretching to the water tanks. They handed along buckets of water to toss over the laboring diggers.

No one noticed the ragged band moving through the smoke toward the main gate. Not even Lieutenant Haverty who was sprinting by them, directing men forward, and shouting orders peppered with profanities.

Lee and Chaz trotted before the others, borrowed rifles in their fists. They followed the interior face of the wall, using tents for cover when they could. Every soldier they passed was running in the opposite direction to battle the fire.

"You know where you're going?" Jimbo called.

"We take the first opening we come to and run like hell," Lee called back.

"I like it," Chaz said.

They reached a sally port along the landward face of the fort. It was set in a smaller version of the main gate, topped by crenelated battlements. Faces spoked from the gaps between the teeth of the ramparts above—soldiers at their posts but curious to know what was happening within the fort. A quartet of uniformed Filipinos stood sentry at the inside post. They raised up on their toes, craning their necks, trying to see the commotion across the other side of the broad parade ground.

One of them, his red turban pinned with a bronze badge of rank, stepped into the Rangers' path and offered a challenge, rifle and bayonet extended.

Chaz batted the bayonet aside and took a fistful of the man's tunic.

"The fire's in the ammo dump!" Chaz shouted in the smaller man's face. "Get your ass out of here! The whole damn place is going to hell!"

The sentry's eyes grew wide, not comprehending all the words but surely understanding the urgency in the enormous black man's voice. He threw down his rifle and ran through the gate for the outside. His comrades took their cue and followed on his heels, flinging their rifles away and howling with fear. Lee and Chaz bolted after them with the others close behind. Jimbo, Bat, and Boats grabbed up discarded rifles. Byrus was satisfied with the curved sword Chaz had put in his eager hands.

The sally port exited onto an apron of land at the foot of a causeway leading over a wide marshy moat for the northern bank of the river. The Filipino soldiers dashed down the causeway, shouting in Tagalog to their brother troops to follow them. Soldiers manning cannons either side of the opening were clambering over their sandbagged embrasures to join the rout. An officer, blond hair under a tall peaked red kepi edged in braid, waved a saber and shouted in German for them to stand in place. He struck a fleeing man across the back with the flat of the blade, but the soldier kept going. He was ignored by his artillery teams who were running full out for the high ground.

The German whirled to see a strange collection of soldiers trotting by out of the smoke. His face twisted in disgust at the state of their filthy uniforms.

"*Wo bist du Piraten gehen? Nach rechts stoppen!*" the officer roared, pointing the tip of his saber at them.

"Fire in the powder room! The whole place is going to go boom!" Chaz shouted as he ran past.

The German stood, riveted in stunned surprise at a *Schwarzer* speaking directly to him in a raised voice.

"Boom!" Chaz repeated, hand cupped to his mouth as the little group pelted onto the surface of the causeway.

"*Boomen?*" he said, perplexed.

The team rested on the banks of a paddy dike watching a tower of smoke rising from the fort behind them. The sky was turning from gray to pink as the sun rose. They drank from their canteens, catching their breath after the five-mile run.

"What now? We're a month from extraction, we're broke, and all we have is what we're carrying," Jimbo said.

"Maybe that Gordon guy will hire us for his Forever Enduring Army," Lee said.

"Ever Victorious Army," Jimbo corrected. "We might work our way upriver as hired guns on a merchant boat."

"Riding shotgun on a cargo of opium?" Bat said from where she squatted in the shallows of a paddy washing the dried mud from her face. Byrus lay floating on his back, fully immersed in the mustard-colored water.

"We got off death row anyway," Chaz said.

"You guys don't know how close we came. When me and Lee were in the tent with Gordon? Prince Kung was there. He's the regent, the current ruler of China," Jimbo said.

"I thought they were run by an emperor," Boats said.

"They are. But the emperor's just a kid now. This Kung guy is ruling in his place until he's old enough. And the guy is one motherfucker I'd rather not meet again," Jimbo said.

"We were gonna get hung, bro," Boats scoffed.

"And that would have been *good* news," Jimbo said. "These Manchus don't let you off that easy. They like flaying, impaling, pressing, scalding, and all other kinds of sick shit where their prisoners take a long time dying. They can keep a man alive for weeks just for the sheer hell of it. One mandarin has a barrel lined with razor blades on the inside. Piss him off, and he has you stuck inside and rolled down a hill."

"This op was a clusterfuck from Day One," Chaz grunted. "We had more friends around us in Afghanistan."

"We need to find food. We need to resupply, rearm, and reorient our asses," Lee said, standing. "This deployment ends when we come back with that fucked-up mailing tube Taan is after. Our only way through this is to continue the op."

The others nodded in grim assent.

"I sewed a few coins into the seam of my jacket," Boats said. "Breakfast is on me."

"We'll order in Chinese," Chaz said to the groans of the others.

"Breakfast might be delayed, guys," Lee said, looking off toward the fort, a hand shading his eyes.

A mile back the way they'd come along the paddy dike, a cloud of ochre dust was rising into the sky. Points of reflected light bobbled in the cloud, the gleam of the rising sun shimmering off the point of lances in the dust raised by the hooves of galloping cavalry.

24

The column of lancers formed a circle about the clutch of escaped prisoners standing atop the paddy dike. Their lances were couched, razor-sharp points swinging in the direction of the six Yankees who were tossing their stolen rifles to the ground. Blue uniforms and white kepis, they were European riders and skilled at that. Their mounts splashed through the shallow water to enclose the sad souls raising their hands in surrender.

No cover, no place to hide, and only miles more of the long stretch of the dike before them. The cavalry would catch up to them before they'd run a hundred yards. Their five rifles were loaded with one shot each. Their bayonets were no match for mounted men with six-foot spears.

Lieutenant Haverty cantered his mount forward to ride through the ring of lancers. He wore a cruel smile as he drew a revolver from the holster at his hip and trained it at Lee Hammond's head.

"The general is most troubled, Yankee, and wishes you to return as his guest." Haverty chuckled. The grim faces of the lancers did not share his humor.

"Gordon still wants to hang us?" Jimbo asked.

"Aye. You'll be lucky to make it to a rope, though. You lot cooked up the lads' rum tot for the next month or two," Haverty said. "You might just as like get a bayonet in the guts for that."

They fell into line to walk back the way they came, escorted by the cavalry, aware every step of the oiled lance points dipping and rising in the grip of the riders.

"You will hang. Indeed, I will see all of you hang," General Gordon said, pacing before his prisoners in full uniform of brocaded black wool, the silver-trimmed scabbard of a sword banging against his leg.

The team was on their knees in the dust before Gordon's grand tent. Their wrists were bound behind them. Ranks of glowering soldiers stood behind them in the open on the parade ground. A haze of smoke swirled in the air. They saw the scorched length of wall as they were marched back into the fort. Coolies were spilling buckets on the still-smoldering timbers of the rampart above. A mixed stench of charred wood and burnt liquor clung to everything. Ash drifted like snow on the breeze.

"As much as I disapprove of strong drink, the destruction of military stores is a grievous act of sedition and of theft. I am sure you are aware that the men under my command had their patience sorely tested. Truth to tell, I am abashed that they brought you back alive rather than skewered on a lance point." Gordon rocked on his heels, looking over the heads of the prisoners to glance at the men under his command with a nod of tacit approval.

"I am tempted to surrender you to the mercy of the Chinese. It is only that I am a Christian man that I do not give into my wrath. Not even for as troublesome a lot as you. Trust me when I say that the gallows is a mercy compared to what the Celestials offer for a choice of punishments." Gordon now seethed, coming to a stop before Lee who was meeting the pasha general's eye without contrition.

"Do you have an explanation for your behavior?" Gordon snapped, eyes boring into Lee's.

"We didn't really agree with your sentence, Gordy," Lee said without a trace of irony.

There was tittering in the ranks behind them, cut short by a yelped order from a non-com. Gordon's brows shot up, and his lips parted, showing teeth clenched to breaking point.

"You swine," Gordon said, voice hoarse with rage. He turned on a heel to reenter his tent, swatting a dusting of falling ash from the sleeve of his immaculate tunic.

A bawled series of orders behind them was answered by the stamp of feet and the sound of creaking belt leather and boots tramping away.

Bat turned her head to see the parade ground emptying as the men marched away. Ten guards were left behind, standing at ease, rifle butts on the ground. Chinese troops in turbans, eyes hard and lips pressed in a tight line. The terrier Haverty strode before the soldiers, studying the backs of the kneeling prisoners.

"What now?" Boats said.

"Maybe it's poor form to hang a man before breakfast," Jimbo said.

Haverty stood shouting orders in Mandarin.

More soldiers, more Chinese troops, came at double-time across the parade ground to lift the prisoners to their feet and return the way they'd come, shoving the team before them with rifle butts. They were trotted to the foot of the gallows. Six nooses swung from the long joist running atop the uprights.

"Lee..." Bat began.

Lee turned to her, his eyes on her but his gaze far away. She nodded and allowed the soldiers to grip her by the arms. They were all pushed and dragged to the platform, eyes on the steps leading upward to the gibbet. But rather than be taken up the thirteen steps, they were shoved back against the support posts. Their bound wrists were secured to the posts by more cording. Another length of cord was cinched about their necks and around the posts, forcing their heads upright. The soldiers stepped back, leaving them standing bound in place. Their guards then took up positions before them, rifles cradled in their arms, and spoke in low voices with one another.

"Maybe you were right about breakfast, Jimmy," Chaz said. "I hope he's a slow eater," Boats said.

Morning passed into afternoon. The sun hammered down on them, the light blinded them. The thongs about their necks prevented them looking away. They leaned their backs into the posts, one foot raised and pressed to the wood, to take the weight from their knees.

The scalding heat, smoky air, and painful light gleaming off the parade ground's sand were making Bat light-headed, that and thirty-six hours without sleep, no food, dehydration, and the stress of an imminent death sentence. She fought to stay conscious. Surrender to a faint, and she'd strangle on the thong around her throat as sure as from one of the nooses swinging above them. As the sun drifted westward, it threw the shadow of the gallows onto the ground before them. She could see the silhouette of dangling ropes projected before her and wondered which one would be hers.

She turned to Lee, bound in place beside her. He had his face forward, eyes on the sentries who either sat in the sand playing games with stones or leaning dozing on rifles.

"Well, there's one question that's answered for me," Bat said in a croaking voice she didn't recognize.

"Yeah?" Lee said without turning.

"About us," she said.

Lee didn't answer.

"I don't have to wonder where you and I are going," she said and smiled to herself.

After a few minutes, Lee spoke.

"This ain't over, baby," he said, voice even, as calm as if he were asking her to pass the salt.

"Wish I could believe that," she said.

"Try praying."

"Is that what you're doing?"

"I was hoping *you* were. Your God seems the right one to pull us out of shit this deep," Lee said, turning his eyes toward hers.

A voice shouted a clipped order that echoed off the walls. Their guards became animated, moving in swift order to stand and come to smart attention, rifles clasped before them. Bat moved her head as much as she could to see the source of the sudden command.

A quartet of figures was walking at a deliberate pace toward them from the grand tent of the general. As they neared, Bat recognized General Gordon walking alongside the officious prick Haverty who was skipping to keep pace with the taller man. And with them walked two uniformed Chinese in flowing green silk robes, faces in the shadow of conical hats of white rattan trimmed in red.

The pasha general had decided to give in to his righteous wrath and hand them over to the mercy of the Manchus.

Bat remembered Jimmy Small's history lesson and shuddered.

25

HOMBRES

"We're going to need water today," Dwayne said, looking to the cargo area of the Toyota. There was one remaining gallon jug of purified water left.

"You think there's water here?" Caroline asked from where she crouched by the fire warming a pan of canned soup.

Rick Renzi was mercifully asleep on the bench seat. N'itha crouched nearby in the shade of the branches of a boojum tree, skinning a jackrabbit she caught in a trap that morning.

"Has to be a spring or a tank somewhere. Wish Jimbo was here. He can always find water." Dwayne shielded his eyes with his hand to scan the cliff face of white rocks above them.

"I will find water," N'itha chirped, wiping her bloody fingers on some leaves before rising.

"I'd feel better if you didn't go alone, honey," Caroline said to Dwayne.

"You sure?" Dwayne said, filling a liter bottle with water for the hike.

"As long as she puts a shirt on," Caroline said, eyeing the near-naked beauty now bent over the slumbering Ricky, delivering a farewell kiss to his forehead.

N'itha led the way along a ledge that broadened as it looped around a sheer face of rock. Dwayne followed behind, a half dozen plastic jugs hanging from his back, a line of rope slung through the handles. At his wife's insistence, N'itha wore one of Ricky's Metallica t-shirts. It would fit her petite frame like a dress if she hadn't cut the lower third of it off and knotted it in the front to expose her midriff.

It must be love, Dwayne thought—Ricky didn't kill her when she took a knife to one of his prized concert shirts.

Below them was a hundred-foot fall to where a tree-covered slope dropped into a valley lined either side by more mountains of green trees broken only by promontories and shelves of rock white as chalk in the high desert sun. Far beyond the peaks was the shimmering endlessness of sand and rock that ran to the Pacific Ocean invisible over the horizon.

The ledge turned downward after a sharp turn and into a deep crevice in the face of the mountain. It was wide enough now to allow a car to pass. N'itha stopped at the edge of a shadow beneath an outcrop high above them. She held up a hand to him, and he stopped behind her. Her face raised, Dwayne could see the girl's nose wrinkling, her nostrils flaring.

She was smelling for water. Something that Jimmy Smalls claimed he could do, but Dwayne always thought was a boast. With this girl, from an epoch long lost to the past, he was a believer. Caroline Tauber suggested to him that N'itha might not be entirely human, at least not one hundred percent *homo sapiens*. She didn't mean it as insult or slight to N'itha, it was a purely scientific observation. Everyone on the team was fond of the girl who was intelligent, spirited, and as tough as anyone they'd ever served with, but there was something feral about her.

Dwayne's estimation of her was only growing as she turned to him, eyes grave. Her hand went to the handle of the sheath knife on her belt. Dwayne set the chain of plastic jugs on the floor of the ledge and followed her around the wall and down into the cleft in the rock.

The pathway widened into a slope dense with trees and hedges of blue-flowered bushes. N'itha moved at a deliberate pace through the thicket without making a sound. Dwayne did his best to follow noiselessly, branches catching on his clothes and hanging him up. The slight girl seemed to glide through the bushes barely stirring a leaf or twig. She stopped and sniffed before cocking an ear. She turned back to him, pointing at her ear. Dwayne listened as well and could hear, somewhere ahead the chuckle of water over rocks. They emerged from the hedgerow onto a slope of gravel that led down to a place where water came out of a crack in the rock face to tumble down into a pool before following a course along a wash and vanishing into the woods below. They moved to the edge of the pool. N'itha stepped into the water and winced. Dwayne dipped fingers in and found the water felt ice cold. Constant evaporation in the desert heat kept the water near freezing.

"It's good. Are you okay here while I go back and get the bottles?" he said.

She nodded eagerly before pulling the t-shirt over her head and tossing it aside. He left her to wade into the chilled water and started up the hill.

The climb back up the slope felt longer than the way down. He found the top of the slope and followed it along the wall of rock to where he left the jugs. He startled some lorikeets on his way down through the hedges. They exploded upward as one, flashes of red and yellow like flames against the enclosing green. He stepped out onto the slope to see N'itha standing in the center of the pool, facing away from him.

Two men stood on the opposite bank, speaking to her. They each had a rifle slung over a shoulder on a strap. A large net bag filled with scuffed gallon plastic jars rested on the rocks at their feet. They wore ragged jeans and worn western yoke shirts with cut off sleeves. He saw a gleam of a gold chain at one of their throats. A Raiders cap with a curved bill on one head. A straw cowboy hat with a creased brim on the other. The most expensive article of clothing on them were their Nikes. Probably Tijuana knock-offs.

"*Que pasa, amigos?*" Dwayne said, walking down to the water's edge. Keeping his tone light. Just another dumb *gabacho*. His back itched where he could feel the butt of the big Colt touching the small of his back.

They looked from him to the girl in the pool, smiles unmoving. N'itha kept facing them, not turning at Dwayne's voice. In her innocence, she was doing nothing to hide her breasts from these *cabrones*.

"*Tu mujer nos estaba diciendo que estás perdido,*" Cowboy Hat said to him.

Good girl, Dwayne thought. She'd told the cowboy they were both lost. And they thought she was Dwayne's wife. No hint that there were others with them.

"Maybe you can point the way back to the fire road," Dwayne replied in gringo Spanish.

"We can show you," the cowboy said. His buddy nodded, returning his gaze to the girl standing in the pool.

"No need. Just point it out. We'll find it," Dwayne said, willing his hand to stay loose, stay away from the gun at his back.

"The trails here are tricky, señor. There is no easy way. You can come with us. We will show you," the cowboy said.

Dwayne started to object, but the guy continued.

"These mountains get cold at night, and your wife is not wearing much clothes. And there are *tigres* here. Very dangerous at night."

I'll bet, Dwayne thought. He shrugged like *What choice do we have?* and whistled to N'itha, tossing her the t-shirt she'd left on the shore.

After filling their jars and bottles with fresh water, they made their way away from the pool along a trail heading north and away from the place where his wife and child and invalid friend were camped. Dwayne weighed his options and the likely outcomes. He might have to kill this pair at some point. They could just be a pair of *campesinos* out on a hunt. Or they could be something else. So long as they were gaining distance from the glade where the Toyota was parked, he could wait.

A glance at N'itha told him that she was running the same odds as he was. He shared a look with her. She lowered her dark eyes to tell him that she would wait to move until he did.

26

BONA FIDES

"Devilish sorry, chaps. There seems to have been a lack of understanding between us," Charles Gordon said, his face twisted in apology.

He'd ordered his prisoners freed. Soldiers were sawing away the thongs at their throats and ankles, releasing them from their cruel bondage to the gallows posts. Haverty was directing the men with hushed commands and gestures. Canteens were offered to them.

The two mandarins stood to the side, faces shaded by their broad conical hats, a tall one with a long horse face and a stouter one, his robe making him look like a fireplug covered with a drape. The one with the horse-face struggled with a smirk, trying to retain his officious demeanor.

It was Shan and Wei, their unwanted chaperones, last seen swimming away into the icy mist of the manifestation field that brought them here.

"I pray you can excuse my actions," Gordon was saying as his men cut the thongs binding the captive's wrists.

"You tried to lynch us," Lee said, massaging his hands to restore circulation.

"You must confess that the nature of your company is unusual even for this mad country. A nigger, a Red Indian, a mad Irishman. I mean, sir..." Gordon trailed off with a smile of camaraderie between old soldiers.

"The general must be excused," Shan said, with a bow of his head. "The Americans can only blame their own impatience. They left without proper documentation."

"Aye. I informed them that travel in Szechuan requires the written approval of a legion of officials. Every step and every transaction necessitates authorizing by the serving mandarin, wang, or doyen. It's deuced inconvenient, but that is how you Celestials play the game," Gordon said.

Shan surrendered to a smile. He held up a vellum folio with a broken wax seal, tied closed with a strand of braided red silk through a silver clasp. It appeared to be packed full of papers.

Gordon began, "Of course, your goods and weapons will be returned to you. If there is any other consideration, I can provide —" Boats, his hands freed, stepped up to Lieutenant Haverty and drove a fist into the officer's face. Haverty plunged to the ground.

"From one mad Irishman to another, prick," Boats said, holding out a hand to help the man up. The lieutenant accepted the hand with a grin, blood in his teeth. "Accepted," Haverty said.

"Shame there's not a brother for *me* to punch," Chaz said to Jimbo under his breath

---

"Mr. Taan was very angry," Shan told Lee Hammond.

"I bet he was," Lee said.

"You would have won that bet," Shan said, frowning.

They were on the gun deck of an ironclad steaming north in the midstream of the river, a vessel of the imperial riverine navy on course to join the siege of Nanking. It was named *The Complete Abundance* in honor of the child emperor. Six twelve-pound guns, three to either side, sat roped in place at their ports. Shan paid passage for himself and his party. The packet of papers impressed the illiterate Han skipper with all its gold seals and stamps and boldly counterfeited signatures.

The crew of the gunboat was Chinese with an Englishman aboard serving to direct the cannon crews, a red-faced York-shireman named Carberry, a man in a perpetual temper. He occupied the ladder to the quarterdeck, leaning on the slats with a clay pipe clamped in his teeth, showing disapproval of the world and everything in it. His gun crews napped on the deck in whatever shade was offered.

The team was inspecting the contents of their crates. Most of their food, ammo, and equipment had been returned along with their gun belts and revolvers. One of the modified imitation Henrys was missing. Morris Tauber was going to have kittens when he found out about that. No one was suggesting another encounter with Gordon or the Ever Victorious Army. They'd trust a century and a half of history to swallow up the rifle.

"We'd be dead if you hadn't come back for us," Lee said, leaning on a gunwale, watching the butter-colored river flow past.

"I was given the transport documents. Mr. Taan did not trust you with them," Shan said.

"Taan is a chess player. He knew if we fucked you guys over, we'd be fucking ourselves," Lee said.

Shan nodded.

"What about Dr. Tauber? Did he freak out when you guys came back?"

"Frick ow?"

"Freak out. He was surprised? Shocked? He wasn't expecting it?"

"Yes, he was most perplexed and excited. Mr. Taan under-stood from this that the doctor knew nothing of our plan," Shan said.

"It was a last-minute inspiration," Lee said.

"Any more such inspirations and Mr. Taan will have your friend shot," Shan said, no trace of a phantom smile on his face.

"Taan understands this operation has its risks, right? You or Wei could catch a bullet."

"Then it is in your interest to see that nothing like that occurs," Shan said, walking away.

They steamed north and west against the current, following the circuitous course of the Yangtze.

The traffic coming toward them, bound for Shanghai, was mostly western vessels flying flags of European monarchies with the occasional Stars and Stripes. Aboard many of them, the decks were packed to the rails with troops. The fighting up north was being left to the Chinese to sort out. Nanking was the last Taiping stronghold. The siege there would be carried through by the Imperial troops, and, once inside, the slaughter would be near-total. The European powers decided they wanted no part of what would be an ugly ending, even for them, to the bloodiest war in human history. It was felt, diplomatically speaking, that it would be best for the regency in Peking to have this victory to themselves in order to restore the dignity stolen from them over the past decade and a half by a war with the English and French and a bloody rebellion from within. So, John Bull and Johnny Crapaud and Billy Yank were steaming back to the coast. Even Pasha Gordon and his mixed army of mercenaries were folding their tents and calling it a win all around.

Down the river roads on either bank marched mile after mile of refugees, wheeling, carrying, and dragging their possessions. The farther north the gunboat traveled, the thicker the press of the forsaken grew. More than once, columns of Imperial cavalry came along the road. Men in lacquered bamboo armor of red and black carrying lances with colorful banners fixed to them and shining shields with brass faces. They whipped a path clear through the wretched parade with the blades of their swords.

Moving toward the battle at Nanking, along with *The Complete Abundance*, were troopships of Imperials, junks loaded with supplies of food, feed, gunpowder, horses, and coolie laborers. All was being fed into the maw of the largest land battle ever fought on the planet. A combined order of battle of a million men set against one another for one final conflict to end the heavenly reign of a man already dead for months.

27

RIVER OF THE DEAD

On their second day upriver, the gunboat rounded a headland to the sounds of gunfire ahead. Carberry bawled his crew to quarters, shrieking what was probably barbaric Mandarin to the ears of his men. His orders were salted with curses in English just as raw. The barefoot men, roused from their naps and highly animated, scurried this way and that to their assigned guns. They loaded the port and starboard guns with powder and grape and rammed the charges home.

"Run out the guns! Run 'em out, ye yellow bastards! God damn yer soulless hides! Buggerin' gong-farmers!"

The team was roused from sightseeing on deck or resting below. They rushed to the quarterdeck, startling the pilot at the wheel, a Kowloon skipper in red silks who wore a sash with a pair of Adams revolvers shoved in it.

Chaz chambered a round in his rifle and watched the point of the headland as more and more of the river beyond was exposed. The crack of rifle fire echoed over the water toward them.

"See anything?" he said to Jimbo, who was sighting through the scope of the long-barreled Whitworth. Byrus was crouched by Jimbo's blind side, gladius drawn and ready in his fist.

"I see gun smoke on the water. I can't see what's making the noise. There's movement in the reeds along the bank," Jimbo said.

"Wish we had more practice with these rifles," Chaz said. The only shakedown they'd been able to give the new weapons was in a makeshift shooting range below decks on the *Raj*. They ran a hundred rounds through each rifle, familiarizing themselves with the weapons. The targets were only fifty feet distant, backed by sacks of sand. Hardly a test of their accuracy.

"Maybe we'll get some now," Boats said, swinging his rifle one-handed by the lever to jack a round home.

"You looked like John Wayne there, sailor," Chaz said.

"The Duke used blanks. It's a good way to shoot yourself in the foot," Jimbo said.

A flurry of shooting sounded from ahead. They all sighted their weapons. Down on the gun deck, Carberry paced behind his crews, urging them in his own fashion to stay steady.

"Ready to port! Ready to starboard. Sight targets and fire on my signal, ye boss-eyed buggers!" he shouted. Following behind him was a Chinese in white pajamas and a black kepi trimmed in white with crossed cannons in gold brocade atop the cap. This man acted as translator, relaying Carberry's barked orders in a soft, almost apologetic, tone to the gun crews.

The prow of the *Abundance* cleared the headland. A hundred yards ahead an ironclad flying the French tricolor was anchored close to shore. Men stood on the upper decks firing muskets into the air. Jimbo lowered his Whitworth and stretched his telescope to fix it on the craft. Through the lens, he saw a thick screen of birds high in the air above the other boat. Ducks. Along the bank, naked coolies were plunging around in the reeds retrieving fallen fowl from the water. They would then swim out to the French gunboat and toss the birds upward in exchange for coins thrown down to them.

"False alarm. The frogs are hunting out of season," Jimbo said, lowering the telescope.

SONS OF HEAVEN

"Doesn't mean we can't have some real target practice," Chaz said and shouldered his rifle. Boats, Lee, and Bat did the same. They banged away at the flock of ducks passing by overhead and brought down a number. Wei joined them, nailing a mallard soaring high above the mast tops. The French hallooed and called out their congratulations as ducks splashed into the muddy water off the port side of the *Abundance*.

Down on the deck, Carberry was shrieking after his gun crew who were, to a man, diving into the water to retrieve the game floating by. His second called after the men, wheedling for them to obey their master. They returned to haul themselves back aboard, tossing duck carcasses to the deck before them. They held them up, all smiles for the Yankees to see, ignoring the apoplectic Englishman going hoarse with rage.

"Anyone for Peking duck?" Bat said, grinning.

They steamed past the first floaters on the morning of the third day.

Bloated corpses, swollen with corruption, came down with the current. Fish swarmed around them, giant carp by the thousands feeding on the rotting flesh. Carrion birds massed along the banks where bodies became trapped in reeds and eddy pools. Unrecognizable collections of rotting flesh that could only be distinguished by size as men, women, or children. All were headless, even infants.

There were human scavengers as well. Peasants, heads wrapped in scarves, waded into the shallows with long staffs to hook bodies. They dragged them to shore where women, with faces covered in mufti, stripped the dead of clothing. Other women spread the sodden garments upon rocks to dry.

As they moved upriver, the number of bodies grew, sometimes gathering in grotesque islands of the dead with ravens

141

perched atop them, gorging. The sheer number of the slain created an unavoidable impasse, their bodies thumping along the hull as the prow of the *Abundance* cut through the mass. The crew bent over the gunwales to clear corpses from the waterline with poles.

They wrapped cloths about their mouths and noses, dousing the cloth in rum to cut the rancid smell. The stink got on their skin and their clothes and clung to every surface. The Chinese crew lit joss sticks and set them along the decks to create a miasma of flowery herbal scents. It only served to take the edge off the stench of decomposition.

Not all the dead were waterborne. In the afternoon, they passed what looked like a black wall running down the eastern bank. As they neared it, the smell of putrefaction came over the water in a noxious fog. The wall was a stack of corpses that looked to be at least eight feet high. It took the gunboat a full ten minutes to pass to the end of the wall—roughly over a mile of decomposing humanity.

The team stood on deck watching the massive heap of dead recede behind them.

"Them poor Chinee buggers," Gunnery Officer Carberry said, a rare note of sympathy in his voice.

"Who did that?" Bat's eyes above the face scarf were rimmed in red. Lee was stoic beside her.

"Taipings. Qing troops. Both. This is a war of annihilation," Jimbo said. "Anyone caught in the middle is collateral. There'll be thirty million dead by the time this is over. Hundreds of cities were erased. Total extermination."

"And we're heading into the heart of it," Bat said, resigned.

"With people, we can't trust," Jimbo said, glancing toward Shan up on the quarterdeck, amused by Wei violently puking over the railing.

"They're as interested in seeing this op succeed as we are. We can trust them on this side of the divide," Lee said.

"Once they get that relic we're after they can fuck us and leave us for dead here in The Then," Chaz said, taking his eyes from a tangle of corpses propelled into an obscene swirling pattern by the bow wave of the *Abundance.*

"We're going to have to get our hands on it first. It's the only bargaining chip we're going to get," Lee said.

"And what's to stop them gunning us down once we get back to the *Raj*? Kill Mo, Quebat, Parviz, Geteye and the whole damn crew," Chaz said.

"That's something we need to work out before we get back to Shanghai. We have advantages here. It's a matter of working out how to use them," Bat said.

"All this for Genghis Khan's diary?" Chaz said.

"I have a feeling it's a whole lot more than that, bro," Jimbo said. "A whole lot more."

The river ahead was broken up by islands at the center. The skipper called orders through a speaking tube set by the steering column. The engine choked and sputtered, The stacks belched black soot, and a high squeal of metal on metal sounded from inside the iron-armored paddle-box as the blades slowed by half. The bow swung to port then righted as the captain turned the wheel to guide them along the broadest channel running along the western bank.

A mate was ordered forward to drop a weighted line into the water at the bow. The end was dipped in sticky tallow. He let loose the knotted rope, calling out the depth at regular intervals. He hauled up the tallow end to eyeball remnants of the riverbed.

"No bottom!" the sounder called back in English. He repeated this three times, holding the rope to trail under the keel. The tallow came back clean each time.

"Deep four!" he shrieked. The skipper repeated the same.

"Half three!" the sounder cried, voice rising higher. It came out as "hoff twee!"

The skipper screamed into the end of the voice pipe, and the rumble of engines dropped to a purr. The walking beam clunked to a stop. The spin of the paddles stopped with a jerk then they were free to turn lazily with the current, moving dead slow. The skipper squawked for help. Two mates leaped to the wheel to help him turn the boat into the center of the narrowing channel. Shan left the stricken Wei to lend a hand, holding the wheel in place against the increasing force of the river. The current was pressing against the bow with greater strength as its way south was forced between the closing banks.

The skipper shrieked an order, and the sounder hauled back his line, counting each knot as it slid between callused fingers.

"Mark three!" the sounder bawled back.

"Jesus, that's three fathoms. We're aground sure if that heathen can't keep the keel centered," Carberry breathed, teeth clamped on the end of his clay pipe.

The sounder called out again. This time it was a gargled cry cut short when he dropped to the deck with the shaft of a long black arrow through his neck. The iron plates rang with the patter of steel arrowheads. More shafts arced down to stick humming in the deck planks. Sparks struck off the iron plating near Boats' head— the shaft caromed away at an angle to lodge in the base of a mast.

"Guns! Guns! To quarters, lads!" Carberry shouted.

Lee and Bat drew side arms and fired through rifle ports set along the port side. The rest of the team scrambled for their rifles, stacked close at hand.

"You see them?" Lee called, levering the big Remington at the near bank, squinting through the gun smoke.

"I damn sure do!" Bat replied.

Horsemen galloped along a broad muddy bank. Hundreds of them in plate armor and helmets that came to a point like a wizard's cap. They were armed with recurve bows, weapons of massive power and astonishing range. As they rode, they loosed a storm of arrows at the ironclad. The black shafts rose in the air to drop down with an unerring trajectory onto the open deck of their target. Not a single missile fell short or long to drop into the river. Bannermen rode along with the archers trailing long ribbons of black cloth and a broad yellow flag with an ornate crimson cross resting on a bench, the symbol of the Heavenly Kingdom.

28

THE COMPOUND

D wayne was wishing he'd taken his own advice, the Lee Hammond approach. That solution wasn't workable now.

It looked like a humble farming village as seen through the trees from above. Rundown hooches of adobe and wood planks. The largest structure was a hangar with a steel roof rusted orange. The whole collection of buildings was nestled in a ravine with one road leading out to the desert. The houses were set up off the ground with crawlspaces beneath, built that way because the rare cloudburst would turn this gully into a river.

He exchanged looks with N'itha the whole way down the trail from the ridgeline, following the two *campesinos* walking ten paces ahead. It was a silent communication, N'itha suspicious and looking to him for direction. His eyes stayed calm, moving from the backs of their escorts to the buildings below.

The place looked innocent enough. A woman was hanging wash outside a shed. Kids played tag in a dirt yard between houses. Dogs slept in the street. Men sat in the shade of porches, drinking beers from a cooler. Music played from a boombox somewhere. Looked like siesta time on the ranchero.

As they were brought farther along the dirt road, the village started looking more like a compound. The kids' game of tag consisted of throwing empty shell casings at one another. The spent brass littered the ground everywhere. The dogs sleeping in the road were pit bulls with chain collars. The men sipping brews in the shade had rifles close at hand. Dwayne saw an AK or two among them. The music Dwayne recognized was a *corrida* celebrating the life of cartel hero El Chapo. The only innocent aspect of the place seemed to be the woman hanging laundry. Dwayne noticed telltale pink stains splashed on the sheets.

The men stepped out from under the porch to meet the newcomers in the center of the street. Four young guys like the pair leading them. A fifth guy, older, the obvious *jefe*, shirtless under a denim vest. He was jangling with gold chains on a broad chest that dropped to a beer gut. One of the young guys was almost as tall as Dwayne and looked mentally challenged, a sloppy grin fixed on his face. More troubling was the AK cradled in his arms like a baby. A sixth man stayed back on the porch, rocking on a chair with a shotgun across his knees.

"That beer looks good," Dwayne said, nodding at the dripping bottle held by one of the men, a skinny guy in snakeskin boots.

They all laughed except *el jefe*. Maybe Dwayne's gringo Spanish amused them. But he knew that wasn't it. He shot N'itha a glance. She tilted her head at him and narrowed her eyes.

Eyes still on his guests, the *jefe* held out a hand to one of his compadres.

"Apple," he said. A guy in a t-shirt, with a faded Estrella beer logo on it, fished in his jeans and came out with an iPhone that he handed over. *El jefe* held the phone aimed at Dwayne then turned his head while the others offered advice on how to use it.

"Stay here no matter what," Dwayne said low to N'itha. He swung the rope running through the jug handles and flung them into the tight knot of Mexicans before turning to run.

He hared over the dusty street toward a tumbled down shack with a collapsed roof and a veranda of sun-bleached wood running before it. There was shouting behind him. And barking dogs. He tensed for a bullet. Or the vise-like clamp of jaws on his leg. He could hear them rushing after him. Dwayne dropped to his belly at the front of the veranda, hoping it looked like he tripped. One of the men chasing him let out a whoop.

Dwayne rolled into the shadows under the slats and into the crawlspace under the shack. He was hidden from sight for a second or two. He could see the boots and sneakers trotting toward him. Ahead of them, a dog's paws kicked up the sand. Dwayne yanked the .45 from his waistband. He laid it on the ground. Before they grabbed him by an ankle, he covered it over with sand. They pulled him into the light.

The *jefe* came jangling up, puffing hard, to deliver a weak kick to Dwayne's side. That started the others kicking. The toes of boots and sneakers swung at him. He rolled with the kicks, giving a yelp with each one. As long as he kept them kicking, they'd leave the dog out of it. The animal was up on back legs, whimpering to get at him. Slobber flew in thick ropes from its snapping teeth. A man with weightlifter muscles and a Pemex ball cap was holding the beast back with a leather strap.

"Get him up! Get him up!" *El jefe* stepped back and aimed the smartphone at Dwayne again.

The others hauled the Ranger to his feet. He could see N'itha standing in the street, her arm locked in the grip of the idiot with the Kalashnikov.

A fist gripped Dwayne's hair and yanked his head back. He could hear the whirr and click from the smartphone as the boss man took snaps of Dwayne's face. They hauled him along back to where *el jefe* took some shots of N'itha. She looked at Dwayne the whole time, eyes open and pupils still.

"How do I do this?" *el jefe* said, leaning to hold the phone up to the guy in the Estrella shirt.

"What are you trying to do?" Estrella said.

"Send these pictures. To this place," *el jefe* said, squinting hard at the screen.

"Let me do it," Estrella said and took the iPhone. His fingers flew over the screen. After a second, he held the phone out to his boss.

"It is sent. See," he said, and the boss nodded, taking the phone back.

In under thirty seconds, all were waiting in the shade of the porch with fresh beers cracked open. The phone came alive in *el jefe's* hand with a few chords of a pop song. He stepped away into the street to hold it to his ear, listening a while, muttering replies. He came back, tossing the phone to Estrella.

"He is one of the ones they want," *el jefe* said, waving a hand at Dwayne.

"And the bitch?" said the weightlifter in the Pemex cap. "They don't know her." *El jefe* shrugged.

The weightlifter was across the porch in a single stride, shouldering another guy to the floor. He snatched N'itha up by the elbow and walked her from the porch toward a shed next door. Dwayne felt the sole of a boot press down on his chest. The men on the porch whistled and stomped.

"Don't break her, Jorgito!"

"She is small! Save some for us!"

From the floor, Dwayne could see through the porch slats. N'itha was being walked away, her toes barely touching the ground. She didn't look back.

"Bossman," Dwayne said in English. The others turned to him. *El jefe* leaned on the porch rail, in the middle of lighting a cigarette. "These men you called. The men coming for me. You don't know them," Dwayne said, returning to Spanish.

"One gringo same as the other." *El jefe* shrugged.

"They're not law or CIA or anything else you think they are. Whatever they promised you is a lie," Dwayne said.

"A lie?" *el jefe* said and stooped to blow a stream of smoke into Dwayne's sweating face.

"They'll take me from you and kill everyone here. Tell me I'm lying."

"You are lying." *El jefe's* smile showed teeth capped in silver.

"We'll see who's lying, motherfucker," Dwayne said, in English, but the other man took his meaning and leaned closer.

"I should believe a coward? A *maricón* like you? These gringos want you alive. But it is many hours until they get here, and my cousins are *muy cachondo*, eh? Maybe they cannot wait until Jorgito is finished with the girlfriend. Maybe I let them have you."

El jefe swiped a hand across Dwayne's face and grunted an order to the others. Two men lifted Dwayne by the arms. They dragged him toward a steel-walled shed across the street.

Dwayne resisted enough to put on a show for them. He looked at the hooch that N'itha had been taken to. No sounds came from inside.

The men hunting him, hunting Caroline as well, wouldn't be here for hours. It would be full dark by then. He knew all he needed to know.

29

AMBUSH

A rrowheads raised a drumming cacophony along the iron hull of *The Complete Abundance.*

"They're Taipings! A cavalry screen to harass reinforcements!" Jimbo called as he sighted the Whitworth through a rifle port. Byrus crouched by his side, sword drawn and useless against the archers on the raised bank.

"Who the hell cares?" Boats said, standing fully exposed to work the lever of his rifle from the hip. He sent a stream of lead at the riders less than a hundred yards away. A shaft came close enough to catch in the cloth of the SEAL's tunic.

"Get down, asshole!" Chaz called from where he was kneeling at a port taking careful aim at the cavalry. The horsemen were matching the speed of the slowing gunboat to send a steady stream of missiles their way. Chaz sighted on a guy standing in his stirrups, sending nocking arrow after arrow from packed quivers hanging either side of his saddle. A squeeze of the trigger and the bowman rolled off the saddle to be trampled by his comrades' mounts.

Jimbo set sights on an officer riding at the lead of the pack. His helmet was rimmed in gold that flashed in the late afternoon sun. The guy was waving a curved sword, his mouth open to call orders, curses, or encouragement. The Whitworth boomed, the barrel rising high with the force of the .50 caliber Minié ball launched from it on a plume of white. He waved a hand to clear the dense fog of sulfur smoke. The guy in the gold helmet was down and had dragged his mount to the ground with him. Riders coming behind rode headlong into the tangle, going down themselves on the muddy bank. Some spilled off the slope to the water. The hail of arrows continued unabated as the column wheeled around the welter of men and beasts to keep stride with the ironclad.

The skipper stayed at the wheel on the exposed quarter-deck. Two of his mates lay on the deck, skewered through with arrows. The skipper had a shaft through his arm but still held fast to the wheel, roaring orders into the voice pipe. Shan and Wei stood to the gunwales firing their rifles, delivering deliberate fire on the mounted archers. The deck around them was a forest of arrow shafts with more missiles tearing the air around them.

A mate ran up and down the main deck banging a gong and shrieking until an arrow through the chest spun him about. A second drove deep into his skull, the point bursting from an eye socket. He dropped to the deck lifeless. The gong rolled away from his dead hand to bounce along the boards.

Up on the quarterdeck, Shan climbed up to sit athwart a section of the iron-armored shielding, working his rifle to send rounds toward horses and men. Arrows spanged off the plating around him. Wei called up to him, cautioning safety. Shan ignored him, levering and firing without heed to the storm of shafts tearing past him. The gunboat was slowing as the current battered against it.

Screaming at the top of his lungs, the skipper called into the voice pipe for speed. A blast of black smoke erupted from the stacks and the paddles, spinning lazily in the streaming water, stalled and banged and reversed to churn the water to froth once more. The ship shuddered in the grip of a violent lurch as the *Abundance* bucked the tide, the bow swinging back midstream.

The sudden forward movement of the ironclad tossed men stumbling to the deck.

Wei's voice rose in alarm from the quarterdeck. He was at the gunwale pointing over the side, calling to the skipper who stood braced at the wheel, eyes fixed on the way ahead. Shan was nowhere to be seen.

Through a gun port, Lee saw a man in the water being carried away into the wake of the gunboat's churning paddles. The Ranger tore off his gun belt and was through the port and into the river, stroking through the yellow water for the man bobbing on the current. Arrows ripped into the water all around him as he swam. Lee kept on, kicking and pulling for Shan, the current pulling him along the hull of the *Abundance*. The man was face-down and showing no sign of movement, drifting away like flotsam.

Bat leaned from the port, watching Lee move farther and farther away behind the ironclad. Chaz yanked her away from the opening as a pair of arrows soared through, ringing off the armor where her head had been.

On the gun deck, Carberry was hurling abuse in English and orders in mangled Mandarin at his crews who were pushing the trucks of their three bearing guns through the ports. His translator lay pinned to the deck with arrows.

"Fire! Fire all guns, ye poxy yellow curs!" the Yorkshireman bellowed.

Under the seismic kick of the three big guns discharging at once the *Abundance* canted starboard, rocking on its keel. The deck was covered at once in a choking, rotten-egg smog of black powder smoke.

On shore, the cavalry faltered when three charges of grapeshot whirled into them from close range. Gouts of river mud geysered upward along the bank. Mixed with the black muck were parts of men and horses mangled by the pitiless rain of thousands of steel balls. The mud boiled under the barrage, water vaporized in the deadly combination of heat and impact. Out of the mist rode what was left of the bowmen. They turned their mounts to climb the slope of the banks and out of the line of fire of the rifle and cannon of the gunboat. A few horses remained at the water's edge including one stamping, mad with pain, in a greasy pile of its own guts. The animal's keening screams echoed through the silence left in the wake of the thunder of the guns.

Jimbo stood and put a round through the suffering creature's head. He did the same for a second horse, limping along the bank trailing the stump of a hind leg.

"What about him?" Bat said, pointing her empty pistol at an archer, both legs shot away at the knees, trying to claw his way up the bank. The man was wailing at the top of his lungs.

"Fuck him," Jimbo said, pushing a fresh cartridge into the Whitworth's breech.

Bat snatched the rifle from the Pima's hands. She sighted on the wounded archer through the scope with all the skill taught her in IDF sniping school at Tze'elim. She put a slug through the man's head. His shrieks were cut off in an instant.

"You know, everyone who we see here was dead before our grandparents were born," Jimbo said, taking the smoking rifle back.

"That doesn't change anything," Bat said.

She leaned far out of the gun port, looking back the way they'd come. Nothing but smoke drifting over the churning wake.

Chaz called to the skipper to stop the engines. Wei was fighting with the captain for the wheel.

Bat ran to starboard to scan the near shore. She could see two small figures, one dragging the other, through the shallows toward the banks of the river island. It was Lee Hammond pulling the still form of Shan behind him.

Shan awoke below deck. He was lying, soaking wet, on a straw mat. His fine silk outfit was caked with stinking mud. The black American was wrapping a bandage about his head. Shan's skull throbbed. Wei stood by watching, his face creased with concern.

"How many fingers?" Chaz said, holding three fingers before Shan's eyes.

"Three."

"You banged your head on something when you fell off the boat. It's going to hurt awhile," Chaz said, tying two strands of the bandage in a knot to secure it in place.

"I went into the river?" Shan said. "I do not remember."

"Hammond went in after you. Saved you from drowning."

"Why would he do that?"

"I guess he thought your sorry ass was worth it," Chaz said and stood to go.

The river widened again once past the archipelago of islets and sand bars. The *Abundance* moved to the center of the current, far out of arrow range from either bank. The broad expanse of the Yangtze stretched like ochre-colored silk under the light of the setting sun before them. The river was dotted here and there by smaller vessels winding north with goods to sell the besieging army.

Shan came up on deck, his head aching the way the American told him it would. His vision was blurred. Probably a concussion. Not his first. He had changed into a shirt and pants he found in the slops of the boat's crew store. He looked across the open deck for the man named Lee Hammond.

The skipper was back at his post, a bandage wrapped tight where the arrow had pierced his forearm. The bodies of dead crewmen were tossed into the water to join the flotsam of dead bound for the sea. The decks were doused with buckets of water to wash the blood out the gunnels. Eager crewmen were in a contest to find as many intact arrows as they could. The decks and masts bristled with them, and each sailor found a bundle of their own.

Shan could see Lee Hammond standing on the forward deck. He was stripped to his underwear and wringing out his uniform over the side. The woman sat on the deck by him, cleaning her rifle.

"They are Tartar arrows," Shan informed Lee as he stepped up. "Each one is worth a pipe of bhang or time with a woman when we reach Nanking."

"I thought the Tartars served the emperor. Those guys were flying rebel colors," Lee said, draping his tunic and trousers over a line to dry.

"The second son of God made a better offer. Or maybe they are rogues. Pirates. It is a time of madness for China." Shan shrugged.

"You know a lot about your country's history?" Bat asked, running an oiled rag down the barrel of her lever action.

"I read all history. A soldier learns from what has come before," Shan said.

"You're a soldier? Not just a gunfighter?" Lee said.

"Lanzhou Night Tigers. China's first and best at counter-terror."

"That's special ops. Elite unit."

"Like you. Rangers," Shan said.

"They just look for the biggest and dumbest and make them Rangers," Lee answered.

Shan nodded sagely. "Same in China."

"Same everywhere, brother," Lee said, taking a seat on the deck by Bat to clean his own weapon.

Shan watched them awhile before leaving them to strip off his own drenched clothing.

"He didn't thank you for saving his life," Bat said.

"Sure he did," Lee said.

30

To the north, a tower of smoke stood miles high on the horizon. It rose into the air, a black, unmoving smear in the morning sky, across the course ahead of the *Abundance*.

By afternoon, they reached the first of a series of pontoon barricades stretched across the river. The ironclad slowed to a stop to queue in behind junks and barges to be inspected before being allowed to continue on to Nanking. Before them, the black cloud of smoke divided the sky in two. They could hear, faintly over the chunder of the idling steam engine below, the boom of artillery. It was a continuous thundering, waxing and waning in frequency but never stopping. The city was still more than ten miles ahead.

To guarantee their passage through the various checkpoints, the skipper showed his own documents, medallions, and certifications to a succession of imperial officers. Each time, a handful of brass coins changed hands before the proper stamps were applied to the official documents, and the *Abundance* was cleared to the next chokepoint.

The final river gate was guarded by a pair of wooden warships with archer towers built amidships. Helmeted bowmen peeped over timber battlements, the necks of their long reflex bows visible over their heads. A mandarin in yellow silks worn under chain mail armor stepped daintily over a gangplank and onto the deck of the *Abundance*. He demanded to know who the *gweilo* were. They'd not seen Europeans this far north in weeks, and he had been told that Pasha Gordon and his army of barbarians had sailed back to Shanghai never to return. It was up to Shan to sell the presence of the strange company of Yankees traveling aboard one of the emperor's gunboats. The mandarin squinted and sniffed at the offered documents before ordering a supernumerary to apply the necessary stamps and embossments.

The environment along the river changed once they drifted past the final gate. The scenery went from the expected mud banks, rice paddies, and escarpments to a maze of piers, wharves, and landings, all packed with either merchant craft or riverine navy vessels. A city of tents spread as far as the eye could see on either side of the river. The smoke of thousands of campfires created a white cotton haze over the river surface. This was home to a half-million soldiers of the emperor's army and double that number of slaves, engineers, butchers, bakers, millers, masons, carpenters, liverymen, gunsmiths, merchants, whores, and the rest of the vast company of camp followers needed to keep a force this size provisioned for an extended siege.

Troops in white coats and pants, trimmed in red, marched with shouldered spears and banners. Cavalry in bamboo armor trotted in long columns, lance points gleaming in the orange light of the lowering sun. At the foot of a wharf, a platoon of men, naked but for loincloths, dragged a siege cannon to shore at the end of ropes. The cannon rested on high iron wheels, its scaled barrel worked into the head of a furious dragon.

The hills rising beyond the banks were bare of trees, the slopes strewn with fresh stumps and tall heaps of deadfall. From the sea of tents, they could hear the rasp and whine of saws working, the ring of hammers striking anvils, and the *tink, tink, tink* of chisels on stone.

Set along one bank, rows of bodies hung like obscene laundry from long cables stretched between poles. The weight of them bowed the cables downward at the midway point, the victims at the center of the spans twisting with feet dangling only inches from the ground. They wore placards in Chinese characters about their necks proclaiming the charges that brought them to the hangmen

————

Before the bow end of the *Abundance*, the column of black smoke filled a third of the sky. From within the dark cloud came flashes of white light that bloomed and died. Threads of white vapor crossed the sky, rockets looping and twisting to explode with muted popping sounds.

Here the sound of the guns grew louder. A ceaseless barrage booming and coughing and sending missiles into the air that trailed sparks on the way to their targets, invisible around a head-land that lay before them.

The Complete Abundance chugged around the final curve that would bring the team to their ultimate destination.

Nanking.

The city rose off the eastern bank behind high walls set before violet hills speckled with flashes of radiance from cannons set in earthworks high on the slopes. Answering fire from guns placed along the battlements created blossoms of sudden light in the gloom. Across an expanse of canal, continuous cannon fire blasted out from an outer fortification. This was Dibai Castle, the Dragon's Neck. It had been captured by the imperial Qing army weeks before, its guns trained now to fire on the city.

Adding to the din were hundreds of mortar barges anchored in chains mid-river. Huge tub-like barrels angled upward from within angled hulls of heavy timbers bolstered with bands of iron. The mortars belched balls the size of grapefruit. These were fashioned from stones dug from a quarry miles away, hauled to the riverside, and worked into lethal rounds of the proper caliber by a legion of coolie laborers. The mortars went off, firing at will, with a monstrous thud, the recoil thrusting the barges deeper in the water to create rings of turbulence that set the vessels about them bobbing. The stones sailed in high wobbling arcs to come down somewhere within the walls of Nanking.

The source of the massive tower of smoke, visible from twenty miles distant, was a huge tower set at the southwest corner of the city's defenses. It was stone and mortar at its base and two city blocks in breadth. The upper part was five stories of timber fortifications and hoardings. It was ablaze now, an inferno that would take days, maybe weeks, to burn.

From the spiked battlements along every wall, sporadic fire lanced out from carronades and jingals. Rockets flashed in the air from the tops of towers to snake down on curving contrails and explode in the air over the earthworks of the besiegers. Answering rocket fire twirled upward from redoubts to either strike the walls with impotent fiery eruptions or drop from the apex of their arcs to fall within the walls where they exploded to project sprays of burning shrapnel.

In addition to the boom of cannons, thunder of mortars, hiss, and pop of rockets, and crackle of heavy muskets, an unceasing racket of horns, gongs, and drums provided a discordant soundtrack.

Everywhere, before the walls of the city, the land lay denuded of plant life. The muddy slopes and flat approaches were gouged with hand-dug entrenchments snaking toward the city on switchback courses that ended in high walls of mud-filled gabions. These forward bunkers were invested with lighter field guns that rained canister on the ramparts of the walls above in an attempt to clear them of defenders. Crews died under the return musket fire raining from the city walls and were quickly replaced with new crews. These men raced up the twisting trenches to pull away the dead and man the cannons until they themselves died or until the cannon was finally rendered mute by withering fire from above.

Between the forward gun emplacements and the cyclopean walls, the ground was carpeted with the bodies of men who'd rushed the walls with ladders weeks before. Their bones showed white through the tatters of rags that were all that was left of their uniforms. The concentration of the dead was highest against the base of the walls—like a black wave frozen at high tide. The ruins of long ladders lay splintered among them. Stone chips from direct artillery hits on the walls rained down to splash in the mud.

The team stood on the deck of the *Abundance*, all eyes on the hellish landscape spread for miles before them above the river's east bank.

"How the fuck are we supposed to get in there?" Boats said, speaking for them all.

31

SHE-WOLF

Through a gap in the steel panels of the shed, Dwayne watched the shadows lengthen. He could hear a generator grind to life somewhere. Lamps atop poles flickered to life, casting down cones of yellow light. The men remained in the dark beneath the porch, smoking and talking. The pair of attack dogs slept in the center of the street. The hooch where he'd last seen N'itha was dark and silent.

The shed that served as his cell was just steel sheets screwed to a wood frame. The door was secured by a stick stuck through the lock hasps. A few kicks and the door would open. The steel sheets were secured with rusting screws in worm-eaten two-by-fours. They'd come free with a good push. It would be noisy. They'd be on him when they heard it. His situation would be unchanged except for a few more bruises on his ribs.

There was nothing in the shed but a litter of ancient corn husks and a pile of backpacks and luggage. This gang preyed on hikers and tourists, gringos who came to Baja and found more adventure than they expected. There were probably graves dug all around this gorge. Graves dug by their victims, probably.

He searched the packs but found nothing of use. Mostly

clothes. Little bottles of hotel shampoos and bags of moldy trail mix and tacky souvenirs. A manicure kit with nothing more dangerous in it than nail clippers. He crouched by the door, keeping an eye to the gap in the panels. An opportunity to break out of here would come. He had to hope it would come before the men searching for him arrived.

The guy in the Estrella t-shirt stepped off the porch into the street. His gait told Dwayne that he was either drunk or high or both. He shambled away from the others who called out to him, laughing. He waved a hand back at them to shush them as he walked. He cupped his hands around his mouth to call into the hooch next door.

"Jorgito... Jorgito..." he called, making a song of it.

A few of the others stepped off the porch and into a pool of light to watch the show. One threw an empty bottle after Estrella, warning him not to awaken the horny bastard. Another added that it was only trouble to get between a dog and his bitch.

Estrella gave them the finger and swung open the screen door of the hooch to stumble inside.

"Jorgito... Jorgito..."

The others returned to the porch, sharing predictions of what Jorgito would do to the poor bastard.

"Jorgito!" Estrella was out of the hooch as if launched. The screen door banged open as he shouldered through it, hands held before him. His hands, fingers splayed, were black in the glow of the pole lamp. He rushed to the others who were off the porch in a rush. The pit bulls were roused by the shouts. They joined the noise, barking and running in circles.

"*Está muerto! Como un cerdo!*" Estrella was shrieking now in a high falsetto, holding out his blood-streaked hands as evidence. The dogs went mad with the scent of it, leaping in the air at the edge of the clutch of men.

"Good girl," Dwayne said as he rushed to the rear wall of the shed. Two good kicks and a steel panel tore loose at one corner.

Wide enough to allow him to squeeze through. He crouched outside in the cool night air, listening to the sound of the shouting men and barking dogs rising in volume. There was a haze of white smoke coming through the trees. It came from the hangar building, dense smoke spilling from under the eaves of the roof like a silent waterfall. The scent of the smoke was pungent and sweet.

N'itha had kakked the weightlifter then slipped away to set fire to their stash of marijuana.

The men were moving toward the hangar. Their shouts were joined by sporadic gunfire. Shooting at shadows or letting off rounds from sheer frustration. These assholes didn't know the first thing about weapons discipline.

Behind him, inside the shed, Dwayne heard the door squealing on its hinges, feet pounding on the wood floor. Dwayne ran low across the alley toward the fallen casa next door. The door of the shed crashed shut. A man called out.

Rounds kicked up fountains of dust behind Dwayne. He dove to the ground and belly-crawled into the crawl space under the veranda. In the bar of light behind him, he saw that two men were racing for him. One had a rifle raised to his shoulder. The other fired single shots from the hip, working the bolt furiously to chamber a new round. A finger of moonlight lanced down through a bullet hole punched through the rotten wood near his head. Then another. He scrambled forward, fingers searching the sand. He found the checkered wooden butt of the .45. A man dropped to hands and knees and poked the barrel of an AK-47 into the dark. The first round took the man under his right eye. The back of his skull showered his crouching amigo with blood and brains. Startled, the second man fell backward out of his crouch to land on his ass. A double flash of light from the shadows under the veranda. Two rounds to the abdomen hammered the second man full onto his back, legs kicking.

Dwayne put another round through each man before clambering out into the smoky moonlight. He snatched up the dropped AK and checked the magazine load. At least fifteen rounds. The second man had the battered old deer rifle. Dwayne left it but pulled a revolver from the waistband of the man's jeans, checked it for loads, and stuck it under his belt. He slung the Kalashnikov over his shoulder.

The gully was filling with white smoke carried away from the burning pot barn by a wind dropping down the rock walls. The building glowed orange from within as flames reached the bales of dried weed. The men were hustling before the hangar and levering the big swing doors open. A gout of fire reached out for them. They stumbled backward, screaming in terror and frustration. The dogs ran yelping from the ball of flame to vanish into the surrounding dark.

Dwayne trotted behind the buildings, away from the fire and the shouting men. He made it into a thick stand of paloverde trees. He turned at a sharp hissing sound.

N'itha separated herself from the shadows to approach him. She was black to the elbows with blood. Her hair was matted with it. The sweat on her face and breasts shone crimson with Jorgito's blood. The Metallica shirt was gone now. Her mouth parted to show a grin of white teeth. In her fist was a bone-handled knife he'd last seen sheathed on Jorgito's belt.

"He died fast for a big man," she said.

Dwayne grabbed her wrist and pulled her to the ground with him. To the west, through the swirling smoke, a white glare was growing in brightness. The glare grew harsher, breaking into wavering blades of light stabbing at them out of the night.

Headlights. A column of vehicles. Heading their way from the desert.

VIEW FROM THE HIGH GROUND

L ee leaned into an embrasure atop Dibai Castle's tallest tower. From his vantage point, he could see a broad grassy slope leading from the opposite bank of the canal below them to the northern expanse of Nanking's outer walls. Puffs of smoke drifted from firing ports all along the defenses as the city answered its attackers with stone shot.

"I say it's a thousand yards thereabouts. You two are the snipers. Distance is your thing," Lee said, sliding from the embrasure. A flurry of tile chips spilled over him from a stray round striking the roof above.

"I make it closer to twelve hundred. But I've only got one eye now. I bow to the lady's estimation," Jimbo said, peering through his telescope in another embrasure. Byrus, his constant companion, stood on tiptoes, craning his neck to see through the narrow gap between the Pima and the stone crenulation.

"Thirteen hundred yards and a skosh. Add another fifty to be sure," Bat said, leaning out to study the stone fortifications. A combination of morning mist and gunsmoke created a fog around the base making the walled city appear to be floating on a swirling cloud.

Despite the constant noise, soldiers in lacquered bamboo armor slept by a rocket battery on the plank floor of the tower's roof. On the broad ramparts beneath the tower artillery crews worked a pair of long siege guns. Stone shot the size of basketballs was slathered with lard and lifted into the muzzle with a rolling block and tackle. The shot was packed down atop cloth bags of powder. Men worked as a team to jam the load in place with plungers twelve feet in length. The cannons were then trundled into their sand-bagged embrasures along iron tracks set on the ancient stone of the castle. The crews fled for cover, hands clapped over ears, as a cannoneer atop a ladder set and lit the fuse. This man leaped from the top of the ladder to bolt back to where the others cowered behind a barrier of sand-filled gabions.

The big siege guns went off one after the other, rumbling back against stops constructed of heavy timbers braced with iron. A blinding smog of gray smoke obscured everything. From their vantage point, Bat and Jimbo could see the stone balls sail upwards in a shallow trajectory toward Nanking's walls. The first struck a round tower about midway up its height. It served to widen and deepen a crater already formed by countless prior shots. The second crashed into the battlements, sending stones and timbers flying as it caromed in a nearly vertical rebound to arc high into the air and tumble down out of sight beyond the walls.

The cannon crews stood atop the walls to peer through the dense fog for signs of where their shot had fallen. When it cleared sufficiently, they cheered and waved banners for their enemy to see. Somewhere gongs were being struck in celebration. But then, day and night, there were always gongs being struck somewhere.

"We need to be here in less than two weeks," Shan said, unfolding a chart that had been prepared with the help of Dr. Wesley Fong. It was rendered on vellum by hand in a style that would not draw attention to it in this period. Just another document in a society already buried in paperwork.

The two Rangers and Bat studied the map. Shan pointed to a section of wall that bowed out between two towers visible to them from their current vantage point.

"The storehouse we are looking for is here," Shan said, laying his forefinger on a rectangle that appeared to be about ten blocks within the inner defensive wall. This wall ran in a concentric ring within the larger ring that formed the outer defensives. This fortress within a fortress protected the city of the Heavenly Kingdom of Peace and its many palaces.

"So, near a quarter mile to get us inside and then, what, another half mile to the storehouse?" Jimbo said.

After a moment to make the rough conversion to metric in his head, Shan said, "That is approximate."

"It's all approximate," Lee said. "We could go through all that out there and find nothing but a solid gold shithouse."

"How far have the tunnels been dug already?" Jimbo asked.

"I have spoken to coolies who tell me they are within a week of finishing a series of three mines leading to the midway point of this wall." Shan's fingers brushed a stretch of wall to the west of the place where they needed to enter.

"What good does that do us?" Lee said.

"There are ten mines in total. They progress toward different destinations. Some serve only as defensive tunnels to prevent counter mines being dug from within the city," Shan said. "One of them, Mogui Gangmen, takes us closest to where we need to be."

"And how do we know that?" Jimbo said.

"You didn't notice, Hawkeye?" Bat said, smirking as she stepped to a broad embrasure and climbed up between the protective stone works. Lee joined her.

"The grass is dead above where they're digging," she said and pointed to the field beyond the canal. Brown areas of grass described the tunnels that lay far below. They looked like road-ways stretching toward the far walls. Some started as one tunnel to branch out in tributaries, all aimed at the city.

"There's tunnels under each dead stretch? Men down there digging? Right now?" Lee said.

"Thousands of men," Shan said.

"We dig?" Byrus said, happy that the conversation has turned to a subject he was familiar with.

"We dig," Jimbo said.

THE WAY DOWN

They drew some attention from the curious as the team moved through the ocean of tents that formed a third massive camp on the slopes beyond Dibai Castle.

For the most part, the imperial troops, peasant conscripts, and coolies greeted them with indifference. *Gweilo* mercenaries were a common enough sight, and these wore the red trim at their collars and cuffs that presented them as in the pay of the emperor. It was at Shan's suggestion that they'd purchased a few yards of red silk and sewn trim to their uniforms in order to blend in.

The only unwanted interest they attracted was from merchants and whores. Hucksters approached them selling knives, clocks, and iron skillets, jade, ivory, lamps, caged birds, and even kites. They trotted along, hawking their wares, faces split by grins marred with black teeth. The pupils of their eyes were blown out like black marbles. Though it was banned by the imperial house in Peking, everyone here seemed high as a kite on opium. The many pans of smoldering incense set here, and there did little to mask the cloying sweet smell of the junk. They even saw kids who looked younger than ten puffing away on clay pipes stained black with tar. Only soldiers seemed immune to the stuff—or at least weren't smoking it in public.

"Guess who won the opium wars," Jimbo said, glancing at a woman seated on the grass before a tent blowing blue smoke into the face of the infant asleep in her arms.

As bold as the merchants were, the prostitutes were worse. The team passed through a lane lined either side by tents painted with ornate depictions of every sex act imaginable. The women lounging in the shade of fringed awnings appeared to be demure as Chinese dolls in painted robes until the Rangers moved closer. The women pulled the robes open to reveal that they were naked beneath the thin layers of silk. They wore white makeup over every exposed inch of their bodies. Lacquered hair, some dyed brilliant red or silvery white, was arranged with combs decorated with pearls or fashioned in the shape of birds, prancing deer, or running rabbits. They each had their feet tied tight in bands of cloth twisted closed with wooden dowels.

Some had piercings of gold hoops in all manner of provocative places that they were happy to expose for potential customers. The only feature they did not display was their mouths, which they covered with fans of paper or trimmed peacock feathers. The ravages of opium left them toothless over time.

"That one's cute. I think she likes you," Boats said, elbowing Chaz.

Chaz turned to meet a pair of eyes circled with lamp black slowly blinking at him over the top of a fan painted with an imaginative picture of a woman being raped by a dragon. The girl was tiny, barely four feet tall. Chaz guessed she was no older than thirteen.

"You could catch something just looking at that poor child," Bat said with a wary shake of her head.

"She love soul brother number one," Jimbo said.

"Love you long time!" Byrus chimed in, recognizing the movie the Pima was quoting.

"Me so hawny!"

The women reclining in the shade tittered at Byrus, and he turned to trot toward them.

"Slow down, Bruce," Jimbo said, grasping Byrus by the collar and yanking him back in line.

They ran the gauntlet of whores to enter under the gate of a stockade of log walls. Within it lay the work camp of the sappers who were digging the tunnels. The place was an anthill of activity.

The pit in the middle of the camp dropped into the ground to a depth of ninety feet. The interior walls of the big dig were lined with scaffolds and ladders to allow the miners access to the floor of the pit via stages of landings and ramp ways of bound bamboo. Over the pit hung a framework supporting a block and tackle system by which a bucket loaded with a ton of soil and rock could be drawn up from below. It was hauled upward by a team of over a hundred bullocks plodding a worn track leading to the north along the river. In addition to animal power, coolies climbed the ladders in an unending stream, all humping baskets loaded with dirt to the surface. Still more coolies worked with carts and shovels to move the soil up roadways that wound in a circle up man-made mountains of mud and rock. These hills were the tailings dug from the miles of tunnels being excavated below.

All the while, officers in red silks raced among the workers shouting abuse and swinging long bamboo flails. Riflemen kept watch from wooden towers surrounding the pit area. Horns blew up and down the line and from deep within the excavation, sending indecipherable signals to the workers. Atop a dais of timbers, a shirtless Mongol beat on a huge kettle drum with a pair of mallets to provide a rhythm for the laborers. And, of course, gongs sounded like wind chimes everywhere.

Shan stepped up to interrupt one of the officers' harangues. They spoke together quietly, the officer shaking his head and Shan pointing to the opening of the excavation. At last, Shan dropped a jingling sack into the officer's hand. The man smiled and nodded and bowed as the sack disappeared into the folds of his tunic.

Taking the lead, Shan walked to a ramp that angled down toward the first ledge of their descent. The team followed. Lee put a hand to Bat's shoulder.

"Not you," Lee said.

"What the hell, Lee?" she said, trying to jerk her arm from his grip.

"You and Wei are staying topside. We need someone to keep an eye out. You're our overwatch."

"You guys knew about this all along," she said, eyes narrowed at Jimbo approaching with his Whitworth rifle and ammo bag held out to her.

"I didn't want to hear your shit any longer than I needed to," Lee said, taking the long rifle from Jimbo and pressing it into Bat's hands.

"You're saying that to make me pissed at you. You could say that you're worried about me," Bat said.

"That too, sweetie-pie," Lee said and bent to kiss her forehead only to dodge Bat's flattened hand swiping an inch from his face.

"Son of a bitch," she said. But she was smiling.

Jimbo relieved her of her repeating rifle and bandolier of cartridges. The remaining men moved off down the ramp, leaving Bat and Wei watching until their comrades were out of sight in the deepening gloom of the pit.

"So, what do we do for fun?" Bat said. Wei blinked, uncomprehending.

3 4

Three big SUVs drove the dirt road and passed where Dwayne and N'itha lay concealed in the shadow of the trees. The vehicles, matte black with deeply tinted windows, cut their headlights and rolled into the compound.

Dwayne watched them pull to a stop in the smoke-filled street. The doors opened, and teams of men emerged, six to a car. They wore black uniforms camo-striped with gray. Hoods, masks, and a type of night vision gear Dwayne had never seen before. With weapons shouldered, they trotted into the pall of smoke in twin "V" formations covering either side of the street.

They were military, but not Mexican army. They were from somewhere much farther away.

He turned to N'itha.

"Go back to Caroline and Ricky. Tell them to pack up and run," he said in a whisper.

"What about you, Du-wane?" she said.

"The plan stays the same. I draw these fuckers away. You understand?"

"You run other way. Fuckers follow you." She nodded.

"That's right. Now don't let them see you," he said, a pat to her leg as she rose to a crouch.

N'itha moved away into the trees, cut north, and was gone into the rocks within seconds.

The sounds of gunfire came out of the haze of smoke enveloping the compound. The boom and blast of shotguns and rifles. It was followed closely by a peculiar burring sound. Dwayne could see threads of brilliant crimson light through the smoke cover. They pulsed like tracers, only brighter and with greater frequency. Any lingering doubts about where these new arrivals had come from were wiped away.

The gunfire died away to silence, followed by a couple of short bursts of the high burring noise. Then nothing.

They'd move in an ever-growing circle to find him. The bulk of them would follow what they believed was his most likely path of escape, the road out. Dwayne had to be sure they followed him and not any tracks left by N'itha.

He rested the AK on the humped root of a paloverde stretching out above him. He set the ring sight on the group of silhouettes moving double time out of the fog between the buildings. He waited until the phalanx shape was clear and set the upright tang on the third man on the right leg of the "V."

The rifle barked and the man in his sights collapsed, a slug in the soft tissue where his leg met his hip. The lead man turned to look back momentarily. Dwayne dropped him with a single round through the ass. The man spun to the ground.

Dwayne rolled from the cover of the root to move low in an ape-like gait for the shelter of bushes to the south, away from N'itha and the camp over the ridgeline.

He was counting on the two wounded men to slow the chase. In the thick of a hedge of berries, he glanced back. The remainder of the phalanx was moving at a run to his last position. They didn't miss a step. Just hopped over their fallen buddies and kept on. The rest of the team would be coming too, breaking into two units to sweep north and south. To flank him. To cut him off.

The AK to his shoulder, he snapped off two shots at the group that was slowing beneath the paloverde to eyeball his spent rounds and look for boot prints. Time for fucking around was over. Dwayne dropped one with a center shot. A double-tap that hurled the man against the bole of the tree. The rest returned fire with that peculiar burring sound. Hot rounds arced close above him, strings of iridescence that buzzed as they crashed through the cold air.

They were shooting high. Not shooting to kill. Driving him. Or trying to scare him into surrender. They wanted him alive.

Distance. All he could do was cover as much ground as he could before they caught up or got ahead of him. Every second he bought N'itha was precious. Dwayne was up and running, breaking through the brittle thorns to stay ahead of the silent men.

35

UP SATAN'S FUNDAMENT

Their eyes adjusted to the dimness while they climbed down deeper into the earth. The way was lit by oil lamps set on shelves spaced along the ramps, ledges, and ladder ways.

"Jesus, it smells like ass down here," Jimbo groused. "Like a *dead man's* ass," Chaz said.

"Like something that died and came out of a dead *whore's* ass," Boats added. When it comes to obscenities, Navy wins every time. The miasma in the air was overpowering with the scent of piss, feces, and sweat. The funk was covered over by the stink from the oil lamps and was turned palpable by the close, humid air trapped in the excavation. In addition, there was the sharp tang of spoiled cabbage everywhere. Cabbage, garlic, and rice was the main diet of the coolies working on the massive dig. The smell of it came from a wooden cookhouse constructed on the floor of the pit. The same odor was also richly coming off the sweating laborers.

Teams of coolies worked a row of giant bellows that drew air from the surface down into the tunnels that branched out from the southern end of the pit. The bellows were constructed of huge leather bags sewn in segments. They collapsed and inflated like giant accordions. Suspended in wooden frames the bags stood twelve feet tall and were operated by a capstan cleverly devised to depress and raise the bag, filling it from oiled cloth hoses strung upward to the surface and expelling the air through pipes of bamboo run down the tunnels, secured to the ceiling beams. The coolies stood atop the frame turning the lateral wheel to the beat of a drum. Ten bellows, one for each tunnel, dominated the large entry chamber to the tunnel complex. The fresh air made work within the tunnels possible. Without it, the men would suffocate in their own exhalations.

"Central air," Chaz said.

"From the Flintstones," Boats said.

Shan led the team deep into a tunnel off to their left. It split into two tunnels, and they stayed to the left at the fork. The tunnels had wooden timber walls and ceilings with matted tree branches set between to further hold back the weight of the surrounding earth. A walkway of planks ran down the center of the burrows.

They passed coolies trotting by, bent under baskets of soil on their backs and other coolies moving down the other way with empty baskets and timbers. In addition, boys, some no older than six, raced back and forth with buckets of drinking water. They slapped aside anyone in their way with their long-handled wooden ladles. Another boy passed them carrying gourds filled with lamp oil, his only job to keep the lanterns filled.

The floors of the tunnels were ankle-deep in muddy water. The passageway widened at intervals where more coolies worked pumps to carry the groundwater up to the open pit, where it was hauled upward along with the loose earth and rocks.

Despite the wisps of fresh air being pumped down to them, the funk in the air grew thicker the lower they went. It was cooler in the deep tunnels which provided some degree of relief from the close atmosphere.

"You okay?" Chaz said to Jimbo. The Pima's one eye was wide and moving side to side. His mouth pressed closed, breath whistling rapidly through his nose.

"Give me some time to get used to this," Jimbo said.

"You were claustrophobic back in basic," Chaz said, recalling an incident when a slit trench collapsed back at Benning.

"Can we stop talking about it? Okay?" Jimbo said and shoved Chaz ahead of him.

Shan stopped at a fork in the tunnel to speak to a work leader who looked like every other muck-covered laborer except for a red turban wrapped about his head. The man pointed down the burrow straight ahead. Shan bowed and motioned for the others to move on.

The floor sloped downward at a sharp angle to where a pool of water had gathered. It reached their hips as they waded to the other side where it inclined upwards again, the floor drier and sandy there. Jimbo touched the ceiling above the pool and felt rock. The diggers had dropped the level of the excavation to burrow under a shelf of granite. He wasn't sure if that made him feel better or worse about his surroundings.

"This is the tunnel we want. *The Mogui Gangmen*," Shan said to Lee.

"They name the tunnels?" Lee said.

"Most peasants are innumerate. No idea about numbers. They can remember names if the names are memorable," Shan said.

"Like what?" Boats called from behind Lee.

"*The Path to Heaven. The Root of Sorrows. The Silken Throat*," Shan said.

"What's this one called?" Lee asked.

"*The Devil's Ass*," Shan said, turning back to them with a crooked grin.

Farther along the tunnel, they found a team of men with mallets hammering lengths of iron pipe into the ceiling. Stacks of pipe rested on a wooden cart. They'd seen the open ends of piping protruding from the ceiling. These were vent holes allowing for passage of air. Deeper down the tunnel they came across another crew hammering solid rods upwards to make pilot holes for other coolies following behind to install the vent pipes.

The work environment was something out of a nightmare, but Jimbo was astounded at the level of ingenuity and the awesome brute force needed to create these mines. Everyone had a job. Everyone understood their role. No one was idle. The tunnel inched closer to the wall with every passing moment because of the combined, machine-like labor of thousands of men.

"*Gung ho*," Jimbo said under his breath. "What you say?" Byrus said, close behind.

"It's the only Chinese I know except for *kung pao*," Jimbo said. "It means 'work together.'"

"*Gung ho*," Byrus said, trying the phrase out. "It is good."

The ring of hammers echoed from the gloom ahead. They reached a crew setting timbers and crossbeams. Ahead of them were the sounds of the digging crew, the chunk of spades, picks, and mattocks working to break the clay soil.

Shan and Lee left the team to find the digging leader. A brawny man in drooping mustaches and a red turban spoke with them. He looked at Shan's chart in the lamplight. The foreman shook his head and barked objections. Shan explained with great patience, but the guy showed no sign of budging. Lee put up a hand to interrupt, fishing in a pocket to produce a single gold coin that he held under the other man's nose. The foreman's mouth clapped shut and his eyes fixed on the gleaming disc.

"You like that?" Lee said and slid his Bowie knife from the sheath. Holding the coin in the palm of his hand, he pressed the blade of the knife into the soft metal to make a crease. The coin snapped in half in his fingers. Lee held the half-coin out to the foreman allowing him to take it.

"Half now. Half later. You feel me?" Lee said, holding up the remaining half of the coin before replacing it in his pocket.

The foreman nodded with vigor, securing the half-coin in a leather purse worn on the belt about his pajama pants. He grinned, showing yellow teeth with a prominent gap in the front.

The man bawled out an order and held his open hand out. A coolie rushed up, bowing and lowering eyes, to place a ball of twine roughly the size of a volleyball in the foreman's hand. The foreman growled and pointed. The coolie took a loose end off the ball and ran back up the tunnel toward the pit, the end of the twine in his fist. As it played out behind the racing coolie, Lee saw that there were knots in the twine, spaced like the depth-meter back on the *Abundance*. The foreman's lips moved, counting the knots as they were plucked from the ball.

They waited, the foreman gripping the shrinking ball of twine until it grew taut in his fists. He bowed his head to them, smiling. Minutes later the coolie returned, panting and bathed in sweat. The foreman barked a question at him, and the coolie gasped a response. The foreman gestured for Shan's chart and placed a filthy finger on the vellum. He marked a spot just shy of the defensive wall at the spot where they wished to enter the city. Shan spoke and placed his own finger at a spot a few inches from the foreman's smudge, a spot well past the wall and under the city proper.

The foreman nodded again, slowly, lips pursed. Then he held up two fingers. Shan turned to Lee.

"I get it. He wants more money. Typical contractor." Lee dug out the half-coin and tossed it to the foreman.

"The same when we're inside Nanking."

Gold broke the language barrier. The foreman bawled orders, and the digging began anew.

It was the morning of July 7th, 1865.

They had twelve days to breach the walls ahead of the imperial army.

36

The leader of the excavation up the Devil's Ass was a man named Choi. A Mongol mother and a Han father made for one tough bastard. He was a ballbuster and a hard-charger and ran his crew like a disciplined machine.

Choi suggested to Shan that he could hire more coolies to speed the work. A sack of copper coins doubled the workforce within hours. Supplies and empty baskets raced down into the hole along the right wall. Laborers burdened with loads of dirt moved up and out along the left wall.

"We dig this much twelve times in a day," Choi said to Shan, holding his hands a distance of four feet.

Shan translated, and Lee did the math in his head. Roughly eight feet an hour. Sixty plus yards every twenty-four hours. They consulted the chart and estimated the burrow would come up near their target in ten days, give or take.

"That's shaving it close," Lee said.

Shan turned to Choi and asked if the work could move faster.

"Tunnel small. Men big," Choi said, holding his palms close together. Only so much room for the men at the head of the dig to swing a pick.

Shan narrowed his eyes, deciphering the foreman's atrocious Mandarin.

"Some dirt is soft. Some is clay. There is dirt. There is rock. Dig fast. Dig slow." Choi shrugged.

"Ten days," Shan said to Lee.

"There's no reason for all of us to be down in this mine all that time," Lee said. "We're just in the way. I say two of us stay down here and the rest go up for now. We can spell each other on eight-hour watches."

Jimbo nodded eagerly. Returning to sunlight and open sky sounded like heaven to him

---

The team, minus Lee and Shan, searched the camp for Bat and Wei. They found them camped in a row of tents along a wall at the back of the stockade. Bat was setting up house with a tent Wei bought for them in the marketplace. It was a red and yellow striped bell tent with enough room for them all to sleep if they didn't mind being chummy. Bat used an improvised sign language and a handful of copper to hire a couple of kids to fetch water and tend a campfire. An iron kettle of water was steaming to a boil over the fire as Jimbo led the others into view.

"Where's Lee?" Bat asked. The team was slathered in mud and already stripping off tunics, boots, and pants. The two hired boys took the clothing and, without instruction, spread them to dry in the sun.

"We're doing shifts in the hole. He took first watch with Horse-face," Jimbo said before dumping a ladle of water over his head.

"What's it like down there?" Bat said.

"Nasty," Chaz said.

"A shithole," Boats said.

190

"Is a good mine. Strong," Byrus said, offering his professional opinion as a former mine slave.

"Will it take us where we need to be?" Bat said. No one had an answer for that.

Lee sat in a niche in the wall, staying out of the traffic moving along the walls of the tunnel. Shan stood by him watching support timbers being handed down the line toward the head of the dig up one side the tunnel. Basket loads of soil and stone were being passed down the other. Water boys trotted from one man to another, offering drinks from ladles.

"I had an uncle who was a tunnel rat," Lee said. "You know what that is?"

"Tunnel rat?" Shan said.

"In Vietnam. The Viet Cong dug all these tunnels. Miles and miles of them. They needed guys to crawl down them and scout them out," Lee said.

"Your uncle?"

"On my mother's side. They're all little guys. Uncle Norton couldn't have been taller than five four."

"He came home from Vietnam?"

"Sure. Two tours. Still lives in the same house he grew up in. The night before I went into the army, he got drunk enough to tell me a story about his last tour."

Shan remained quiet.

"They dropped him down a hole so tight his shoulders touched either side. Just him, a .38 revolver and a flashlight. He crawled and crawled, going deeper into this hillside. What he didn't know, and what his unit CO didn't know, was that there was an airstrike called in on the opposite face of the hill. My uncle's down there when the loads start dropping. Tunnel collapses, and he's buried alive."

"What did he do?" Shan asked.

"He did like he was taught. Dropped face down with his hands cupped either side of his face." Lee mimicked the motion. "Laid there with a thousand pounds of dirt on him. Wondering how long two handfuls of air would last him. Then he hears digging. Someone's coming for him. He feels hands on him, and he's hauled out of the dirt. Only it was by two V.C. A man and a woman. He said he didn't know who was more surprised by that."

"They took him prisoner?"

"He shot them dead, both of them. Then he found his way out of there."

"I see," Shan said.

"My mom says, after Uncle Nort came home, he didn't sleep indoors for more than a year," Lee said. "Spent the nights, rain or not, in a hammock in the back yard."

Both men were silent for a while, watching the ceaseless march of the laborers moving past.

"One can never know who might save one's life," Shan said. "Or how to reward them for the favor."

"Yeah. My uncle said that gratitude only goes so far," Lee said.

"Yes," Shan said, his face turned away from Lee.

QUARRY

The hunters were moving more deliberately now, widening their hunt for Dwayne out to the edges of the woods where the desert began.

Dwayne lay on the lee side of a dune, watching the men spreading out in a circle at the opening of a ravine. They'd moved past him where he hid covered in brambles and shadow. He was inside their search ring with a plan to double back. Get to one of their vehicles, fuck the other rides up, and take off for any road heading away from here.

It was almost dawn, the sky lightening behind the ridgeline above him. He'd managed to keep them on the move for hours, drawing them away from the compound and away from Caroline. N'itha would have reached the camp before now. By this time, they were all inside the SUV and moving farther east into the *Lagunas*. He had no idea what sort of array was visible to the hunters through their NODs gear. Light enhancement, sure. Maybe thermals. The tech was unknown to him. Maybe unknown to anyone this side of whatever manifestation field they blew in through. He was left with the age-old conundrum of whether to keep moving, keeping the terrain between him and the hunters, or sticking in place to let them move on by.

He watched through a notch in the sand at the top of the dune, lying sideways with one eye on the broadening half-circle of men. He waited until the nearest one stepped behind the tower of a cirio cactus. At a half crawl, he moved fast along the shadows on the floor of the gully between the two dunes. He reached the mouth of the depression and rose to his feet, rushing bent-kneed for the cover of rocks at the base of the ravine. From there, it was a sprint for the trees. He made it into the palo verdes just ahead of the aurora of pink light glowing off the desert. The dawn sky bloomed behind the mountain.

Dwayne raced through the blue shadows of the woods toward the smoke-filled canyon where the three vehicles were parked. Racing into a clearing between the trees, he ran nearly headlong into a figure in camo black and gray.

The man raised the bug-eyes of his vision gear and stalled for one precious half-second in surprise. He lifted his rifle. Too late. Dwayne, still moving full out, struck the man with all his weight gathered behind the steel butt of the AK. They went down together, tumbling along the sandy soil.

The blow from the rifle butt shattered the gear on the man's face. Dwayne brought the rifle down two more times, feeling bone give way with wet snaps.

A shift of movement through the trees. Dwayne rolled to the scant cover of a young tree. Streaks of red pulsed close by. The sand steamed where the rounds struck between himself and the body of the man he brought down. The ozone smell of electrical fire hung in the air.

The hunters had left a reserve force back at the compound. He'd either lost count of the pursuers, or they'd called for back-up. The men searching for him on the desert would be coming back this way. He was trapped between two forces in a ravine with only two ways out, both blocked.

There was another way out. It required sideways thinking, and he didn't like it. But it could put a span of distance between him and the men after him.

Dwayne reached an arm around the tree and let off a long rip of fire from the AK. He tossed it aside, bolt locked back on an empty magazine. Red streaks cut the night behind him as he launched himself for the body of the man he'd butt stroked. He rolled, grabbing fistfuls of the man's uniform, pulling the corpse atop him.

The body juddered over him as hot rounds punched into it. One lanced across the meat of his calf, feeling like he'd been struck there with a ball bat. They were still trying to take him in one piece. He could hear boots pounding on sand. The squawk of a radio transmission grew louder as the ring of men drew tighter. Dwayne freed an arm to let off random rounds into the dark from the .45. Dwayne's other hand found the steel bracelet on the man's wrist and fumbled his fingers along its interior face. A display lit up iridescent blue on the smooth metal. He ran the tips of his fingers over the face the way he'd seen Samuel Renzi do. He had no clear idea of what he was attempting. Dwayne only knew that this was a swear-to-Jesus forlorn hope of a longshot, and he was taking it. The voices of men neared, speaking hushed. The clink of equipment. The tramp of boots on sand. A light grew over him. A white cloud spread to engulf him. Searchlights and gas?

He realized that the source of the brilliant light was the device on the wrist of the dead man. The chilled mist was thickening, dropping over him like a freezing blanket. His stomach heaved. His vision swam. All was cold air and white radiance.

Dwayne's eyes fluttered open to a painful light above him. He shoved the body off him and sat up, his vision moving in and out of focus.

The night was gone. Replaced by a desert sun high in the sky. The paloverde trees were gone as well. He lay on a field of rock scree between the ridgelines of the ravine. The rocks above were the only thing that remained unchanged from only a few seconds before.

He was in the same place but not in the same place. And not in the same time.

Whenever he was, Caroline was far away and free to escape. He rolled onto his hands and knees and puked until he was dry.

3 8

Boats had dozed off and came around to find that he was not on a beach at Oahu with that cute chick from the insurance commercial. "Shit," he hissed and looked around to see silent shadows moving through guttering lamplight. The air was close and heavy with the scent of sweat and cabbage. Men were passing baskets filled with dirt one way and empty baskets the opposite way. He was still in the tunnel.

He looked up to see Wei's broad face grinning down at him.

"I fell asleep. Fuck you, okay?" Boats said, rising to his feet to tower over the other man.

Wei's grin only widened. "Yeah. So, what did I miss?" Wei's head tilted.

"Shoulda learned more Chinese than 'How much for the beer?' and 'Does she have a sister?'" Boats grumped before taking a swig from a canteen and spitting it out in a long stream. He poured a splash over his head.

Voices reached him from up at the head of the tunnel. He heard an exchange in rapid-fire Mandarin. Angry words. The clink and chop of tools had ceased. The laborers slowed their work and then stopped entirely, looking to one another with wide, frightened eyes.

Boats moved at a crouch up the tunnel, parting coolies as he went. Wei scurried in his wake.

Choi, the excavation foreman, was in a heated discussion with a guy who could not have looked more out of place in the mine. An official-looking dude in midnight blue silk pajamas and slippers of brocaded gold cloth, now caked with mud. The dude wore one of those caps that looked like a little lampshade worn upside-down on the shaved crown of his head. His long queue of braided hair was bound in silver cords. His manicured hands were encrusted with rings of gold studded with gems. The peacock feather in his silly cap was bent double against the low ceiling beams of the tunnel. And the dude was *pissed*.

Two soldiers with rifles and sheathed long swords stood with him looking either displeased at what they were hearing or unhappy to be this far up the Devil's Ass. They turned baleful eyes and gleaming bayonets toward Boats and Wei.

Boats grasped the gist of the argument from the gestures of the little mandarin. He was asking where Choi got the balls to draw so many coolies to *this* particular tunnel? He threw a handful of copper coins into Choi's darkening face. Someone talked. The mandarin knew all about the hostile takeover of his digging operation. He turned and met Boats' eyes with a combined expression of disdain and disgust. The mandarin pointed a folded fan at the giant SEAL and hissed orders between clenched teeth.

Boats felt Wei close by him. Wei had undone the flap of his holster and was closing his fingers on the butt of the Remington. Boats gripped him by the wrist.

"Slow your roll, Wang," Boats hissed.

Wei's eyes grew wide in his sweating face.

The tough little fireplug understood the mandarin's words and was scared shitless. Boats wished that he knew what the mandarin was saying. Then he realized that he should be glad he didn't know

Jimbo and Chaz trotted down the branching tunnel to reach the fork where the Devil's Ass began. It was their turn in the hole. Byrus followed behind Jimmy Smalls' eternal shadow.

"You seem to be dealing with this better, bro," Chaz said.

"I've convinced myself that I'm not going to die here," Jimbo said.

"That right?"

"This is no place for an Indian to die."

"God has other plans for you?"

"That's what I'm counting on."

"And how *does* a Pima brave go out? With a war cry?"

"At eighty years old, humping one of those chicks from the blackjack tables down at the casino," Jimbo said.

Chaz chuckled. "I don't think that's in God's plan, Cochise."

"It is if God wants me to be happy," Jimbo said, coming to a stop where the tunnel became too congested with coolies for passage. They tried making their way through, pulling men aside to make way. One of the men turned to them, eyes wild with fear. Jimbo began to speak. The coolie reached out to press his mouth closed with callused hands.

None of the laborers was speaking. They were listening with rolling eyes. Jimbo turned to Chaz, a finger to his lips. His brother Ranger unshouldered his rifle and jacked a round into the chamber. Byrus drew his gladius from its scabbard.

In the hushed silence, Jimbo could hear a metallic sound coming faintly from somewhere ahead and above them, a chipping, scraping noise. He moved to the wall and pressed his ear to a timber. The vibrations came to him through the wood. Digging.

Jimbo hissed sharply, and the laborers turned to him. He

gestured for them to move up the tunnel behind him, to run for the surface. The jam of men broke up, dropping tools and baskets, to run past the Rangers toward the tunnel entrance. The way ahead was clear now but for a handful of workers who remained, eyes cast upward toward the sounds of excavation. They held tools, now weapons, in their fists. Jimbo drew his revolver with one hand and thumbed back the hammer. With his other hand, he slid his seven-inch Bowie from its sheath.

Twenty feet before them, a section between two ceiling beams crashed to the tunnel floor followed by a stream of soil and rocks. A pair of shadows dropped through the fresh opening and rushed toward them. Two men, naked but for filthy loincloths, eyes gleaming in faces black with muck. They swung axes before them as they charged the laborers blocking their way with mallets and picks.

Jimbo put out an arm to stop Byrus from running to meet the attackers. Chaz raised his rifle and put a slug into the face of the lead axman. The noise was painfully loud in the confined space. The man was hurled back, half his head gone. The second ax-man planted his ax in the ribs of a screaming coolie before being brought down by a mallet to the head. The other laborers chopped at the fallen man with picks.

"There's more of them!" Jimbo shouted and held his Remington outstretched in his arm.

More figures dropped through the hole opening in the ceiling along with part of a tunnel wall. The Taiping counter-mine had struck the Devil's Ass at a downward angle. The men approached at a run, shrieking, curved swords in their fists. They crashed into the small knot of armed coolies creating a fierce tangle of fighting men that choked the way ahead, blotting out the lantern light. They chopped their way through the laborers only to meet the guns of the two Rangers.

Jimbo fired the Remington until it went dry. Chaz pumped

the lever of the rifle. They filled the narrow space of the tunnel with light, smoke, and noise. The press of swordsmen folded under the rapid gunfire. They had nowhere to run but into the teeth of the fusillade. The front rank went down followed by a second. A third clambered over the bodies of their comrades, howling vengeance, only to be gunned down to create a growing blockage of dead and wounded men that plugged the tunnel.

Chaz kept up a tattoo of rapid fire to cover Jimbo. The Pima holstered the long pistol and secured his knife under his belt to swing his rifle into play. The pair knelt on the sodden planks and kept up a withering fire into the counter-miners who were struggling to clear a way through their own dead and dying. Behind the Rangers, Byrus crouched, his face contorted with fury. The little Macedonian was waiting to be unleashed.

A boom like summer thunder filled the tunnel followed by a fog of sulfur smoke propelled by a spray of white sparks. Somewhere behind the bunker of flesh, a big bore musket fired. One of the jingals, a portable cannon capable of firing loads of grapeshot or a projectile the size of a billiard ball.

Just above Chaz' head, a section of support beam vanished in a shower of splinters. Dirt rained down from the ceiling with the concussive blast of the weapon.

"Don't give them time to reload!" Jimbo shouted to be heard through ringing ears. He stood up to drive a stream of .44 slugs toward the source of the flash as fast as he could work the lever. Next to him, Chaz had drawn his revolver, fanning the hammer, roaring with rage.

A second boom vibrated the walls and floor. A big stone ball whistled between them, inches from Byrus' head, to explode in shards somewhere far behind them.

"Reloading! Reloading!" Jimbo bawled, backed away as he pulled the loading tube free to feed in cartridges from his bandolier. He felt the other Ranger's hand push him back up the tunnel. Chaz raised the revolver to pump rounds into a mad-eyed swordsman slithering through a gap created in the mass of dead that was blocking the tunnel. His final two slugs took the man through the chest and mouth. The swordsman slid to the floor, convulsing in a gush of his own blood. Two more men shouldered through in his wake, collapsing a section of the grisly barricade before them.

"Reloaded! Engaging!" Jimbo called as he dogged home the tube on his second magazine. Chaz dropped behind him to charge his own weapon. Jimbo worked the lever and put rounds, center mass, into two swordsmen in the lead. The pair of attackers stumbled only to be shoved aside by two more. And three more behind them. Swordsmen were being replaced by men wielding fat-barreled flintlock pistols that sent embers and shot down the tunnel. In their frenzy, one of the pistoleers put a ball through the neck of another attacker. The man's throat exploded before he fell in a heap to trip up his comrades.

A wild shot struck a timber near Chaz' head. Jagged needles of wood appeared in the flesh down one side of his face, forcing him to stagger back. He shook blood from his eyes and worked the rifle, the hexagon barrel glowing red like a poker. The press of men in the tunnel was growing. Wave after wave leaped their own dead to get at the pair of barbarians. More and more ball and shot flew from the mass of fanatical Taipings.

Jimbo, Chaz, and the little Macedonian dropped back as they emptied their rifles at the rising tide of attackers. They reached a place where the tunnel curved just before joining the mother tunnel that led back to the floor of the pit. Chaz tore off his tunic to wrap around the steaming barrel of his rifle. He gripped it to use as a club. Jimbo crouched, his knife in one fist, his revolver held like a club in the other. Byrus' face was twisted in a wicked grin, his gladius held ready in one hand, a mallet in the other.

"Looks like God gets the last laugh, Cochise. I don't see any hoochie-mama blackjack dealers here." Chaz laughed as the tunnel before them filled with shrieking men and flashing blades.

Jimbo didn't hear Chaz, only the beat of his heart, steady and slow as a war drum.

39

THE IMPASSE

Swordsmen rushed up the tunnel in a constant pulse. The attackers came two and three at a time with more of their number crushing in behind.

There was no room to swing his rifle. Chaz held it to his shoulder, driving the brass butt plate like a piston into skulls or turning it to parry the blades of swords. Jimbo drove men to the ground with blows from the butt of the big revolver. He slashed at exposed arms and leg with the blade of his Bowie. Byrus crouched between the Rangers, stabbing out with the point of his sword, bringing the mallet down on the heads of the fallen.

They fought for breath in the furnace heat created by the massed, struggling bodies in the cramped space. Their advantage was size and reach. The attackers were smaller men, picked for size to allow them to worm through the tunnels of counter-mines. They made up for their size with sheer ferocity, their eyes wide with opiates or adrenaline or animal fury or all three.

The Rangers and the pit fighter were backed to the neck of the curve. A heap of flesh was before them with more men clambering over the fallen to get at the three barbarians blocking their way to the surface. The impasse of the dead slowed the assault for only a heartbeat.

"Reload your rifle, bro!" Jimbo shouted. "We'll slow them down!"

Chaz backed away, reluctantly, to recharge the magazine tubes of his rifle. His hands were slippery with sweat. The butt of the rifle was caked with blood and hair. Jimbo and Byrus rushed to meet the next surge of swordsmen. The attack staggered as the Pima and the pit-fighter carved their way forward buying Chaz time to bring his rifle to bear.

The thud of boots on the floor planks in the tunnel behind him made Chaz turn. A voice called a cadence in Chinese, growing louder. The rifle loaded now and held to his hip, and the Ranger braced for a new assault from a second breach at their backs.

Men came around the turn in the tunnel, long rifles with gleaming bayonets affixed. They wore deep blue uniforms, trimmed in red under black lacquered bamboo chest plates and red conical hats. An officer called time. He was in a red turban and armor painted in gold, a straight-bladed sword in his fist. The character for the Qing dynasty was painted on his chest in white.

Imperial troops. The fleeing coolies had sounded the alarm.

Chaz pressed back against the wall of the burrow to allow the troops to pass.

"Jimmy! Clear the range!" Chaz bawled.

The emperor's soldiers, in response to the officer's yipped orders, formed triple ranks in the narrow confines of the tunnel. The front rank threw themselves prone to the mud, the second dropped to a knee, the third stood upright.

Downrange, the attack seized up at the sight of the rifle barrels trained their way. Jimbo shoved Byrus to the ground and dropped on top of him a half-second before the combined firepower of the three ranks exploded to fill the tunnel with light and sound.

The Taipings dropped in heaps under the first fusillade. The crush behind them swarmed forward to meet a second dose of lead that slashed them down like wheat before a scythe. All their momentum was lost as the tide of attackers halted then receded back toward the breach until they stalled against the clutch of their comrades still pouring down from the counter-mine.

The imperial officer shrieked an order, and, to a man, the riflemen charged down the tunnel for the Taiping wretches. They went to work on the attackers with bayonet points. Sinking the long triangular blades into ribs and guts, twisting, pulling, and spearing out again. They worked silently but for the roaring of their officer urging them on. The attackers' cries of defiance and threats turned to shrieks of pain and terror as the hacking wicket of blades drew blood and pierced flesh with mechanical efficiency. The combat moved farther down the tunnel, driven by the emperor's troops in a ghastly peristalsis that left a bloody carpet of dead and dying rebels.

Jimbo, bruised by the boot soles of his rescuers, rose from the muck. He pulled Byrus up with him. The little Macedonian, painted over with mud, was grinning and nodding. He was bleeding from a deep cut across the back of one hand but otherwise unharmed.

Chaz approached, holding out Jimbo's rifle.

"Boats is still waiting on us," Chaz said. Blood ran from the splinters embedded in his face and neck.

They trotted after the imperials, leaping and scrambling over the tunnel floor covered from wall to wall with the slain.

At the excavation end of the tunnel, the mandarin was quailing in fear.

Boats and Wei joined the mandarin's bodyguards to aim rifles into the dark. Choi stood behind with his gang of laborers, each armed with tools and ready to fight with their backs to the wall.

Coolies had come fleeing down to the dig site ahead of the sounds of gunfire up the tunnel.

The mandarin was wailing like a child, mouth working wetly, pale hands waving.

The SEAL sighted over the barrel of the lever-action, watching the spots of light from oil lamps stretching away to blackness. One after another, the lamps seemed to go out, their illumination snuffed. There were men coming toward them. The sound of feet splashing through mud, the glimmer of blades in the gloom.

Boats fired a round toward the first face he saw emerging out of the black. He advanced up the tunnel, jacking and firing as he went. The others followed. The air filled with smoke, and they walked through the haze, firing blind. The muzzle flashes from their weapons lanced out to create a crazed pattern of dark and light in which they could see men falling over one another before them.

Less an assault than a rout in reverse, the rebel attack petered out, leaving only the groaning wounded and silent dead. The tunnel rang with the sound of fighting, but no more rebels showed up. A Taiping, no older than twelve, cast his sword down and knelt in the guttering light, hands clasped together. He mewled at them, eyes searching, pleading. The men lowered their rifles.

The mandarin, his courage restored now that the threat had evaporated, strode forward, yapping orders. His bodyguards stood unmoving, eyes on the quivering boy. The mandarin snatched a rifle from one of them and marched down the tunnel to plant the point of the bayonet in the young rebel's throat. The boy collapsed, seizing and gurgling as he drowned in his own blood. The mandarin turned, grinning back at the company. He jerked the blade free. Boats put a .44 through the man's skull. The silly hat went flying up on a gout of blood and bone, the peacock feather twirling. The mandarin dropped as though legless into the wet mud. The SEAL jacked a new round and turned his eyes to the bodyguards.

"Do we have a problem?" he said.

The bodyguards provided an answer by rushing to the fallen mandarin and yanking the rings from his fingers.

A VEXING INCONVENIENCE

S ir Neal Harnesh chose to wait in the back of his limo while his jet was fueled. Better to sit in the heated confines of the Mercedes stretch rather than in the garish architectural atrocity that served as the executive waiting area at Kyzylorda Airport near the capital of Khazakstan.

He was soul weary rather than physically fatigued. *Weltschmerz*. The Germans had a word for everything. Sir Neal had endured a dinner party the night before that seemed to last an eternity. He'd been seated between the Khazak dictator's mistress, a former Miss Khazakstan—and a former president of the United States. He presumed he was positioned as a buffer between the famously lecherous former president and the shapely young supermodel. The dictator sat at the head of the table with his wife seated by him.

The whole event was ghastly, the food greasy, the champagne poor, the conversation tedious and the entertainment, frankly, appalling. But suffering through all of it was a sacrifice that Sir Neal was willing to make to secure mineral rights to a large portion of the country's rich uranium fields. The American president was there to make certain that the deal went through. In exchange for a generous donation, two hundred million dollars through Canadian shell companies, to his library, foundation, and very private account in Cuba.

Sir Neal was annoyed at the waste of his valuable time. Time he would never get back. Though he realized with a wry smile, that last was not necessarily true for him.

There was a tap on the tinted window by his head. He tabbed the window key, and the pane slid down to allow in the frigid, dry air from without.

Augustus Martin, collar up against the cold, bowed to speak to his master through the narrow gap. Martin appeared to be a fit man in his mid-twenties but his eyes, cold and hard, betrayed that first impression. Today, his eyes were colder and harder than usual.

"We believe that we've found the device," Martin said.

"Device?"

"The property stolen from our facility in Nevada."

Sir Neal came out of his ennui, his full attention on his supernumerary.

"Join me on the plane, Gus," Sir Neal said and raised the window.

At thirty-five thousand feet over Russian airspace, Sir Neal and Gus Martin continued their conversation over drinks. The multi-billionaire enjoyed a Dom Perignon '98 and his aide a room temperature lager.

"How was this done? Did you find the Taubers as well?" Sir Neal asked, accepting a warm towel from an attendant who made Miss Khazakstan look like a washerwoman.

"To answer your first question," Martin said, "we turned up satellite photos of a weather anomaly at the mouth of the

Yangtze. It was a curiously isolated lightning storm, accompanied by a thick white fog, occurring a few weeks ago."

"It is the device. China? How the devil did they get there? How the devil did they get halfway across the world with an unregistered nuclear reactor?" Sir Neal sat forward in his chair, eager for details.

"Apparently, it's aboard a ship, a cargo container ship leased from a global shipping company and registered in Egypt. The *Ocean Raj*. It's how they got to China. It's how they were able to reach the Mediterranean to interfere with the Judean operation," Martin said, grateful for his master's full attention. He was also pleased, for the moment, to have the upper hand. At least as far as information went.

"And why are they in Shanghai?"

"They're moored offshore for now, but intelligence we gathered on the ground tells us that they have been anchored for nearly two months in a berth belonging to Fei-Tong Freightage. That's a subsidiary of another company that ultimately is controlled by Jason Taan."

"I'm not familiar with him."

"One of the new Chinese billionaires. Some of your own shell companies had business with him in Malaysia a few years back, Sir Neal."

"And the Taubers?"

"There have been two activations of the device two days apart. I think it's safe to assume that one or more of the Taubers is aboard."

"They remain at anchor?"

"We're keeping an eye on them. No one on our watch list has left the ship. Only normal activity on board. As much as we can observe, anyway. They have the ship moored inside a shelter they constructed for the purpose of concealing their actions. There's armed security. Private."

Sir Neal watched the tops of clouds drift by below. His finger tapped the edge of his champagne goblet, causing the crystal to ring like a distant temple bell. He shifted his gaze to Gus Martin and spoke.

"I want the full itinerary of this container ship back to the first day of their lease. A full sweep based on what we find. Who do we have in Asia who can move immediately?"

"Franck is in Ho Chi Minh City. Quan is on Java."

"Get them both. I want a team ready to board that ship on a moment's notice. That ship is waiting for a reason. They have a team in the field somewhen. It will be there until the team has accomplished its objective. We strike while the field is open, catch them while their attention is focused elsewhere."

"And the orders for Franck and Quan?"

"I want the Taubers taken alive, and everyone else eliminated."

"Simple enough."

"And I want Visvamitra put to work on this. Search for any further anomalies and changes occurring across the chronal spectrum in the Yangtze valley. Anything out of place. Any time and place where the timeline has been buggered about."

"Yes, Sir Neal."

"And the other operation? Where was that? Mexico?"

"In Baja, sir. That is ongoing. No word yet."

"Perhaps you need to take a hand in that, Gus."

"Consider it done. Consider it resolved," Gus Martin said, wiping away a lager mustache from his upper lip with the corner of a damask napkin.

O ver two hundred dead Taiping rebels and laborers were hauled from the tunnel.

Sappers crawled up into the counter-mine to pack it with rags and brambles that were lit with oil. The burrow was angled sharply upward with only enough clearance for one man at a time. The resulting fire prevented a follow-up attack. The blaze created a draft drawing air down into the pit and up the tunnel and up the counter-mine like a flue, feeding the fire until it built to an inferno. At risk to their lives, sappers stoked the fire with fresh kindling. The support timbers of the approach to the counter-mine eventually burned through. They collapsed, bringing hundreds of tons of dirt down with them to extinguish the fire and block the counter-mine from further attacks.

Coolies closed the remaining gap with stacks of earth-filled baskets. Carpenters walled over the breach with timbers. Nothing was said of the unfortunate death of the mandarin, and his naked body was tossed into a mass grave on a slope above Dibai Castle along with rebels and coolies alike.

The outlaw excavation was now considered cursed. The coolies demanded higher wages. Shan suggested doubling their pay to two copper coins a day. The workforce returned, and the tunnel continued at twice the pace of the neighboring digs. The curse had the added benefit of keeping any more mandarins from snooping around. After all, this was the hole that swallowed one of their privileged class, never to be seen again.

The work of digging went on. The Devil's Ass cleft deeper into the heart of the hillside.

The next three days brought the tunnel under the foundations of the northern wall. For a stretch of forty feet, the ceiling of the burrow was enormous base stones on a bed of gravel and flaking lime mortar. The digging went faster since no bracing was needed. They were above the groundwater line as well.

Now the tunnel would angle upward at a ten percent gradient on a straight line two degrees off true north. That would bring them to within striking distance of their target with an easy vertical dig to the surface that could be accomplished in one night of work.

"We come up before dawn on the nineteenth. The histories all agree that the imperials blow their main tunnel at noon on that day," Jimbo told the others back at their camp in the stockade—absent Wei and Boats doing their spell in the dig. The team was sharing boiled mystery meat and rice. Byrus confirmed that it was horse. He'd eaten his share in the past.

"It gives us time to find the storehouse, get in and locate the prize," Lee said. "We find a place to hole up until the wall blows and the Imperials come in to loot the shit out of the place. We mix in with the melee and find our way out."

"Then back to the sea and we're home," Chaz said. "You almost make it sound easy," Bat said.

"What could go wrong?" Lee said. All but Shan laughed.

"We're getting close. I think we need to double the number of us at the point of the spear. Overlapping watches so there's always a minimum of four guns in the tunnel. We don't want to get this close and lose the dig to another breach," Lee said, and everyone nodded.

"You know, we've been lucky so far. There's so much chaos here that no one's paying attention to us," Bat said. "But do I have to tell you that it all changes when that wall comes down. This army will go feral for a few days. Their generals will allow that."

"What's that mean to us?" Chaz said.

"You really need to read more history," Jimbo said. "When we won a fight, we got some downtime to sleep, write emails, and catch up on Halo. But for these guys, it's going to be party time medieval style. Rape, looting, murder."

"And evening scores," Bat said. "We're barbarians to them. You guys have been focused on the dig. I've been up here the whole time. This place is fucked up."

"What?" Chaz said.

Bat cleared her throat and spat a wad of gristle into the fire. "Yesterday? The coolies and soldiers were worked up like it was spring break. They left the stockade to go down to the edge of the river. Banging gongs and tooting horns and like that. I followed along. I wish I hadn't. They had all these people locked up in a big iron cage up on a boat dock. Women and kids too. A hundred, maybe. I didn't notice at first, but the cage was on wheels that ran on wooden rails. The banks are mobbed with lookie-loos. Soldiers, workers, whores. Some asshole in black stands on the back of a cart and reads off a list from a scroll. Then coolies run forward out of the mob and begin pushing the cage down the tracks and down the ramp at the end into the water. The people inside are mashed against the bars as the water comes up around them. I saw a woman trying to get her baby through the bars. They were both crushed by the others before the water covered the whole cage. You could still hear them all screaming through the water."

"Sweet Jesus," Chaz said for them all.

"And the crowd didn't make a sound except to bang those fucking gongs," Bat said. "They just stood smiling until the last bubbles broke the surface. Then they went back to their posts, and their tools like nothing happened. They ran out a team of oxen and hooked them up to ropes tied to the cage. I didn't stay to watch the cage pulled out of the water. So, all's I'm saying is that someone's idea of fun might be killing some Yankees. We'd better watch our asses until we're back on the *Raj*."

"And after that," Lee said, meeting Shan's indifferent gaze.

WORLDS APART

Caroline drove through rain that streaked the windshield like dirty tears. The barren desertscape of San Felipe stretched like a tabletop before her, gray sky meeting gray earth.

The seat beside her was empty. She glanced at it again and again, praying to see Dwayne there.

Rick Renzi reclined in the back seat with N'itha, cushioning his cast with a rolled sleeping bag. Stephen was strapped into his car seat, sucking on the head of a Cookie Monster teether. His eyes studied the animated rivulets of rain dancing across the window by his head.

She'd known this day was coming. She knew with certainty that she would be separated from Dwayne at some point. She knew as sure as she knew anything that he would see her again. It could be January of 1871 on a snowy street in Paris. Yes, he would see her again, but she had already been there. That moment was in her past and in his future. For her, their last meeting was yesterday afternoon when he went to get them water.

Caroline drove the heel of her hand across her eyes to wipe them dry.

Dwayne found the pool right where he had been the day before. Or a million years ago or a century from now.

There were no signs of human habitation. No contrails trailing behind jets in the sky above. No litter on the ground. No footprint but his own. He saw no wildlife. The air was free of birds. There were biting horseflies, the only sign of life other than himself.

The pool lay among a tangle of gorse. It was shallower now. The water falling from above had not yet gouged the rock to the depth he remembered. What did that mean in geologic time? How many years did it take for erosion to create a wading pond from the inches-deep pan before him now? In the loose dirt around the edge of the pool were prints. The tiny hooves of deer? Pads of rabbits and larger animals. Predators. Coyotes, maybe.

He lay on his belly and drank the cool water. He stripped down to boxers and washed the blood from his shirt and jeans before laying them on a rock to dry.

His inventory consisted of the clothes on his back, the .45 Colt with three rounds left in the mag and one in the chamber, a revolver with five loads and the rifle he took off the guy he rode to this place on. He found a release on the body of the strange rifle that revealed a kind of canister drum containing what looked like thousands of needle-like projectiles. Ballistic speed, or greater than ballistic speed, darts.

Slipping on his boots, he hiked back to the hedge of grease-wood where he'd left the body of the hunter.

The cloth uniform was a synthetic but felt like it breathed. The tunic and pants were reinforced at the elbows, chest, and knees with an extra layer of fabric that had a mesh feel to them. The clothes would fit him well enough—he was roughly the same size as the dead man. He pulled away the smashed eye gear and helmet to reveal the face of a man in his late twenties maybe. The man's face was locked in an eternal sneer. One eye was black with an eight-ball hemorrhage from Dwayne braining him with the butt of the Kalashnikov.

The dead man was of mixed race. High cheekbones with mocha latte skin fading gray now with death. His one eye was olive-colored without an epicanthic fold. His military cut hair was raven black.

Unlike the uniform, the boots were a dead loss. They were more than a size too small for Dwayne. He pulled off the laces since they might be of some use later. The uniform stripped off, the dead man wore a black t-shirt and briefs of an unknown net-woven fabric and design. No manufacturing labels or markings.

The equipment belt held a canteen flask, penlight, clasp knife, flares, two more ammo canisters of the darts and some kind of wafer-thin device of blue metal. It looked like a smaller version of a smartphone, but Dwayne couldn't find a way to power it up. There were no buttons or pads anywhere on its surface. There were absolutely no personal items anywhere on this guy. A tattoo high on his arm featured a running stick figure like one from a traffic sign. Beneath it was a row of stylized characters that could be letters or numbers.

He had the guy stripped naked but for one item. The bracelet.

Dwayne searched for a clasp or even a break in the surface and found nothing. He sat on the sand, sipping from the dead man's canteen and tried to make up his mind about a number of things. The liquid in the canteen had a citrus taste and a touch of sweetness, dry like ginger ale.

His thoughts all came back to that ring of steel around the hunter's wrist.

Should he destroy the bracelet? *Could* he destroy it? Or should he gear up and use it to zap himself somewhere else? He wasn't sure how he'd set it to bring him when he was now, whenever it was. Using the device again might just zap him back into the arms of the assholes he'd just escaped from. Could they use it to track him? If that were true, wouldn't they already be here? Or, given the vagaries of time travel, would they arrive here six months from now? Or the day before? Or arrived yesterday and were even now watching him from the surrounding rocks?

Back in basic, they taught him that the days of linear, old school combat were over. No marching to take an objective from the bad guy and holding it. The new battlefield was liquid and moveable with bad guys three-sixty, twenty-four/seven. His world now made counterinsurgency warfare seem so simple.

In the end, he decided that he needed the bracelet.

And, since he didn't plan on dragging a rotting corpse along with him, he set about the work of freeing it from the dead man's wrist.

43

The digging men spoke only in whispers now. They chipped at the earth foot by foot, lengthening the tunnel by the hour. The earth was loose and dry, allowing them to work soundlessly with spades. The carpenters sweated to keep up, hammering boards in place with mallet heads wrapped in layers of cloth. Through the soil above them came the muffled blare of horns and even voices. Their enemy, the mad followers of the second son of God, marched just over their heads.

Jimbo crouched in the bell-shaped chamber at the foot of the final stretch of the Devil's Ass and drew with a splinter of wood in the loose soil. Chaz was by him. Wei looked on, trying to comprehend the drawings the Pima was making. Byrus slept against a wall of the tunnel, coolies stepping over him to carry baskets of dirt away.

"We could be in there tonight. By my measurements, anyway. It's daytime, right?" Jimbo said, finishing his rough diagram showing the tunnel's progress under the walls of Nanking and the palace of the East King within the walls of the inner fortress.

"Afternoon by my best guess." Chaz shrugged.

"By the end of our watch we'll be at the entry point," Jimbo said. He held up five fingers then one to Wei. He pointed to his wrist then up the tunnel. Wei understood. Infiltration in six hours. Jimbo woke Byrus and sent him back up the tunnel to Lee Hammond with the message.

"Bullshit. I'm part of this team, or I'm not," Bathsheba Jaffe said, the spray of freckles across her nose darkening as her rage stoked.

Boats and Shan geared up, ignoring the lovers' spat that looked to turn lethal given the weaponry available.

"You are. But we need someone topside, babe," Lee said, slipping a second bandolier of ammo over his shoulder.

"Bullshit. Bullshit. Bullshit. You think I can't deal with what's ahead?" Bat said.

"I don't even *know* what's ahead," Lee said.

"Even more reason to not be down by one gun," she seethed, picking up her rifle and bandoliers.

"I worry about you, okay?"

"I never asked you to."

"It's going to get rough, babe. We're going eyeball to eyeball."

"And you think I can't hack that? Do I have to kick *your* ass to prove that I can?"

Lee threw up his hands. Bat moved past him, delivering a shoulder check to force him out her way as she marched toward the pit. Boats grinned and winked at Lee as he and Shan followed the girl to war. Byrus trotted after them with an ax he'd picked up somewhere resting on his shoulder. He was anxious to lead them back to Jimbo at the head of the dig.

"You never should have stopped dating waitresses, brother," Lee sighed to himself and picked up his rifle to bring up the rear.

———

Far up the Devil's Ass, a rupture opened.

It began as a trickle of sludge that flooded the floor of the tunnel into a swampy mess. The leak came from the place where the counter-mine had broken through five days earlier. The trickle became a sudden storm of evil-smelling water spraying between the timbers that were hammered in place to shore up the break. The weight pressed on the barricade of gabions until it broke and gave way, loosing a violent torrent that swept up and down the tunnel in a noxious brown tide.

The Taipings had diverted their sewage to run down the counter-mine. The weight against the blockage built until the pressure pushed the plug free.

The scream of the coolies in the lowest part of the dig was cut short as the city's wastewater flooded the tunnel to the ceiling. The current smashed them against the walls, killing them with blunt force rather than drowning, a mercy in its own way. The poisonous river tore away timbers as it flowed to find the lowest places in the excavation. It raced down the tunnel like a hose, sweeping laborers along with it, on its way to the leading point of the mine. As the passageway filled, the water surged upward toward the entrance. Coolies threw down their tools and their burdens and clambered over one another to escape the wave swiftly filling the tunnel.

The overpowering stink of it reached Lee and the others as they made their way toward the rest of the team waiting somewhere ahead. The shrieks of panicked men echoed up the throat of the tunnel. Laborers, coated in reeking muck, clawed their way past. Behind them, the tunnel way grew dark as the river of sewage extinguished the oil lamps.

The team turned to follow the coolies to the light. Boats took Byrus by the arm and dragged him along. The little Macedonian, loyal unto death, was willing to swim the length of a tunnel of shit to reach the side of Jimmy Smalls.

The mine flooded to just shy of where it forked off the main tunnel. The putrid water swirled there, the way beyond filled to capacity. The battered bodies of coolies bobbed up to the surface to come to rest at the edge of the lapping brown surf.

"My God, could Jimbo and Chaz still be alive?" Bat said, heaving for breath after the frantic run into the open air of the pit.

"The dig angles up at their end. Maybe they got far enough to be above the highest level," Lee said, dropping to sit on the dirt.

"What now?" Boats said.

"We go in with the soldiers when the wall comes down tomorrow," Shan said, his eyes as hard as stones.

"You son of a bitch," Boats said, stepping up to the other man, hands fisted into twin clubs. Shan stood his ground, regarding the huge SEAL without a change in expression.

"He's right, sailor." Lee sighed. "There's nothing we can do for Jimbo and Chaz. We go on like they made it and link up at the treasure house."

"*That's* the brilliant plan?" Boats locked eyes with Shan but stepped back.

"No, it's a clusterfuck. But like you Navy assholes say, better a bad plan..." Lee said.

"Than no plan at all," Boats said and sank to sit by the Ranger.

Bat turned from them to hide the hot tears coursing twin paths through the dirt caked on her face.

44

POISON TIDE

Where the tunnel angled up from below, the shallow pool of water had turned to a lake then boiled up the mine toward them. Coolies climbed upwards to escape the crush of water. Jimbo and Chaz pulled Wei along with them as the bell-shaped chamber filled to knee height and kept rising. They backed away, all eyes on the level of toxic sludge bubbling to pursue them. The coolies wailed in horror and pummeled one another to reach the highest point above the deluge.

Choi barked orders and battered at his terrified laborers with his fists. They settled down to scrabble silently up the slope of the mine. The Rangers and Wei followed, the sewage eddying at their heels. The current peaked, then receded a few yards.

They were left with roughly fifty feet of dry tunnel above the high-water mark. Close to a hundred men crammed into the confines of a tunnel too low for Jimbo or Chaz to stand and too narrow for them to hold their arms at full length to either side.

"Fuck. Fuck. Motherfucking fuck," Chaz hissed.

"That sums it up nicely." Jimbo was fighting down the grip of his phobia.

He wasn't reassured when a section of tunnel ceiling collapsed into the water with a splash. Wei scrambled back, eyes darting wildly as if seeking a heretofore unseen exit from this hell.

"All right. Fuck it. Only way out is up," Chaz said, slapping the back of Jimbo's head. "Same plan but we dig our asses out now."

"Yeah. Yeah." The Pima was staring back at the pulsing surface of muck sealing the tunnel below.

"Now," Chaz repeated. "We're only going to have so much air. You feel that? In your ears? The flood pushed air ahead of it. The pressure's up in the tunnel. But it won't be breathable forever."

Jimbo could feel it, the sensation that his head was full like in a plane taking off on a rapid ascent. He followed Chaz forward with Wei behind them. They picked up shovels and joined the coolies who were hacking a way forward under Choi's barked commands. Those without tools loaded baskets with fill using their bare hands. The baskets were handed along to be dumped into the flooded tunnel. They were extending the tunnel without increasing the interior space. The work proceeded at greater speed. The number of men was sufficient to fill baskets, hand the full loads back in a chain with another chain to return the empty baskets in an unbroken ring.

"Like moles," Chaz grunted, loading a shovel and pitching the contents behind him.

Like rats, Jimbo thought, chopping at the loose soil with feverish energy.

Lee and the others climbed the ladders to the surface and made their way back to camp to wash the literal shit storm from their uniforms. Boats remained behind at the mouth of the pit to watch the preparations going on there.

Bullock carts loaded with barrels of gunpowder were drawn up to the opening. Coolies dampened the ground before the pit with bucket after bucket of river water to prevent the possibility of sparks. A path of damp straw was spread under the feet of the laborers hauling the barrels from the carts toward the bed of the lift. Each load was secured tightly with wet ropes before being swung out over the pit and lowered, slow and careful, on squealing block and tackle lines.

On the pit floor, more coolies unloaded the barrels and made their way into the entrances of two tunnels. Ten carts were unloaded this way, and the explosives carted into the depths and along the half miles to where they would be bedded in a big chamber scooped out beneath the foundations of the north wall.

Boats, a keen judge of all that goes boom, estimated that each of those holes was loaded with ten tons of black powder. Enough to create an instantaneous sinkhole and bring down the walls and ramparts above the twin blast points. The entire painfully slow process took until well after dark. All was done under constant hectoring from mandarins dressed in their party best. But the orders were delivered in hushed voices as if any loud utterance would release the fury of the massive amount of powder they'd stuffed down the tunnels. Even the ever-present gongs and bugles were silent.

Following the powder came more bullock carts stacked with bales of straw. The bales were lowered and hauled down the mines to pack the powder-packed chambers full to the ceiling. The straw would burn and ignite the powder. A trail of powder down the walking planks of the tunnels would serve as a fuse.

Boats grew bored with this part of the preparations and made his way back to the tents. Lee and Shan were stripped down to undies, oiling and cleaning their weapons and leather. Byrus was bringing a fresh razor edge to his sword with a whetstone. A pair of hired coolies were pressing the moisture from their uniforms, fresh from a washtub of boiling water. Boats assumed that Bat was doing the same in the concealment of their tent.

Soldiers gathered to watch the strange company at their ablutions. They pointed and remarked on the tattoos displayed on Lee Hammond's scarred hide. A rattlesnake was inked on his right arm, coiled up from just above his wrist, wrapping around the corded muscles to end in a gaping mouth of dripping fangs on his shoulder. On his left arm, a dagger through a grinning skull. An American flag unfurling across his biceps. His chest was emblazoned with a Celtic cross and on his back a pair of crossed M4 rifles with a scroll reading, *Rangers Lead The Way* across a map of Iraq.

"They're working up to the big blow tomorrow," Boats said, stripping out of his own filthy uniform, showing off the spread-winged eagle and anchor under the thick mat of red hair on his chest.

"Right on schedule like the history books say," Lee said, pulling an oiled patch of cloth up the barrel of his rifle.

"We're going in with the mob?" Boats said, handing off his clothes to a coolie who bowed and grinned.

"We'll let the first and second waves take the lead for once," Lee said. "Fong's paper on the battle says the Taipings put up stiff resistance through the afternoon. We have no dog in this fight. We stay clear of any contact. We're here for one thing."

"But we must beat the looters to the prize," Shan said.

Lee turned to Shan with some heat. "Thanks for the input, Captain Obvious. But Jimbo and Chaz will be there waiting for us."

"How can you be certain of this?" Shan sniffed.

"Because I've seen them in tighter spots than this. That one-eyed Indian and that hardcore, stone-cold brother aren't going to drown in some shithole in this shithole country and this shithole war," Lee said slamming the ramrod home in his rifle.

"Zim not dead. Byrus will not let him die," Byrus said between clenched teeth, emphasizing his words with strokes of the stone along the blade of his gladius.

"And that's the last word on that," Lee said and stood to walk to the tent.

45

GOING DOWNTOWN

W ithin the walls of Nanking, a peasant family was awakened from fitful sleep by an unknown hissing sound.

They had taken shelter in what was once a horse stable that housed mounts for the cavalry of the Shield King, one of the cohort of lower kings who served the Heavenly King, ruler of the Land of Eternal Peace. A mother, father, elderly grandmother, and seven children had taken a stall in the stables as their home when their own house burned to the ground in the first weeks of the siege. There was room in the stables now—all the fine Arabian stallions of the elite mounted regiment known as God's Vengeful Fury had been butchered and eaten months before as famine swept the city. Even the floors were clean, swept of every grain and stalk of straw to be ground to meal and used as filler in the loaves of bread parceled out as meager rations.

The youngest son was the first to waken after dreaming of a giant serpent with glowing eyes and poison breath. When he realized that the hissing sound of his dreams was real and very near, he roused the others. The father hushed the others and crept toward the susurrating sound coming from within one of

233

the abandoned horse stalls. He paused, swiping a hand through the air before his face. The air was filling with a nauseating outhouse scent. The father gagged but kept on.

The hissing sound was dying away now. The father stood in stunned disbelief as a flagstone in the floor began to rise from its place all by itself. More amazed when a glow of muted light projected from beneath the shifting stone. When it was moved aside, a beam of light shot upward from a hole in the floor of the stall. He drew closer, then stepped back. The head of a mallet struck upward from the hole, widening it and unseating the flagstones around it. The hole collapsed, becoming a crater and the voices of men, cursing, rose from below. The father turned to run, to move his family to flee and to raise the alarm. A filthy hand gripped his sleeve. An arm slid around his throat from behind. He was thrown to the floor, a sandaled foot on his chest. Above him, a demon from hell, smeared dark with mud, raised a shovel to bring the blade down on his head.

The demon was tossed aside by the biggest man the father had ever seen. A man with skin as black as ebony. Near him was a second man with one eye covered by a leather patch. They exchanged words that the father could not understand. The black man gripped the father's hand and pulled him to his feet before shoving him away. More men were emerging from the hole in the floor. Coolies, their nearly naked bodies caked with foul-smelling muck, eyes staring and mouths panting.

The black man shoved the father away once more. The father turned to find his family and flee, his only thought to get his loved ones far from this gate to Hell.

"I guess this is the only luck we're gonna get tonight. Could have come up in the middle of a barracks," Chaz said. He put a finger to his nose to press one and then the other nostril closed and blow out streams of muddy mucous.

Jimbo said nothing. He stood bent, hands on knees, and filled his lungs with clean air, pressure relieved to be free from the tomb of the tunnel. His inner ears crackled adjusting to the change in atmosphere.

Wei was forming up the coolies who were beginning to wander off toward the moonlight beyond the stable doors. He had a hushed exchange with Choi that ended with Wei making *stay* gestures with open palms.

"Good idea. These guys should stay out of sight," Chaz said to the uncomprehending Wei. Chaz gave him a thumbs up, and Wei nodded with enthusiasm and returned the sign.

Jimbo raised his head from where he'd dunked it in a stone horse trough. He shook the water from his hair in a spray and stripped off his feces-encrusted tunic to toss it to the floor. He stood, leaning on the trough, eyes closed, mouth moving in silent thanks.

"Think you can find this place?" Chaz said after giving his friend a moment.

Jimbo turned and sat on the edge of the trough. He picked up his rifle, checked that the action and barrel were clear of mud then rose.

"How hard can it be? It's a palace, right?" Jimbo sighed and rose to lead them into the night of the enemy city.

———

The Rangers had been on enough night ops behind enemy lines to know that skulking around drew more attention than boldly walking in plain sight. Wei fell in behind them, strolling as if he belonged there.

They walked steady and with purpose along a lane that Jimbo figured would take them to the concentric wall ringing the inner city where the big shots lived. The streets were dark, and the alleys black with shadow, probably from a shortage of lamp oil. There was no one on the streets and not even the sound of barking dogs. Jimbo surmised they'd all been eaten long ago.

Troops were concentrated on the outer defenses. There were no patrols within the city. There was nothing left to loot. Awnings drooped over market stalls standing open and empty.

Many buildings, once grand homes or businesses, were blackened skeletons where they'd been set ablaze by rockets or balls of heated cannon shot. Others lay collapsed in upon themselves, victims of the stone balls fired from mortars. These derelicts stood by buildings that remained untouched by the siege. Many of the streets were torn up, leaving only the bare soil beneath. The stones paving the street had been pulled up to create shot for the many cannons defending the city.

The trio came at last to the three-story wall that served to separate the Heavenly King and his most loyal acolytes from the unwashed masses of greater Nanking. They followed it along a frontage road toward a gate. From the shadows of a ruined home, they considered the tall gatehouse topped by timber ramparts covered with a tiled roof. Loitering before the gate, under guttering torchlight, was a gang of men in black silks and turbans. They were armed with axes and swords. Some leaned on muskets. They were sharing a pot of some kind of gruel bubbling over a fire built on the cobbles before the gate.

"True believers," Jimbo whispered.

"No bullshitting our way past them," Chaz replied. Wei shook his head slowly at them, eyes hard.

They turned at a creak of rusting metal. Across the lane from where they crouched concealed, a vertical bar of radiance grew wider within a shadowed recess of the wall. It was a doorway cleverly concealed in a niche. As it opened, it revealed the light of a lantern reflecting off the street cobbles.

Jimbo met Chaz' eyes. His brother Ranger nodded, and they moved to the light in time to find a man dumping out buckets of wet slop into a gutter at the curb. A second man held a lantern high to provide light.

The Rangers struck the pair, driving them back into a narrow corridor built within the base of the twenty-foot thick wall. The servants crashed to the floor. The buckets of piss and feces they were dumping spilled across the cobbles. The lantern fell into the spreading puddle with a hiss, the flame dying. The pair of men struggled and were still. Jimbo heard the man under him mewl in protest and go silent. His eyes adjusted to the gloom to see the man grinning from a new mouth slashed across his throat. He heard a rustle of cloth and a grunt from Chaz Raleigh. The Ranger was shoving Wei against the wall. At their feet, the second servant lay kicking out the last of his life, his throat sliced open like the other. A knife, gleaming black with blood, fell from Wei's hand.

Jimbo pulled Chaz away from the smaller man. "He killed them," Chaz snapped.

"It had to be done," he said through his teeth.

"But I wanted it to be my idea," Chaz growled back, a last cuff to Wei's shoulder as they parted.

"Now *he* owns it," Jimbo said and pushed Chaz along down the corridor.

Wei stooped to wipe the blade of his knife on the tunic of one of the servants then rose to follow the Americans toward the uncertain lights of the City of Heavenly Contentment.

46

AN EMBARRASSMENT OF RICHES

A s it turned out, there were a lot of palaces on the grounds of the inner city.

They were set back behind decorative curtain walls along cobbled streets once lined with flowering trees. The steep angles of tiled rooftops could be seen over the tops of the walls. Hand-carved beams atop the crests were fashioned in the shapes of dragons, tigers, and angels, all accented in gold leaf. The only remnant of the trees along the lane were stumps where they'd been cut down for firewood.

"Damn. This map's no good," Jimbo cursed, the chart created by Dr. Fong in his hands illuminated by the flickering light of an oil lamp held by Wei.

"What's the trouble?" Chaz said.

"I don't see how it relates to where we are."

"We're gonna need to ask for directions," Chaz said, looking the length of the long street and seeing not a single living thing.

Jimbo held the map up to Wei and stabbed a finger at the location that Wesley Fong marked as the likely location for the East King's palace. Wei nodded, first at the map and then at the two Rangers. He trotted down the broad pebbled street.

The Rangers stepped into the shadows of a shrine set in the niche of a wall. They took a seat on a bench within the enclosure. A jade statue stood against the back wall of the closet-sized shrine. It was unmistakably Jesus Christ.

"That would look good in my man cave," said Jimbo.

"That ain't no Jesus I've ever seen," Chaz said, eyeing the idol depicting the messiah battling a dog-faced demon, a sword in his fist and an expression of righteous fury on his face.

"I don't have a man cave anyway." Jimbo shrugged.

"You're not that kind of asshole."

"What kind of asshole am I?"

The Rangers heard the tramp of boot soles on gravel. The clack of bamboo armor and the creak of leather reached them as the glow of an oil lamp loomed on the street outside the entrance of the shrine. A patrol of about twenty men clothed in black armor marched by. They shouldered long spears and curved swords in scabbards swung at their hips. A bannerman led the way, a lamp held on a pole before him. Fists gripping their rifles, the Rangers watched the parade go past and the street fall into darkness again.

A few moments passed before they heard a sharp hissing sound from the darkness. It was Wei trying to get their attention from a niche in the wall two palaces down. The Rangers trotted to meet him and found him at a cleverly disguised gateway hidden in a recess. Wei had a feebly struggling man in a choke-hold, a chubby guy in yellow and black striped silk pajamas and brocaded shoes with pointed toes. The captive's eyes rolled toward Jimbo and Chaz, the pupils swirling.

"He knows the way?" Jimbo said, hushed. He jabbed a finger at the folded map.

Wei nodded and jerked his prisoner upright. The guy's face darkened, his eyes turning up to show the whites. Jimbo pulled on Wei's arm, and the prisoner fell to the ground.

"Who's this dude?" Chaz asked.

"A palace eunuch," Jimbo said and crouched to gently slap the man's face until he responded with a yelp.

"That mean what I think it means?"

"Yeah. No balls."

The guy came around with a gasp. Jimbo placed the barrel of the Remington against his forehead and cocked the hammer. The Pima placed a finger to first his own lips and then to the eunuch's. The smaller man grunted and nodded his assent. Wei barked at him in Mandarin and kicked him to his feet.

They followed the eunuch along a maze of decorative walls and across open areas of weed-choked dirt between dry garden ponds. Statues in marble and bronze stood on plinths depicting animals or saints. Dark structures loomed above them. High peaked rooftops, windows covered in ornate latticework and tiers of balconies rising toward the night sky. The sounds of the siege seemed far away here, the guns and rockets muffled by distance and the concentric defensive walls that encircled the city of the kings of Heaven on Earth.

The eunuch led them to a pair of massive doors of lacquered green fortified with bronze bands. He shook with tremors that set his flab to quivering. His eyes blinked at them, sweat beading on his face. Jimbo shoved him aside. Chaz raised his rifle to follow. The Pima shook his head and slid his broad-bladed knife from the sheath at his waist. Chaz slung his rifle and drew his own blade. Together they shouldered the door open in a rush.

Two more eunuchs were startled from where they leaned, dozing on pikestaffs within a broad foyer lit by braziers. Jimbo slapped a hand over the mouth of one while, in the same motion, slamming the point of his knife upward behind the man's chin. The blade bit in with a series of crunching sounds and the man went limp. Chaz had his man in a chokehold, lifting the guard's feet kicking from the tiles. He drove the spade point of his knife at an angle into the man's skull where it met the top of the spine. Chaz twisted the blade once, and the man's arms and legs ceased their dance. The sharp stink of urine filled the air. Chaz tossed the dead man aside. Wei dragged his captive inside, the little eunuch's eyes staring, his neck turned at an obscene angle.

Together they swung the big armored doors closed and dropped a stout timber into the cross braces. The high-ceilinged foyer was lined either side by pillars of black marble streaked with red. The tiled floor was set in a pattern of large and small squares engraved with Chinese characters along with stylized crosses inlaid with onyx. At the end of the foyer was a broad staircase of carved stone leading to a higher level. Over the steps hung silk banners depicting Hong Xiuquan, the Heavenly King, and Jesus Christ seated on thrones of gold. Hong held what looked like a diamond the size of a cantaloupe in the palm of his hand while Christ seemed to be petting a tiger cub resting on his lap.

"I've seen better velvet paintings of Elvis for sale at gas stations," Chaz grunted.

Jimbo agreed. "All the money in the world and their taste in their ass."

They followed Wei up the long flight of stairs to a level that ended in a mezzanine with walls papered in hand-painted silk depicting intertwined branches of rose bushes from which peeped stylized monkeys with white fur and disturbingly human eyes. The mezzanine ran along three walls around an area open to the foyer below. The only opening off the mezzanine was a pair of heavy doors set in an arched opening. The door was forged in bronze with relief sculptures of doves and dragonflies in flight. Wei tested the ornamental handles, fashioned in the shape of a pair of leaping salmon, with a push. They swung inward easily and without a sound. The Rangers raised their rifles, hammers cocked.

Beyond the massive doors was a huge black space. The fall of their boots echoed as they advanced over the tiles. Wei snatched a brazier from the mezzanine and led them in. They found other braziers and lit them with the embers from the first. The light illuminated an area around them but failed to reach either the walls or the ceiling. The chamber was enormous, supported by rows of pillars wider around than a man's arms could encircle. They were of the same ebon marble shot through with red as the pillars in the foyer below.

Between the pillars, and stretching back into the gloom, were row after row of tables covered in silk cloths. And upon these tables were arranged an assembly of objects that shimmered and gleamed in the dancing light of the braziers.

"Shit the bed," Chaz breathed. His voice echoed against the walls of the invisible vastness of the chamber.

"Beats the hell out of one of Saddam's palaces, for damn sure," Jimbo said in hushed wonder.

The three soldiers entered the treasure house of the East King. Statues, miniatures, dishware, combs, scepters, and crowns of gold and silver inlaid with rubies, emeralds, and opals were spread in either direction off a center lane. One table held nothing, but toy-sized animals carved in jade and gold-inlaid ivory. Another was stacked with mechanical clocks of all sizes fashioned from obsidian, malachite, and gold. Tables were piled six feet high with bolts of silk of every color imaginable. Another broad table was dominated by a three-dimensional map of the Heavenly City of Peace, the buildings fashioned from gold and encrusted with gems. There was a table of hand-painted silk fans with spines of carved ivory, Another of hairbrushes cleverly fashioned from jade and obsidian in the shape of the same animals the bristles had been derived from, horses, pigs, bears, and camels. Beyond the tables were stacks of chests loaded with gems and coins. Row after row of immaculate balls of crystalline glass the size of basketballs rested on stands of carved mahogany inlaid with jade and silver and furniture carved over every surface with images of animals or figures from Chinese mythology and legend stood against the walls.

Two rows of sedan chairs, carts, and rickshaws stood as if they were on a showroom floor. These were no common conveyances but were fashioned of silk-covered wood and trimmed in either solid gold or gold leaf. The wood was heavily lacquered, and much of it was carved in intricate patterns. The velvet upholstery was accented with gems in place of buttons.

Wooden chests reinforced with bands of iron or bronze were laden with coins of gold and silver. Bullion wrapped in paper rested in pyramid stacks on pallets. There were bottles of fine porcelain in crates packed with straw; each bottle was painted with graphic pornographic images of men and women, women and women, and men and men. And more chests were amassed in piles ten feet high and packed with blocks of sticky black tar wrapped in translucent paper.

Opium.

"Pray all Sunday, sin all week," Chaz said, shaking his head.

"And this was the stash of one of the *minor* kings," Jimbo said. He raised a brazier over his head.

Chaz tsk-ed. "They looted this country dry, bro. All those people looking like they don't have a handful of rice between them and these motherfuckers living like dot com billionaires."

Wei was staring with wide eyes and slack jaw at the landscape of treasures as far as the glow of their braziers could reach. He spoke to himself in whispers.

"How the hell are we going to find this thing we're looking for? There's miles of this shit here," Chaz said, picking up a jade statue of a naked woman astride a charging tiger.

"We have until noon tomorrow. I'm guessing that's about eight hours from now give or take," Jimbo said. "That's when the mine blows. Even more time before the imperial army fights its way this far. We should have time to locate it and get our asses clear."

"Let's go shopping," Chaz said with a grin.

"We'll start at the back and work forward," Jimbo said,

holding the brazier high and searching the dark for the limits of the vast chamber.

The Rangers and Wei headed for the back wall of the treasure room. They froze in mid-step. From below them came a rhythmic booming sound. It was the big doors on the first level. Someone was knocking.

47

THE GENERAL

The pounding on the doors increased in frequency and volume. Rather than a fist, it sounded like the doors were being struck with a blunt object, the butt of a pike or the pommel of a sword. A voice, muted but discernibly emphatic, could be heard even through the thickness of the wood. The impacts stopped after moments of steady banging. The voice could no longer be heard.

Jimbo and Chaz stood at the top of the long staircase, Wei behind them in the open doorway of the treasure vault.

"They went away. Nobody home." Chaz sighed.

"They'll be back," Jimbo said.

The door below shuddered under the weight of something on the other side. A rumbling boom echoed up to them. The timber bar stayed in place, but the doors trembled under the blow. The impact was repeated and continued with the steady cadence of a heartbeat.

"Somebody went and got a ram," Jimbo said.

"A lot of somebodies," Chaz said, checking his rifle for a load and thumbing back the hammer.

"That's some serious doors. They'll be a while busting in."

"I'll keep an eye out. You and Wei look for the booby prize," Chaz said, handing his rifle to Jimbo.

"And a back door," Jimbo said, moving back into the vault with Wei following.

"We're gonna need one of them too," Chaz said, turning to the doors below, quaking in their hinges under the relentless assault from without.

The sun rose to the thunder of drums.

The entire siege camp was roused to wakefulness by the beat provided by a company of men hammering in time on rows of kettle drums six feet across.

An area was cleared on the broad field used as a parade ground at the center of the sea of tents. Bawling bannermen raced across the trampled grass, swinging their silk flags and shouting words to rouse the martial spirits. Soldiers, sappers, coolies, merchants, and whores gathered in deep ranks along the edges of the field to witness the arrival of the general who had been commanding the siege effort. Even the artillery went silent, the gun crews, black with expelled powder, watching with ramrods in hand.

Bat stuck close by Lee as the Ranger wended through the crowd toward the front rows. They'd lost Boats and Byrus somewhere behind them.

"What do you think this is?" She shouted to be heard over the babble of voices.

"Final orders," Lee said. "This whole thing kicks off in a few hours."

They got within ten rows of the open field, close enough to see over the heads of the shorter men standing before them. The crowd was hushing now, turning in anticipation to the end of the field.

The big man rode onto the field, astride a massive white stallion that made him appear child-sized in comparison. General Hsui Shen Sang wore leather armor the color of flames, trimmed in high polished gold with gold bucklers studded across every surface. Atop his head was a tall conical helmet ending in a curved point and festooned in black ostrich feathers. Behind him trotted his lieutenants in armor only slightly less resplendent. Behind them rode a thousand or more Tartar archers in fur-trimmed armor. To either flank sprinted thousands more bannermen, holding aloft a forest of streaming flags and banners. They took up positions along the edges of the crowd that lined the field and glowered with cold menace at the onlookers.

The General made no speech, no promises of victory. He reined in his horse and sat tall in the saddle, or as tall as he could manage, for all to take in his bellicose magnificence.

From somewhere in his entourage, a voice shrieked an order. The ocean of pressed humanity shouted back, repeating the phrase as if from one throat. The invisible crier screamed another order, and the response was delivered with even more gusto from a half a million throats. Bat held her hands over her ears to cut out the din that went on and on, call and response after call and response. The mob around her grew more passionate as the ceremony went on. They went from indifference to howling in fury, shrieking madly, faces dark with rage and weapons held over their heads in fists with knuckles turned white. Bat saw a man from the cook tents standing with a stirring paddle raised to the sky in warlike fervor.

The general wheeled his horse around to gallop back the way he came. Silence fell over the field. His entourage of officers and bodyguard of bowmen turned to follow their leader, sending clods of dirt flying through a growing pall of yellow dust. The bannermen followed, double-timing after the cavalry in rank after rank.

This parade was followed by coolies dragging hundreds of

carts onto the field. The carts were loaded with rice balls bound in leaves. These were tossed to the eager crowd who were, moments before, roaring with the rage of caged beasts but were now laughing like children in anticipation of the general's munificent treat. Some giggled like schoolgirls when their first mouthful of sweetened rice revealed a copper coin hidden within.

"They'll die with a full belly and a penny in their pockets," Lee said, taking Bat's arm to pull her from the path of a particularly eager favor seeker.

"I don't know who I feel sorrier for, this bloodthirsty bunch or the poor bastards who don't know that their hometown is going to get shit on today," Bat said, moving to stand close by the Ranger while the party crowd around them grew more raucous.

"Not our fight, baby," Lee said, resisting the urge to put his hand in her hair and draw her nearer. "Not our fight."

48

A SWIG IN HELL

The heavy doors shook in the frame and crashed to the floor followed close by a stumbling crew of eunuchs gripping the cannon barrel they had been using as a ram.

They spilled to the floor. The bronze cannon barrel hit the tiles, ringing like a gong. A dozen more eunuchs, armed with long swords and longer pikes, stormed in behind them.

Jimbo sighted on the biggest and pressed the trigger home. The others stared in momentary bewilderment as one of their number flew in the air as though slipping on a slick surface. A second spun to the ground atop the first, clawing and shrieking with a slug in his guts. A third collapsed clutching a spurting wound to his throat.

The gang of eunuchs turned their fury to the source of their punishment. They charged up the long flight of stairs toward the man standing at the top in a haze of black powder smoke. A high-pitched ululating cry rose from them as they rushed to the mezzanine, spears thrust before them.

Their advance was slowed as first one, then another fell under Jimbo's rifle fire. The eunuchs tripped over the tumbling corpses and fell in a tangle of limbs and weaponry back the way they'd

CHUCK DIXON

come. Jimbo pumped round after round into the pack, dropping men before they could rise again. The rest backed off toward the open doorway and out of sight, leaving behind a writhing mass of wounded at the foot of the stairs.

The Pima blinked through the thick, acrid smoke at the carnage below. As he reloaded, he could hear the sound of gongs from outside. The alarm was raised. The next attack would be soldiers, the fanatical personal guard of the Kingdom Of Heavenly Peace and Contentment.

Chaz was beside him, handing over one of his bandoliers of ammo.

"You okay out here?" he said.

"I can hack. Any luck inside?"

"No joy. There's a lot of shit to look through in there," Chaz said, shaking his head.

"Find a back door out of here?"

"Not yet, brother. You may be covering the only exit."

"Rangers lead the way. Right into a corner." Jimbo wore a grim smile and jacked a fresh round home.

From below, the sound of clashing gongs grew louder. It was joined by the trudge of boots on gravel. A crush of men exploded through the open doorway, pounding over the fallen doors, leaping the bodies of Jimbo's victims. These were soldiers in leather armor studded with iron and heads topped with conical helmets. They were armed with spears and axes and moved to the foot of the stairs and climbed with a fearful silence, four men across, up the steps. The column stretched back to the doorway and beyond in what looked like an endless stream.

The Rangers opened up on the mass rising toward them. The front ranks dropped only to vanish beneath the boots of the men pressing behind. Rifle fire poured into the soldiers, punching holes through armor and flesh. The advance didn't seem to slow, only rippled like a serpent while the onrushing men climbed over the dead. The front rank loomed close enough for the Rangers to see black eyes and gnashed teeth and the shining spear points wavering ahead of them.

A long shriek of what they recognized as obscenities in Mandarin caused Jimbo and Chaz to step apart. Wei exploded from the doorway of the treasure chamber, pushing one of those decorated rickshaws. He'd piled it with glittering junk including a life-size brass statue of Confucius. Howling dire threats, the fireplug of a man launched the rickshaw to roll bouncing down the steps, the weight of it fracturing tiles.

The half-ton load smashed into the ascending soldiers, striking flesh and bone with terrible force. The upward charge halted and reversed. Soldiers crashed into the ranks behind them in a panic to escape the blunt force of the trea-sure-laden cart. The clot of routed soldiers grew wider and deeper until men were falling from either side of the staircase to drop two stories to the floor below. As the soldiers receded down the stairs, the rickshaw followed, bumping on the steps and fallen bodies, becoming airborne. It came to rest on its side at the foot of the steps. The way above it was carpeted with dead men. More were wounded and crawling and dropping away, slowed by broken limbs and crushed organs.

Jimbo and Chaz kept up a withering fire from their rifles until the magazines were empty and barrels glowed an angry red. They kept up the punishing fusillade with their handguns. Wei joined them and worked the lever of his rifle, picking off any man who still stood. The spearmen had retreated back to the doorway but stubbornly refused to leave. They stood in a hedge of spear points. Each man that fell to gunfire was replaced by a new man.

"They're working up the balls for another charge!" Chaz roared to be heard over the ringing in their ears from the racket of constant gunfire.

"More like they're holding the line!" Jimbo said, feeding

rounds into the magazine tubes of his rifle, the steel burning hot to the touch.

"For what?" Chaz shouted.

He had his answer within seconds. The wicket of spears parted to allow in a crowd of men in white bamboo armor. The newcomers formed two ranks even as bullets from above ripped into them.

The first rank dropped to a knee and, within seconds, two dozen fat muskets were trained up the steps at the invaders.

The Rangers dropped to the floor, and Wei leaped backward. A boom erupted from below. Heavy lead balls struck the railings either side of the steps, punching holes in the masonry. More lead tore into the ceiling, dropping chunks of plaster down on them.

Jimbo belly crawled to the edge of the steps and trained his rifle down into the fog of creamy smoke spreading out at the foot of the stairway. He sent rounds into men reloading muskets with astonishing speed. He dropped two, and Chaz dropped a third before he saw a rear rank of men joining the firing line.

Jingals.

The third file was made up of men armed with muskets that fired either canisters packed with round shot or lead balls an inch across. Jingals were mini-cannons that required two men to fire. One at the trigger and a second to support the heavy barrel on his shoulder.

The Rangers were rolling away when the third rank let loose in one thunderous volley. Sprays of shot and lead balls turned the air into a storm of debris. The lethal shower ripped into walls and ceiling. The head of a statue, a crouching temple dog, was torn away to clang across the tiles. The twin ranks of musket men followed the jingals in a combined barrage. Balls whistled by the Rangers scrabbling back toward the doorway. They could feel rather than hear the steady tramp of boots as soldiers rushed up the steps under cover of the hail of lead.

The first row of spearmen was in sight at the top of the staircase when the Rangers and Wei pressed the big brass doors closed. Their quarry within reach, the soldiers let out a rolling growl and came on at a run, spear points lowered and steady.

They swung the doors shut and dropped the crossbar into place. The first spear butts struck on the other side. The treasure chamber echoed with the booms of the pounding fists and weapons of the enraged fanatics eager to get at the barbarians who dared despoil their sacred place. The doors held and would hold for a while. The chains on the thick, iron-banded cross bar jingled in their places.

"Sweet Jesus, I'm thirsty," Jimbo said, panting.

"Me and Wei found the wine collection back there," Chaz said, jerking a thumb into the gloom of the treasure vault.

49

THE FORLORN HOPE

The sun rose toward its apex over the towers of Nanking.

The guns along the walls continued their regular cannonade, the occasional stone ball reaching the outer lines of the besiegers' camp. But the mortars and cannons of the emperor remained silent throughout the morning. Sensing a change in the current of battle, the artillery crews on the walls of the city stopped their labors. A hush fell over the open field between the enemies.

"Almost noon. This is about to get real," Boats said, squinting up at the sun through wisps of rising smoke.

"It's too real for me already," Bat breathed, eyes on the city walls. She leaned on the long Whitworth rifle, the butt resting in the grass.

The team stood upon a slope of raised ground behind the stockade walls to watch the coming show. Lee stood by Bat, sighting through his telescope. Byrus paced like a dog, anxious for the hunt. Shan climbed the slope to join them.

"Do you ever get used to this?" he asked no one in particular.

"Get used to what?" Lee said.

"Knowing what is to happen next. Seeing the future by

reading the past," Shan said, turning to join the vigil of the tableau below them.

"Trust me, the history books are bullshit. Nothing is a sure thing," Lee said.

"You may think it amusing, but I find that reassuring," Shan said.

"No. I get that." Lee nodded.

The ground heaved under their feet. Birds rose into the sky in droves.

The caches of gunpowder, in their burrows deep beneath the wall of the city, ignited seconds apart from one another.

In a mighty rush of dust and debris, the mouth of the pit vomited up a brown tower of dust that shot hundreds of feet in the air within seconds before collapsing to cover the siege camp in a suffocating miasma. Midday became dusk as the gritty cloud shut out the sun. Visibility was reduced to an arm's length. The endless ranks of men, bunched for the assault in their thousands, were suddenly alone in a world where they were blind to anything but the man on either side of them.

At the base of the city walls, a massive dome of earth rose and doubled in size with the force of the second blast from the belly of the foundation. The concussive wave from the twin explosions could be felt thousands of yards away. An evil gust, tinged with the rotten eggs stink of sulfur, caused banners and flags to unfurl for an instant in a gale-force wind. Then the city of Nanking was invisible behind a dense, swirling cloud of dust and smoke. From within the cloud came a rumbling, grinding sound like a monstrous approaching wave.

All was silent except for the sounds of men coughing to clear their throats of the cloying powder of atomized dirt that had settled over everything in a shroud.

The silence was broken by the clash of gongs. They were joined by hundreds of others being struck in a rising emphatic din. Trumpets sounded from all around the camp. Men spat to clear their mouths of the cloying dust. They gripped weapons and tensed for what came next, all while straining their tearing eyes to see through the curtain of smoke that separated them from their goal.

After what seemed like hours, the dust began to settle and the air to clear across the no-man's-land between the walls of the city and the earthworks of the besiegers. All eyes were upon the crest of the falling tide of smoke to see if the walls still stood in place. At first, they saw nothing and then, as a man, they realized that nothing was precisely what they wished to see. Instead of a two-hundred-yard stretch of unbroken battlements between two stout towers, there was now a wide gap as though some unimaginably enormous beast had taken a bite from the wall. At the bottom of the bite lay a steep hillock of scree that would act as a ramp into the gap. The wall had collapsed in on itself to fill the man-made sinkhole created by tons of gunpowder. The unassailable defenses were now gored. The city lay beyond, through that ragged tear in its armor, to be plundered.

The first wave of assault companies broke ranks and rushed up the slope to the walls, their officers trailing behind shouting unheeded orders. Bannermen followed in the rear of the attack rather than leading the charge. The mass of sprinting peasant soldiers converged in a point like an arrowhead aimed at the breach in the walls. The first lines of professional soldiers swayed but held their ranks at the sharp commands of their officers riding on ponies before them and swinging whips. All were eager to get at the imagined treasures within the walls. The mandarins were content to allow the rabble of armed coolies to be the first in.

They could kindly be called auxiliary infantry, barefoot and armed with farm implements and cheap swords of hammered iron. They were nothing more than livestock to the mandarins. Perhaps less. How better to test the defenses?

The mob of peasants raced across the rough hill of broken

masonry and timbers that now filled the moat between the glacis and the base of the ruined wall. They clambered upward on hands and knees. The walls and towers above remained mute until the first of the auxiliaries reached the crest of the rubble and perhaps caught a glimpse of the wonders of the city beyond before all hell opened up.

Along the walls, puffs of smoke bloomed from muskets, jingals, and carronades. Rockets soared in the air in twisting spirals to explode harmlessly in the sky. But a few dropped among the rear of the attackers. The rockets exploded, creating blasts of razor-sharp shrapnel that shredded men to bloody rags. The assault staggered, slowed, and came to a stop at the top of the rubble heap. Musket balls tore into the front ranks from the ramparts and towers. The peasant soldiers were routed under the murderous hail of lead and stone shot and turned to flee. The lethal rain continued, cutting down men as they tumbled off the hill of scree and ran across the open land toward the siege camp. The hillock of ruins was now carpeted with the dead.

The besiegers answered with their own artillery. Cannon opened up from embrasures dug close to the walls. Stone shot and gravel raked the ramparts in an effort to clear them of defenders. The reply from Nanking was a storm of rockets that filled the sky with snaking contrails of smoke and sparks. Most of the rockets landed to discharge on empty ground. They did little but spur the fleeing survivors of the first assault to greater speed.

But one tube dropped by the slimmest of chances into the powder magazine of the nearest gun embrasure. The blast vaporized the gun crew and sent the cannon barrel spinning high into the air like a stick tossed for a dog. It crashed to the earth, warped and smoking, a few yards forward of the first rank of imperial troops. Smoke drifted from the dragon's mouth forged at the end of the barrel. The shock of the impact caused a horse to rear, pitching an officer to the ground.

A trumpet blared and the imperial troops, in fine black lacquered bamboo armor and bearing long spears in their fists, surged forward in rank after rank, moving in time to beating drums. They streamed toward the break in the walls across the open ground. They marched in perfect discipline, formed in squares of a thousand men each. And behind them, by fifty yards, a second wave marched followed by a third and fourth. Officers cantered their mounts forward along the flanks. Bannermen trotted, long streams of colorful regimental flags fluttering behind. Peasant boys ran alongside, banging on gongs and squealing encouragement as if on a playing field rather than a killing ground.

Steady fire pelted down from the walls either side of the breach. The first column of men was already leaving bits of itself behind. Either still or writhing, victims of the muskets and carronades along the ramparts, men in black armor sprawled on the ground behind the advancing regiment. The following ranks marched over them, only another obstacle in the path to brace their enemy in his lair.

The army of the boy emperor meant to exploit the chink in the city's defense through sheer blunt force. General Sang would spend as many men as it took until his army was invested in the city and the houses there put to the torch and the defenders put to the sword.

"I think I understand what Chaz was saying," Bat said, eyes fixed on the mass of men walking in orderly procession directly into the withering fire from the walls.

"Yeah? What was he saying?" Lee asked, eye to a telescope.

"I feel like I've never really been to war before," she said, throat suddenly dry.

50

LONELY PLANET

He stood on the beach, watching lazy white rollers coming off the Pacific. Gulls wheeled in the air. Egrets and terns stalked tidal pools hunting for fish and crabs.

It took him three days of hard hiking to reach the coast. On the way, he saw not one single sign of any kind of human habitation. Not a campfire, structure, or even any rubbish left behind. The ocean to the horizon was free of any kind of vessel.

As far as he knew, he was alone on the planet.

Not entirely alone. There was wildlife, rabbits, lizards, birds, and deer. There were coyotes though he never saw one. He heard their yips in the night when he camped and their tracks crisscrossed the sand between the dunes.

He saw no species that were unfamiliar to the time period he called home. So, whenever he was, it was within the last ten thousand years.

The way Dwayne Roenbach saw it, there were two ways ahead open to him, travel through time or travel through space.

Playing with the bracelet was dangerous for now. Activating it probably registered somewhere with the guys sent to find him and Caroline. Open a field, and they might be drawn right to him. Take a jump himself, and the bracelet might be programmed to take him back where he started and straight into their hands. He'd have to make some distance before trying it again.

So, he'd make his initial move through space. His plan was to make it to the coast and march north up the thousand-mile-long peninsula of the Baja to the California border. That would allow him to jump forward to someplace more familiar, that was if he could figure out how to program the bracelet without a manual. Mostly, all he could do was get the tiny monitor field to light up with numbers and symbols that were unknown to him. Until he worked it out, he wasn't willing to jump blind.

The hike to San Diego would take a month if he made a steady thirty miles a day. It would be more since he'd need to hunt or fish and find sources of water. Food would not present a problem, the land was rich with game. He'd used the needle gun to bring down a pair of rabbits and a small doe on his way to the ocean.

Water could be gathered from any springs or streams he found or, in a pinch, from the barrel cactus that dotted the dunes above the beach. The flask he picked off the hunter didn't hold enough for long hikes. He fashioned a water bag by slashing a sleeve from the jacket he'd stripped off the dead man and tying either end with a bootlace. The fabric of the hunter's uniform was watertight and made a decent makeshift CamelBak.

Dwayne was used to living rough both from a childhood spent mostly outdoors and his Ranger training. The hike would be no hardship on him, but the isolation would wear thin, that and concern about what was happening back in The Now. His thoughts returned again and again to whether N'itha got away from the hunters if she reached Caroline ahead of them. He knew Caroline would know to run. But there was only so much N'itha could convey to her about the threat.

He tried to put those thoughts aside and concentrate on his current situation. He was no help to Caroline and Stephen if he made decisions out of desperation. As pressing as time seemed to be on him, he knew it was an illusion, an irrelevancy. The bracelet that hung about his neck on a length of bootlace made time his bitch, but a fickle bitch. If he could figure out how to operate it.

He walked down to the water's edge and put the sun off his left shoulder and set off north along the hard sand. Dwayne drew his focus down to the long way ahead and whether or not to have fish or fowl for dinner.

51

THE LIST

The temblor rocked the treasure house of the East King.

The floor shifted, and the walls shimmied as the concussive wave swept from the blast point across the underbelly of Nanking. Chaz leaped clear of a stack of heavy chests caving in and bursting, sending an avalanche of gold coins to the floor. In other places around the room, cabinets collapsed. Tall stacks of dishware and shelves of porcelain crashed and shattered on the tile floor.

The rhythmic hammering on the doors paused while the tremor subsided. Then the pounding resumed its insistent tattoo.

"That means it's noon," Jimbo called from somewhere in the recesses of the chamber.

"Roger that!" Chaz responded and took his place again behind a barricade built of opium casks.

He manned the bunker they'd constructed to cover the pair of bronze doors. The doors were fortified with the weight of cartloads of statues, heavy furniture, and chests of coins. The load was pressing the doors closed even as the frame began to give away at the hinges. The relentless pounding of a pair of rams rang against the bronze. They'd been doing so for hours. First one boomed, and then the other, without interruption. The brass-bound crossbar was creaking with the strain. The soldiers would make it through. It was only a matter of time until the doorway filled with spear points and muskets.

Chaz stood, eyes locked on the door through a haze of falling dust. He had all three rifles fully loaded and arrayed before him. The palace guard would get through, but he'd make sure it was damned expensive for them

---

At the rear of the treasure room, Jimbo found a collection of books and scrolls. Wei lit oil lamps to create enough illumination to read by. Shelves groaned under leather-bound volumes trimmed in gilt. Latticed cabinets were packed with scrolls of vellum and parchment tied with silk. There were further cases stuffed with literature in countless languages. Jimbo realized that he was looking at a priceless library. He also realized that few, if any, of these works would survive the sacking of the city. The illiterate peasant army that would soon stream in through the breach in the wall would carry away only what they knew to be of value. These books and scrolls would be trampled underfoot by looters or, more likely, burned to ashes.

After hours of pulling down books and scrolls, Jimbo decided that the ivory reliquary was not among the volumes in the library. If the scroll of the great Khan was here, then why wasn't it among the other literary valuables?

"Where would you hide Genghis Khan's diary?" Jimbo said to Wei, who only blinked at him.

There was no sophisticated system of sorting applied to the treasure chamber beyond the obvious. Dishes with dishes, coins with coins, dolls with dolls, clocks with clocks, and on and on. Probably the duty of eunuchs who saw the riches as dross to be stacked and counted and inventoried.

An inventory.

The Manchus' madness for recording data and deep bureaucracy would be shared by the Taipings. The whole bloodthirsty rebellion was inspired by a failed civil servant. It was a culturally shared obsession, the irresistible urge to record the significant and the trivial in writing. Somewhere in this room, there would have to be a list of the items in the collection.

Jimbo searched his mind for anything that seemed out of place. Any anomaly in the room they'd systematically searched in the hours they'd been here.

The Pima set off into the gloom between the glittering aisles.

Wei followed, running to keep the Ranger in sight.

A simple wooden podium sat against a wall. Its enameled surface was scored and scratched. A humble writing desk set among the extravagances of the royal treasures. Atop the desk rested a large open book bound in rough leather with thousands of pages. A pot of ink sat in a well encrusted with dried ink. Brushes of varying sizes lay in a sill at the bottom of the angled top. The open pages were covered in neat rows of characters.

"What is this? Is this an inventory? A list?" Jimbo said, handing the open book to Wei.

Wei studied the open pages before leafing through the book, eyes dancing over the lines of script and numbers. He looked up to Jimbo, nodding.

"Find the scroll! Find. The. Scroll. Read this!" Jimbo said, stabbing a finger on a page of the book. Wei winced in annoyance and pulled the book away with a muttered string of abuse in his own language.

"And read fast," Jimbo said. His eyes turned upward. Somewhere in the darkness above, he heard the sounds of feet running across the roof.

52

A MORTAL WOUND

The broad breach in the wall filled from side to side with ranks of musketeers standing five deep. They trained their weapons on the columns of men charging the base of the mountain of rubble. Looking down their barrels, they rested the front sights on attackers clawing over the heaped corpses of the first failed assault. A cry went up followed by the sounding of a horn.

The first two rows of muskets exploded simultaneously. The musketeers handed back spent weapons to accept loaded ones brought forward from the rows behind.

On the heap of broken stone below, lead, and stone balls ripped through the attackers, dropping hundreds of them in a single blow. They fell, dead or dying, only to be clambered over by their fellows coming up behind. Though covered in armor, these were still peasants, shock troops, impelled forward by a discipline thrashed into them. It was not only the threat of punishment that gave them courage. These were men whose entire lives could be changed with the possession of one gold coin, and the dreams of the riches contained within Nanking had driven them mad with avarice.

Those dreams died with the next hail of fire from above. The armor was useless against the firearms blasting away above. Balls punched through layers of lacquered bamboo as though through slices of bread. Hundreds fell to join the hill of the dead. Still more rushed over them, crawling over the slain like beasts, pushed from behind by more and more soldiers anxious to reach the promises that lay beyond the break in the wall.

Concentrated fire erupted from the tops of towers either side of the break. Carronades swept the attackers with chain shot and stone shot. Jingals boomed. Muskets cracked. The forward momentum of the assault faltered and stumbled and stopped entirely when the third volley blasted a storm of balls into the massed peasants. Men were dismembered and beheaded under the merciless fusillade. A single stone ball from a jingal ripped a coolie nearly in half, continuing on through the unfortunate's divided torso to take the leg from a bannerman. A near-continuous fire rained down on the attackers as they ran, rolled, and slid downward to escape the hell of flying death. Few made it clear of the devastating punishment, and soon the rocky slope, and the ground before it, was empty of life.

Cheers went up along the wall, and gongs sounded as the defenders gave voice to victory. The victory was short-lived. A whistling sound rose from somewhere above the pall of gun smoke that cloaked the walls in a gray fog. Some of the men along the breach looked up into the hazy sunlight in consternation. Others, more experienced soldiers, were already breaking rank to seek cover.

Arrows by the thousands crashed down on the packed ranks of musketeers. They dropped down with lethal force from the top of an arc hundreds of feet above. Shafts drove into upturned faces. They pierced cloth and armor and flesh. Some men fell with as many as six arrows embedded in them. The arrows sounded like hail striking a rooftop.

Thousands of Tartar bowmen raced to the bottom of the hill of ruins, loosing shafts as swiftly as they could nock and release a fresh arrow. Their ponies charged forward, controlled only by the knees of their riders leaving hands free to deliver their deadly torrent. Their blind volley fire was concentrated on the men blocking the breach. Calculating the arcs with expert skill, they sent shafts high into the sky to fall upon the defenders. As they neared the wall, they could see individual targets more clearly, tiny figures along the bottom of the break. The Tartars trained their eyes on these men, sending shafts upward and away on flat trajectories at chosen targets.

The results were devastating. The full power of the mighty reflex bows sank shafts deep into the front ranks of musketeers before they could bring their weapons to bear. Such was the clout of the Tartar bows that some defenders were shot through, the arrows continuing on to wound men behind them. The ranks behind shrank back to escape the shafts ripping in among them.

Even the continuous fire from the towers above failed to drive off the mounted bowmen. The mass of men and beasts below swirled at the foot of the hill beneath the tear in the wall like boiling water in a pot. Each man kept his mount in constant movement all the while keeping his arrows winging toward the massed men blocking the way into the city.

Some of the Tartars broke from the throng to ride along the foot of the towers, galloping along the top of the glacis above the moat. These riders sent shafts flying up at the cannoneers and jingal crews atop the towers. The arrows clattered impotently against the battlements or glanced off the slopes of the heavy timber roofs. The shower caused musketeers to shrink from their gun ports until harangued back in place by shrieks and blows from battery officers.

In one of the towers, a shaft stabbed through the eye of a soldier steadying the barrel of a jingal even as the man behind him pressed home the trigger. The end of the barrel swayed, and the ball crashed against the inner wall of the tower to carom around the interior with deadly results. A half dozen men were cut down in an instant by either the golf-ball-sized round or flying flinders of stone. One man lay rolling and howling on the flagstone floor, clutching a spurting stump where the ball ripped his leg away at the knee.

The Tartars kept peppering the defenders, driving all but the most courageous from the ramparts and creating a break within the breach. Some of them even urged their mounts to climb the steep face of the hillock of ruins to send shafts buzzing into the broken gap in the wall.

From trenches dug close to the walls rose a wave of bannermen with fluttering streaming black flags. They were followed by a fresh mass of armored men approaching the wall at a rush. The defenders peeped through ports along the ramparts to witness a sea of spears closing toward the breach under cover of the lethal blizzard of arrows dropping all along the walls.

Musketeers and gun crews fired down into the dense tide of attackers as fast as they could reload their weapons. The meaning of the black flags was understood by all, a universal signal that there would be no mercy for the vanquished, no quarter, and no prisoners. Nanking would be put to the flame and its every inhabitant to the sword or rope or worse. The crews fired in silent desperation, without pausing to aim, certain their charges would strike at their enemies, so densely packed was the assault. Gaps were ripped in the ranks of the charging imperial troops only to be filled in at once, momentary eddies in the current.

From within the city, a growing stream of arrows was launched into the sky in answer to the Tartar's barrage. Mongol bowmen massed in the lane behind the breach and atop the ramparts in greater and greater numbers until the sky was shadowed by the intersecting arcs of shafts. An age-old rivalry between warriors of the steppe was being rekindled as Mongol and Tartar competed for targets.

Armor bristling with broken shafts, the imperial troops surged up the hillock of ruins, a massive human battering ram. Officers in tall conical helmets urged them on into the maw with whirling bullwhips. They were over the crest and charging down the inner slope of the breach and into the teeth of massed muskets and field cannons. The first rows of spear and bannermen absorbed a horrific bombardment from grapeshot and ball and arrows. But the momentum of the massed attack would not be denied. The elite of General Sang pressed into the gap and beyond, splashed with the blood of their comrades, in a headlong charge for the line of guns arrayed before them. Behind the spearmen came rifle companies, at first firing at will and then forming ranks that blazed away in coordinated volleys. Both lines of fire, separated by less than fifty yards, chewed away at one another, fogging the area at the back of the breach with blinding smoke that made the opposing sides invisible to one another except for the spitting flames of their weaponry. The gunners and bowmen atop the walls and towers could no longer find targets in the dense haze.

The imperials, with their faster loading bolt action rifles, gained supremacy. The firing ranks of the defenders withered in number and finally broke. With bayonets affixed, Sang's troops charged into the last of the defenders before them. Wave after wave of soldiers and conscripts followed to spread through the streets into the city, defied only by a few steadfast fanatics. These were swiftly overrun. The bulk of the disheartened Taiping defenders was now in full rout. There was nowhere to run.

Ladders were run up and leaned against sections of wall that had been abandoned in order to reinforce the area around the breach. Sappers swiftly scurried up the ladders one behind the other to infest the walls and towers where they set off gunpowder charges and set fires. Within moments the timber tower tops were ablaze, and the defenders on the ramparts found themselves locked in combat with swordsmen and axmen appearing blackened from the smoke and wailing like demons.

The dam had burst, and the killing tide was flooding in. The emperor's vengeance was upon Nanking.

53

THE DRAGON'S MOUTH

Full night had fallen.

Lee Hammond gave the high sign, and the team moved out toward the city.

Shan was all for going in before sunset. Lee shut him down and refused to discuss tactics any further.

"There's still heavy fighting in the streets. You really want to jump into a shitstorm like that? Be my guest, fucko," Lee said before turning his back and entering the tent.

"You're never gonna convince him," Boats cautioned Shan.

Shan's orders from Jason Taan were clear. Get the scroll at all and any costs. But he needed the cooperation and the guns of the Americans to reach the palace of the East King. He sat in the shade of the tent awning and watched the sun sink low in the smoky sky.

Two towers were on fire when they approached. Burning roofs and ramparts created colossal torches to light the night. There were more fires from within the walls, rooftops ablaze. The flickering light of the fires and the cloying stink of sulfur formed the backdrop for the hellish scene the team found on the open no man's land that lay between the walls of the city and the siege camp.

The bodies of men were everywhere. Some lay where they'd died. Others, closer to the camp, expired where they'd managed to crawl from the range of the terrible enfilade coming off the walls. Soldiers and peasants littered the ground where their withdrawal+ to safety stopped when their lives ended. Some were missing limbs, leaving snail trails of bloody ground behind them.

Worse than the dead were the injured. They lay unheeded and unaided. No one looked their way or responded to their cries for help. Walking wounded limped past them without a glance. Peasants lumbered with loot back to the city of tents. Men carried carpets, furniture, and bolts of cloth past others beseeching them for mercy. One coolie struggled to haul a cart weighed down with a pile of copper pots. He growled at anyone who offered to help pull his load.

Near the walls, the bodies grew in number and density until they formed a carpet all the way to the base of the breach. It grew impossible to move around the heaps of dead. Eventually, with no ground visible, there was no way forward but to walk upon the corpses of men and horses. The mélange beneath them was an unending mass of pulped flesh and bone after the soles of thousands of boots, hooves and the wheels of heavy guns had marched, stamped, and rolled over them. One body was indistinguishable from another—they were all crushed to form a ghastly roadway toward the city walls.

Bat kept her eyes on Lee's back and sipped shallow breaths, doing her best to ignore the yielding surface under her feet. She swore to herself, as she'd sworn on the operations to Roman Judea and prehistoric Nevada that this would be her last trip in the Wayback Machine. You can have history, fuck the past, she thought.

They fell in behind a column of riflemen marching up the hill of ruins and into the breach in the wall. The way ahead was illuminated by torches. Bat looked back across the field and could see the beetle-backs of more troops gleaming under the firelight as they moved toward a gateway that had been forced open. In the other direction, more soldiers climbed row after row of ladders up onto the walls. The city was being fully invested by the regiments of Sang and the other generals, moving in to make the city theirs.

She imagined that similar incursions were happening all around the circumference of Nanking.

It reminded her of columns of ants moving to and fro from the carcass of roadkill.

Then they were down the lee of the heap of broken stone and into the city.

Musket fire popped in an unceasing cacophony from the streets beyond. Wood smoke drifted everywhere. The stars above were replaced with a skein of swirling embers against towers of black smoke.

"Which way?" Boats said. Byrus stood by the SEAL looking about anxiously as though he might catch a glimpse of Jimmy Smalls somewhere in the press of humanity.

"The shortest route to the inner city that carries us around any firefights," Lee said. A series of booms from within the city cut him off. They held position until the barrage passed.

"That will be cannons trained on the sanctuary walls," Shan said. "The imperial troops will be on the palace grounds before dawn."

"Stick close. Eyes on me. We fight when we have to. But only when we have to," Lee said and turned to trot into the widest lane leading off the area back of the breach.

There were more bodies. More and more of them civilians. Women and children, even infants, lay along the curbs and building fronts. Skulls dashed to pulp. Some without heads. Most of the women, young and old, were naked, and their white flesh was black with bruises. Bat looked away, not wanting to see any more. She was grateful they hadn't come in daylight. Above the crackle of muskets and boom of explosions, she could hear the high peals of women screaming. She wanted to stop her ears with her hands but resisted the urge.

A market square, much like the one they'd hurried through back in Shanghai, was in utter turmoil. Soldiers and peasants were openly looting warehouses and stalls. Some stooped to pick valuables from corpses. The dead lay everywhere. A Tartar, bow and quiver slung over his back, was crouched by a pile of severed heads. He was prying teeth out of the jaws with the edge of a knife and dropping them into his fur-lined cap resting on the ground.

Some soldiers, in the bucklered leather skirts of the emperor, were arguing over a girl who looked to Bat to be no more than twelve. The girl's eyes were dead with shock. The soldiers were giggling and jeering as they plucked her from each other's grasp like a toy.

"Not our fight, babe," Lee said, suddenly at Bat's side with a hand gripping her arm to keep her in step.

"I know," she whispered, voice hoarse. This was all in the past. This had already happened, and there was no changing it. Everyone within her sight had been dead for a hundred years before she was born. Still, to her, it was happening now. This was, as crazy as it seemed, her present.

Bathsheba Jaffe was no stranger to the bestial nature of man.

It was a suicide bombing during a visit to Jerusalem that convinced her to move to Israel and enlist in the IDF. A dance club was ripped to pieces by a Hamas 'martyr.' She was outside talking to friends when it happened. She still awoke from night-mares imagining that she was once again painted in the sticky wash of blood and ephemera that sprayed her and her friends in the blast. One of the girls Bat was talking to died when a single piece of shrapnel drilled through the girl's skull. She learned later that it was a common house key probably from the deadly mix of projectiles the bomber packed into pockets on his explosive vest.

But this, Nanking, was stupefying in the scale of its brutality. Everywhere she looked, she could see humanity reduced to its animal elements of slaughter and fear. And she knew that, all across this city, the same scenes were repeated with banal constancy. Man unleashed, a synergy of evil feeding upon itself. This was a world without order or boundaries or even the most common kindness. Beyond the market, they reached a wide lane where Imperial troops were raking a makeshift barricade with rifle fire. The Taiping defenders had erected a wall of carts, bales, and furniture and were laying down musket fire from behind the fragile defensive position. Lee waved the team into an embrasure in the wall of a building with a marble façade.

"This road makes a beeline to the main gate of the inner city," he shouted over the rolling explosion of muskets and rifles.

"What is your idea?" Shan called back.

"We follow these guys in once they've cleared this mess. Beats getting lost in a tangle of back alleys," Lee said. The others nodded and dropped back into the shadowed doorway to watch.

The imperial riflemen laid down regular fire from three ranks, but the return fire from the barricade didn't slow. The firing line of imperials was being reduced, man by man, by shot from hidden guns. An officer waving a length of bamboo rod strode the ranks bullying the men to keep up the fusillade without heed to the balls whistling by his head. He stumbled to the ground, a leg brushed from under him, the bamboo greave on his leg suddenly running with blood through a ragged hole. A soldier supported him and helped him stand. All the while, the officer kept up a stream of commands, even smacking at the helmets of the nearest riflemen with his flail.

Under the withering fire from the Taipings, the soldiers stood as one, dropping the butts of their rifles to the cobbled street with a crash and whipping out needle-shaped bayonets a foot and a half in length. At the wounded officer's shrieked directions, they snapped the bayonets in place even as men fell from the ranks under the grueling fire.

The imperial troops charged the barricades, bayonets before them. The officer hobbled along with them, hopping on one leg, and whipping that bamboo stick around to thrash the men to greater speed.

"I think we picked a winner," Boats shouted with a broad grin, jacking a round into his rifle. He broke from the shadowed doorway to chase after the charging mass that was closing on the barricade. Gladius drawn, Byrus was right on his heels.

"Fucking Navy," Lee seethed and ran to the guns, with Shan and Bat close behind.

54

CUL DE SAC

The chunk-chunk of axes and hammers continued above. A section of the roof collapsed. Timbers crashed down into the treasure room followed by a shower of broken boards and tiles. Knotted ropes dropped into a blinding shaft of sunlight streaming through the gap. Men moved into beams of light casting huge shadows. They slid down the ropes, swinging in pendulum arcs as they descended. Sword blades glinted on their backs. They were easy targets for the two Rangers waiting in the cover of the East King's plunder hoard. The rifles boomed. Men pitched off the ropes to tumble into shelves of pottery and racks of silk kites. More swordsmen followed. A heap of dead men rose on the floor in the brilliant cone of light from above. They were naked but for loincloths. Their skin was rubbed with lampblack to conceal them in the dark. A swordsman swung his rope to bring him to a landing atop a roof beam. Jimbo shot him off the perch. The man fell spinning and landed with a crash of breaking porcelain.

Releasing the ropes, other swordsmen chose to leap through the hole in the roof unaided. They landed on their wounded and dead comrades, breaking bones in the thirty-foot fall. Their suffering was brief as they fell under the rifle fire coming out of the dark.

A man hurled to the pile of the slain and rose to his feet despite a shattered femur, the jagged end of white bone jutting through blackened flesh. He held a sword in his fist and lunged from the circle of light. Jimbo dropped him with a round through the head.

"They're gooned out!" Jimbo called.

"High as motherfuckers!" Chaz replied.

The assassins were flying on opium. Their fanaticism made them fearless, the bhang made them numb to pain.

The attack from above slowed, allowing Chaz and Jimbo to train rifle fire on the hole in the ceiling. Footfalls fell on the roof as the suppression fire caused the assassins to retreat. Chaz' face creased in a bitter smile at the sound of bodies tumbling and voices screaming. Attackers fell from the high pitched roof.

The pounding at the double doors, the rhythmic work of the rams, continued. Though the doors remained in place, the masonry around the frame was showing cracks. If the attackers couldn't bring down the door, they'd bring down the walls.

"We are seriously fucked here," Chaz said, panting.

"There's got to be a back door. A secret passage or some shit," Jimbo said, feeding rounds into his rifle's magazine tubes.

"If there were, these assholes would be using it. This is a vault, son. One door."

"How are you for ammo?"

"All I have is already in my rifle and sidearm," Chaz said, patting his empty bandolier.

"I have maybe forty rounds total," Jimbo said, eyes turned upward. There were men moving on the roof again.

Wei rushed to them from out of the shadows. He had the inventory book in his arms and was babbling in rapid-fire Mandarin. He pulled Jimbo to him, holding up the open book and stabbing a finger at an entry. The columns of neatly drawn characters were broken by an intricate brush drawing of a horse.

"We don't have time for this, bro," Chaz said, eyeing the circle of sunlight above them.

"This is what we came for, Chaz. This is the operation objective," Jimbo said.

"And what good is it when these fuckers get in here?"

"Hold the fort." Jimbo set his rifle and bandolier down by Chaz to chase after Wei. Their babbling chaperone was wending his way through the labyrinth of treasures.

"An Apache telling me to hold the fort. Shit," Chaz said to himself, jacking a fresh round as the patter of feet above converged on the hole in the ceiling.

Jimbo caught up with Wei who was pointing at a magnificent statue of a trotting warhorse. The statue was life-sized and cast in highly polished brass. The teeth in its snarling mouth were faced with mother-of-pearl. Its eyes were opals. A leather saddle with a high crown rested on the horse's back. The leather of the saddle was trimmed in gold. The bridle was worked with buckles of gold and studded with gems. Straps of leather armor draped the hindquarters and chest with silver bucklers worked along their length. The saddle and tack were old but well cared for. The leather was a rich deep umber with years of oil rubbed into it.

The whole statue had to weigh a ton or more. It stood bolted onto a marble plinth that was two tons or more on its own. The base under the horse's hooves was carved to imitate trampled grass. Wei dropped to hands and knees and felt along the base of the plinth. He barked at Jimbo, jerking his head at the base as he worked his way around. At first, Jimbo thought the man was trying to shift the weight aside on his own. Then he realized that Wei was looking for something—a concealed latch or spring.

Jimbo got to his knees and felt along the base with his fingertips. There was a recess an inch deep above the floor that ran all around the inside of the base of the plinth. He worked one way while Wei worked the other.

From the dark behind them, Chaz' rifle boomed. The radiance from the beam of sunlight was interrupted by bodies dropping through the break in the ceiling.

The Pima's fingers, greasy with sweat, found a small plate set in a place where the recess deepened. It was set level with the underside of the base with a nearly imperceptible gap around it. He called a "yo" to Wei and pressed upward.

The plate gave way, sliding into place within an indentation with a tolerance of a mere fraction of an inch around the plate. The grinding of gears and clink of chains came from within the torso of the gleaming warhorse. A counterweight clunked to a stop somewhere under the floor beneath their feet. An exhalation of air was released from the bottom of the base. Dust swirled over the tiles. The expelled air had the scent of lavender. Jimbo and Wei stepped back and looked at one another.

Jimbo reached out a hand to shove against the haunch of the statue. The entire structure, horse and plinth, skated away from his hand as easily as though on oiled bearings. He and Wei pushed together, and the statue moved aside to reveal an open hatch in the floor with stone steps leading down into a well of darkness. The smell of lavender grew stronger.

"Chaz! This way!" Jimbo called.

Wei descended into the dark, the book under one arm and an oil lamp held up in his fist.

Chaz was working the lever of Jimbo's rifle. His own weapon lay on the floor empty. The pile of dead in the ring of smoky sunlight was becoming a mountain as swordsmen dropped howling from above. He turned, eyes red with fury, to see Jimbo yanking on his elbow. The Pima was shouting at him, pulling him away. Chaz has nearly deaf, his ears ringing with the sound of gunfire, shrieking men and the drumbeat of rams.

Together, the two Rangers backed into the shadows, firing

pistols as they moved. More men leaped down through the ceiling break to land on the hill of the dead. They tumbled away to run blindly into the surrounding dark. Others swung to the rafters where they leaped from one beam to another, searching the gloom below for their prey.

At the far end of the chamber, the bronze doors crashed inward along with a broad section of wall either side. The floor shuddered with the impact. That end of the room lit up with the glow of torches from the opening bashed in the wall. The treasure vault was awash in dust-streaked light. The shadows came alive with soldiers erupting from the open doorway, boots drumming on the massive doors. They charged inward in a flood to join the swordsmen descending in greater numbers from the ceiling.

Jimbo and Chaz ran full out, the Pima leading his friend to the open hatch that was concealed by the plinth. They dropped inside, sliding down the stone steps toward the glow of an oil lantern. Wei stood at the base of the steps, his hand on an iron lever. As they cleared the gap above, Wei shoved the lever forward. Gears moved. A counterweight rose on chains and, above their heads, the three tons of brass and marble trundled back into place, shutting out the murderous cries of the men above.

"We needed a back door. I found us a back door," Jimbo said, grinning.

"Or a grave," Chaz said with a deep frown, looking about the narrow confines of a silent corridor of fitted stone walls.

55

CARRION

On the twenty-eighth day of his hike to the north, Dwayne came across his first sign of humanity.

Ahead of him along the wet sand, a column of sea birds rose swirling into the brilliant blue sky. As he neared them, he saw they were gathered in two areas on the sand, squawking, nipping, then flapping clear to land somewhere else in the mob.

The birds were gathered to feed on crabs that were, in turn, feeding on the flesh of two corpses lying partially buried in the sand at the water's edge. Dwayne shooed the birds away. They rose into the sky laughing and cawing to settle in a broad ring around him. He kicked at crabs to scatter them off one of the bodies.

It was a man, or what the water and feasting crustaceans had left of a man. He lay face up and eyeless. Much of the tissue on his face had been pulled away, leaving a grinning skull staring from a torn mask of skin. His fingers were stripped to white bone as were his feet. Strands of black hair clung to his water-logged scalp. The figure was no taller than five feet and naked. Despite the swell of corruption, the man showed signs of starvation. His skeletal structure was visible through the skin.

Dwayne placed the toe of a sneaker under the man and flipped him over. The corpse's back was crisscrossed with raised bands of scar tissue. He'd been beaten, flogged. And from the look and pattern, it had happened many times. The man's wrists were covered in gray callus as were his ankles. He'd been shackled, possibly for years. Dwayne knew the signs well after his time as a galley slave aboard a Phoenician pirate ship two years or two thousand years ago depending on how he read the calendar.

Dwayne made his way to the second body. The birds and crabs returned to the first corpse. This man was much like the first except that he lay face down. The same build, same signs of malnutrition, and same telltale stripes across his back. When turned over, his facial features were bloated but intact. The man was dark, not from the sun but from birth. His features weren't African or aborigine. He looked more like an Asian Indian. Dwayne noticed that both men were free of body hair except at the groin.

He shaded his eyes to search the horizon for sails or masts and saw nothing. These two either escaped from or were tossed overboard from, a boat of some kind. The vessel could be miles at sea in any direction. The dead men could have drifted hundreds of miles south with the current. But the evidence told him otherwise. If they'd been in the water longer than a few days, then more of their skin would have been consumed by fish. Dwayne could assume that, wherever these men came from, there were other men within a day's travel.

And they were men who kept others captive as slaves, slaves they did not see value in. They saw them as beasts to be exploited and beaten and then discarded when their use was at an end.

He wouldn't be able to use the beach as a trail anymore. He'd have to move inland, using foliage and terrain for cover.

This world, whenever it was, became a more dangerous place with the presence of men.

56

THE GILDED ABATTOIR

The sun set over the hilltops west of Nanking, shifting the dusk created by the smoke of torched buildings into true darkness. The emperor's army blasted the fortified gate to the inner city to rubble with cannons pushed into position by the brute strength of teams of coolies under the whips of Tartar cavalry. Soldiers and peasants alike swarmed in to help themselves to the plunder of gold and flesh. A final defense of eunuchs and bodyguards was swept aside in a hail of bullets and a hedge of bayonets. Their bodies were mashed to pulp under the heels of the invading horde.

Courtiers of the kings of the Heavenly Kingdom were treated brutally, dragged from hiding and either beheaded or impaled on spears to the delighted jeers of the invaders. Royal concubines, of which there were thousands, were assaulted inside the shelter of their seraglios. Many of them had lived their entire lives within the haven of the palaces of God's other son. They knew only the pampered life of perfumed air, fine silks, and the rarefied existence of prized creatures born to serve the desires of one man. Now they were at the mercy of a throng of men filthy with soot and blood, men who pawed at them like beasts and subjected them to unimaginable outrages.

There were still pockets of resistance within the city of palaces. Fighting raged across once magnificent gardens and into courtyards. The paradise on Earth constructed by the Taipings became a slaughterhouse as knots of musketeers and spearmen fought with frantic devotion to defend the homes of their masters. The attackers pressed forward, driven by avarice and revenge, and brushed the holdouts away.

The team moved in well behind the first wave that rushed through the conquered gate. They were all exhausted and hurting from a long afternoon of the street-to-street fighting that brought them to their goal. They'd come miles through streets and lanes, fighting all the way.

Boats wore a blood-stained rag wrapped around his head to staunch the flow from a deep cut on his scalp. Lee was limping from a spent musket ball that struck his knee. Shan had taken a grazing hit from a spear point and had a rough bandage tied about his forearm. One side of Byrus' face was purple with bruises where a hurled rock had collided with his face. Only Bat Jaffe remained untouched except for some cuts from stone shards to her face, neck, and arms.

"Anyone know where to find the place we're looking for?" Boats said, his back to a garden wall. The team sheltered out of the line of fire of stray shots that were flying everywhere.

"Beats the shit out of me," Lee said, watching a soldier rush by, shoulders draped in layers of silk robes looted from some wardrobe. He saw the man spin when musket balls struck him, the silk fanning out like a rainbow-hued gown before the soldier fell to the ground where he lay still in a spreading pool of blood.

Shan bolted from the group to leap the wall of a pond and charge to where a soldier was forcing a eunuch in yellow livery to his knees. The soldier, in armor crusted with spatters of dried blood, pressed the mewling eunuch to the ground with a booted foot between his shoulders. He raised a curved sword to take off the servant's head.

Not slowing his rush, Shan struck the soldier full in the face with his fist. The soldier stumbled back, dropping his sword, knees buckling. Shan was on the man as he crashed to the tiles. A boot heel drove into the man's throat. The soldier let out a gurgle from his crushed windpipe and then lay still. Shan returned to the team with a hand locked on the back of the eunuch's neck, trotting the terrified man before him.

Shan hurled the eunuch against the garden wall and shouted a stream of Mandarin at the man. The eunuch squeaked out a burbling torrent, raising a hand to point the way, nodding madly. A swift kick to the ass set the eunuch running with the team following.

They reached a complex of buildings with high angled rooftops. At the rear of the decorative gardens was a windowless structure, the front doors bashed in. Inside, heaps of dead lay in a broad foyer room and at the bottom of a long flight of steps leading to a mezzanine above. Among the dead lay the wreckage of a fancy cart and pieces of broken statuary. The brass barrel of a cannon lay under a pile of corpses.

The eunuch pointed the way up the steps. Shan kicked at him with a hissed curse. The eunuch ran away through the doors and into the night.

"They were here," Bat said from where she'd climbed the steps past the pile of bodies. She held a spent brass cartridge between her fingers. She tossed it to Lee, who snatched it from the air.

"Damn," Lee said, examining the cartridge. A .44 round stamped with the markings of the munitions factory in Chizhou.

"Zim! Zim!" Byrus cried as he raced up the steps, his gladius in one fist and a round Tartar shield he'd appropriated somewhere on the other arm.

The team charged after him. The little Macedonian leaped through an open doorway at the top of the steps and over fallen doors and broken masonry. Guns up, the rest sprinted to keep him in sight. Bat noticed a pair of heavy wooden rams wrapped in hemp ropes lying in the wreckage of the door.

The vast chamber was empty. A pile of dead men lay on the floor around a patch of moonlight coming through a jagged hole in the ceiling. There were brass casings everywhere. Boats found one of the team's modified rifles leaning on a barricade of furniture and what looked like treasure chests.

"They made it this far," the SEAL said, slinging the found rifle over his shoulder.

Byrus ran up and down the corridors of plunder calling Jimbo's name.

Shan lit oil lamps and handed them to the others to begin the grim search for the missing men.

Lee searched the dead while the others spread out across the treasure house. All he found were the bodies of near-naked men with some kind of black substance rubbed into the skin. Swords and axes lay around them. All showed signs of gunshot wounds, puckered entry wounds and exit wounds the size of coffee saucers. The hollow points were man stoppers.

Jimbo and Chaz weren't anywhere in the killing field.

He found long trails of blood, black in the moonlight, smeared across the tiles toward the door. There had been more men here at some point, men who took their wounded with them. Or prisoners. In the dust, and in the blood trails, he saw prints from boots. There had been soldiers in addition to the naked swordsmen. They were either driven off or were called away when the palaces of the inner city became infested with imperial troops.

Bat was quickly lost in the maze of astonishing riches piled everywhere she looked. She searched the floor as she ran and called the names of the Rangers. The others were calling out as well. Her rifle raised to her shoulder, she scanned the way before her over the front sights.

<del>footer</del>
<del></del>

294

The absolute quantity of wealth was hard to comprehend. She was struck by the triviality of things like clocks fashioned in the shape of elephants and tigers against the horrors of what was going on outside. All of this misery was caused by effete tyrants more interested in their own amusements and affluence than in the welfare of their followers. She knew the same could be said of the mandarins in Peking. This was a war with no good guys and no bad guys. Two men who claimed to be the Son of Heaven battling to maintain their lofty place, both dead now. This was a war with only suffering for those unfortunate enough to be born to lower castes. A pointless conflict. No wonder history chose to forget it.

She felt the pangs of fatigue climbing her legs and into her hips. The adrenaline rush of battle was fading. The fighting seemed far away from this museum, surrounded by gold, silver, gems, and pearls. Bat leaned back against a seated Buddha statue twice life-size. It was carved of some kind of smooth green stone streaked with pink. Buddha smiled at her benignly, hands clasped together. Gold earrings fixed in his ears, gold rings on his fingers.

Somewhere out in the dark Boats was yelling for Jimbo and Chaz. Shan barked Wei's name. Byrus was farther away, his voice calling plaintively, "Zim! Zim!"

Bat sank to the floor and regretted it. Sitting would only make it that much harder to get up. All the aches and pains of the previous weeks gripped her at once. She kept up with the Rangers and the SEAL and could almost match Byrus for energy level. But there was a limit to her conditioning and toughness, and she was feeling herself drawing near to it. It wasn't so much what she'd done as what she'd seen.

There'd been suffering in her past. She'd witnessed what men could do to one another. She knew what she could do herself if pushed to it. At night, the faces of the men she'd killed came back to her. Not as flat images seen through the lens of her scope, targets too far from her hide to be visible to the naked eye.

Instead, she saw them in her dreams as if they were within reach of her hands, in the same room with her. Their faces, their eyes, their smiles, and scowls were imagined, of course. The men whose lives she'd ended were only seen fleetingly as they passed through the reticles into the kill zone. She did not feel remorse at killing them. It was war. It was for her people. The men she killed threatened the fragile peace of her adopted homeland. What she regretted was that it had to be her who pulled the trigger. It was a task she now wished had fallen to another.

And now the scale of the horrors she'd seen on this latest trip back into The Then. She'd witnessed sights that she was certain would replace the faces in her dreams. She'd walked, unheeding, through the misery all around her. There'd be a price to pay for that. There'd be no unseeing those sights. They would only become more vivid in her memories. Just as the faceless men who dropped in her scope took on the clear visages they wore in her dreams.

The men called the names of their friends with no answer. Their voices faded away in the vastness of the treasure house. She dropped her face to her hands and heaved a sharp sigh. There were no tears though her eyes burned. Bat sipped in air and held it in her lungs. A brief respite. A moment of quiet all her own and then she'd resume the search with the others. Though she felt the search was pointless. How could three men alone have survived the slaughter here?

In the momentary silence, she heard a recurring tapping. A metallic scraping, muted but regular from somewhere near her.

Clink. Clink. Clink. Pause.

Clink. Clink. Clink.

"Guys!" she shouted, standing with eyes searching the gloom.

THE LOOTERS

L ee came upon the curious sight of Bat Jaffe and Boats kneeling side by side each with an ear to the floor.

"What the hell—" he started.

"Shh!" Bat and the SEAL shushed him in unison.

"Is it Morse Code?" Bat whispered.

Clink. Clink. Clink. Pause.

Clink. Clink. Clink.

"Naw," Boats said, eyes moving as he listened to the tapping resonating through the tiles, his hand cupped about his ear.

"Then what is it?" Bat said.

"'Jingle Bells,'" Boats said and pulled his combat knife from its sheath to rap the butt on the floor.

Tap. Tap. Tap. Pause. *Tap. Tap.*

A metallic grinding sound vibrated through the floor beneath them. Ten feet before where they knelt, down a lane between life-sized statues of real and fanciful beasts, a bronze war horse seemed to come to life. It shifted sideways to reveal a bar of yellow light rising from a gap in the floor.

"That better be you up there, motherfuckers!" Chaz' voice boomed from somewhere below.

Jimbo was the last to step out of the trap in the floor. He held a thick roll of camel skin cradled in his arms. He unraveled it to show the others a curved tube of ivory capped on one end with a golden swan and on the other with a crouching frog. It was damned close to the computer model Wesley Fong showed them back on the *Raj*. The whole thing was roughly the size of a muffler off an army truck.

There was a lot of back pounding. Byrus embraced the Pima about the waist and had to be pried off. It was all smiles except for Shan and Wei who looked on without speaking.

"How'd you find it?" Boats asked.

"I found a manifest book. Remember what Gordon told us about these guys being crazy for paperwork." Jimbo grinned. "Wei found it listed in a secret vault. It was down there with a stuffed dog and a porno collection."

"You're shitting us," Lee said.

"No lie. A taxidermied Pekinese and a bunch of paintings that would make Larry Flynt blush," Jimbo said. "Wei has the inventory book. We'll bring it along for Dr. Fong. He'll be in Heaven."

"Too bad we couldn't bring back some pictures for him," Chaz said.

"That's a hell-no," Lee said. There was a strict 'no cameras' rule for anyone going through the Tauber Tube.

The sounds of voices and footfalls echoed up from the open foyer below. The looters had reached the treasure hoard of the East King. Boots and bare feet pounded up the steps toward them in a hurry. The sound of hoots and cries of delight resounded across the vault as the newcomers took in the golden sea of valuables before them.

A collection of rough men with wild eyes braced the team. From the smell, a lot of them had been drinking heavily. Their armor and clothing were black with spilled blood. Shan approached them with hands open before him and speaking steady, reasoned words to the suspicious bunch. The pillagers decided in the end, distracted by the riches spread about in all directions, that there was enough to go around and drifted off to begin sacking the treasure house to the bare walls.

Outside, the sun was coming up in an angry sky streaked black with the smoke of burning homes. The air was foul with the smell of blood. As the air warmed flies were beginning to gather in clouds. Across the courtyards and gardens, bodies lay like piles of rubbish, mutilated and stripped of clothing. Drunken soldiers and conscripts stumbled in mobs among the palaces or lay sleeping wherever the alcohol finally overcame them. From over the rooftops came the occasional report of a musket. The battle was over. The rape of the city was only beginning.

"We need to find a place to hole up," Lee said. Bat gripped his arm.

"I know we're all beat to shit. God knows I hate the thought of taking another step," she said to him, eyes red. "But can we please get away from here? Sleep somewhere on clean grass?"

Lee looked to the others who nodded in silent agreement.

With their prize stowed in a rucksack on Jimbo's back, they hiked back the way they came on the shortest route out of Hell they could manage.

58

VISITORS

The day was gray overcast and the sky hung low enough that the tops of the tall cargo cranes disappeared into an opaque cloud ceiling. The launch cut across the water with all running lights blazing to ward off any river traffic that might cross its course to the sheltered anchorage where the *Ocean Raj* lay.

Jason Taan brushed aside all assistance in finding his way down through the ship to the chamber where the time travel device was housed. This was the latest of his trips out to the *Raj*. Each one ended in disappointment. It had been a full six months since he sent his two operatives back to pursue the team of mad Americans. He was growing impatient with waiting and weary of Morris Tauber's excuses. Most of all, he was tired of the physicist's condescending explanations on the relativity of time travel.

He wanted the team back today. He wanted the prize he'd already spent a fortune for, today. Right now.

"Another false alarm?" Taan growled, storming into the control room. Morris Tauber sat at the array of monitors on which numbers and three-dimensional models morphed and scrolled with dizzying speed. These were the dense calculations for aiming and manipulating the gigawatt energy needed to power the device in the chamber below, visible through the wall of glass.

"I've had a transmission from our operatives. I'm a few hours from getting an accurate fix on their chronal position," Tauber said, himself weary of Taan's impatient tantrums. "You said you wanted to be here when they returned."

"I was in a meeting," Taan groused, pacing. Actually, he was glad to be able to cut the meeting short. It was a tedious teleconference with the execs of an Italian engineering firm. He hated dealing with Italians. They were the only people, other than the Chinese, who took so long to come to a decision and even longer to act on it.

"There's tea and raisin buns," Tauber said and turned back to his keyboard.

Taan threw himself into a chair and glared down at the array of carbon steel rings in the manifestation chamber. They were already sheathed in a casing of frost preparatory to being activated.

It was almost midnight when the new transmission came through. "Op team to central control. You reading this? Op team to central control." It was Lee Hammond's drawl coming from the speakers.

"This is Mo. We have you with crystal clarity. Come back," Morris said, standing at the control console. Taan was standing, looking down into the manifestation chamber, the floor invisible in a chilly mist.

"We're within range. Port of Shanghai. You have a fix?"

"Give me a minute to make adjustments, fine-tune things, okay?" Morris said.

"Ask them if they have it!" Taan shouted, turning from the

glass.

"What's your situation? What do you need us to prepare for your return?" Morris said, ignoring the billionaire's furious gaze.

"We lost a man. We're banged up but no need for urgent medical attention."

"Heat up a pizza!" Boats' voice in the background of the transmission.

"And ice some beer!" That was Chaz Raleigh.

Morris wondered who they lost. He turned to check the signal profile, matching it to his projected aiming point. He'd know soon enough.

"Do they have it?" Taan roared. All his polished cool was gone.

"Tell him we have it. It was right where Fong said it would be." After a pause, Lee added, "Almost."

"Bring them back! Bring them back now!" Taan said, stabbing a finger at the tube chamber.

Morris Tauber tapped a series of commands on his keyboard. The arctic fog about the rings of the manifestation array rose to spread fractal ice patterns across the observation glass

A bank of mist spread across the waters of the channel off Changxingxiang Island. It swelled outward and upward until it touched either bank of the Yangtze River mouth and mingled with the low cloud cover above. The epicenter of the sudden veil of cold fog appeared to be the recently constructed boat shelter erected mid-current almost a year before. The shelter and the big container ship within were soon invisible in the cloaking haze.

The strange weather phenomenon was keenly observed from a train of barges anchored at a berth along a slip at the Yuanshagang Yards at the southern foot of the island.

Maurice Franck watched through binoculars. The growing blob of white extended out across the river just as he'd been told it would happen. He touched a tab wired to the collar of his windbreaker.

"It is happening. We are 'go.' We go now," he said in a voice that rasped from scarred vocal cords.

Within minutes five Zodiac inflatable boats were removed from hiding and lowered into the water by the barges. Armed men, five to a boat, dropped down into the boats. Within seconds they were off, powered over the water by twin outboards. The bows of the boats lifted from the water. The men on board made last-minute checks of night vision gear, weapons, and body armor. They were being well paid for tonight's operation and all were anxious to reach the center of the mysterious fog and get to work.

Quan Ho hunkered at the prow of the lead boat, an MP-5 clutched in gloved hands. His eyes were locked, through the lenses of an advanced NODs device, on the growing digitized silhouette of the shelter that contained the *Ocean Raj*, their primary target.

A blinding flash came through the lenses, searing his eyes with white light. Quan tore the NODs from his face with an irritated snarl.

Within the column of fog, a brilliant nimbus of light appeared for a moment. It glowed within the haze with solar intensity, turning the tops of the water silver. The sky went dark again, leaving only the lingering ghost shape of the ball of light on the retinas of the men on the boats.

A loud squawk of commands through his earpiece caused Quan to wince. Franck was shouting questions and directions in his barbaric Cantonese. Quan turned to the man at the helm of the Zodiac and barked a command. The man pressed the control arm down, and the prow of the inflatable rose higher off the water as the screws of the mighty outboards dug in. The rest of the boats matched the speed and followed to soar up the river toward the heart of the frigid mist.

CONTACT

The journey back down the Yangtze took half as long as the voyage to Nanking. For a fistful of silver tales, the team booked space on a barge piled with loot for the mandarins heading downriver. Coolies worked the long poles, walking them bow to stern, to propel them along the current and around other craft.

Once back in Shanghai, they purchased a skiff they could row out into the channel. It was skunky with barnacles and weed but was solid enough. It would take them out to the *Ocean Raj* waiting at mid-river a century and a half away.

Boats found the stone pier where they'd scuttled the longboat marked with the *USS Pennock's* name. Shan and Lee watched the SEAL strip off his shirt and dive into the brown water, vanishing in the murk. He surfaced moments later with a small wooden box in his fist.

"Is it intact?" Lee asked, helping Boats back onto the pier. "The casing is still watertight," Boats said, handing the small carton over. Its surface was slick with river muck over a thick waxy covering.

"I did not know of this," Shan said as they walked up the pier, wending their way between stacks of cargo and fish traps.

"This is how we coordinate with the *Raj* to get back to The Now," Lee said. "A concession to the twenty-first century. A modified radio transmitter."

"It's sealed in paraffin to keep it temporarily waterproofed," Boats said. "The seal would wear away in six months or so, and the transmitter would rust away over time."

"That way, if we didn't make it back, the radio wouldn't cause a ripple in the continuum," Lee said. "Though I don't understand what all that really means, the Taubers get all pissy about it."

"And without it, we could not return," Shan said.

"Without it, we'd need you to teach us all Chinese," Boats said with a snort.

Back on the skiff that Chaz had christened *The Rusty Turd*, Lee broke the waxen seal on the box to remove the transmitter. It powered up, speaker crackling.

"Op team to central control. Op team to central control," Lee said, settling down on a bench below deck. It might take time to reach the *Raj*. On low power, Morris Tauber could keep the field open just enough to allow a transmission through. A pinhole in time, not enough for anything physical to pop through. From past experience, they knew the transmission field was twitchy and unreliable.

Members of the team poked their heads over the lip of the open hatch above him, curious and anxious to see if he'd made contact. More than an hour later, he received an answering squawk followed by Morris' voice.

"Who's there? Who am I speaking to?"

"It's Lee Hammond, Mo. You have a fix on us?" Lee said. He heard footfalls on the deck above. Shadows fell over him from above as everyone gathered to listen.

"It's weak," came Morris' brittle reply through the hiss. "Give me time to amp up the signal. Be ready to move."

"Roger. Out," Lee said and turned the gain down to conserve the transmitter's battery. He looked up to see the others looking down at him.

"Get this shitbox seaworthy. We're going home," Lee said.

As evening fell, *The Rusty Turd* made its sluggish way through the maze of junks and barges anchored in the harbor. Boats stood at the tiller calling time for the rest of the team working the long sweeps. He noticed that there were more masts and stacks of merchant ships visible along the harbor quays than when they left a month before. The wars were over, and it was back to business.

They anchored the skiff out on the open river and took turns watching the water rising in swells as the ocean's tide pushed against the Yangtze's current. The night was clear with a near-full moon.

Lee and Bat sat on the bench below decks. Near them, Byrus was sound asleep on coils of musty rope. A hanging lantern swayed while the boat rolled gently side to side. Lee pulled the ivory reliquary from the rucksack and examined it in the lamplight.

"You think Genghis Khan's last words are really in here?" Lee said.

"All this crap for something I'd probably have walked right past at a garage sale." Bat shrugged.

"Who gives a shit. It's what Tann sent us back for, and we got it."

Lee held one end of the tube up and examined the golden lid.

He found a place below the head of a golden swan where there was a gap that went all the way around the curved neck. He pulled it, and the head came free, connected to the neck by a rod with serrations worked in it.

"You're going to break it," Bat said, hushed.

"It's just a pimped-out mailing tube. It's what's inside that makes it valuable." Turning the head clockwise, Lee heard some catches release inside the cap. He yanked, and the lid came free in his hand with a hiss.

He tipped the tube, and a roll of vellum dropped from the carved out hollow of the tusk. It was a scroll tied with a ribbon of silk. Lee pulled the ribbon free of the wax seal and unrolled the vellum easily. It was still supple even after centuries in the air-tight reliquary.

"This is the big man's diary?" Lee said, examining row after row of tiny, precisely penned characters.

"He wasn't that big, actually," Bat said, taking the free end of the scroll to marvel at the penmanship of whoever served as the Khan's stenographer.

"Big enough to take over half the known world," Lee said and continued unraveling. He stopped when he reached a series of drawings. Lines and squiggles done in the same skilled hand as the characters. Alongside the drawings was a grid containing symbols that were not part of the Chinese alphabet.

"That's a key, right? It looks to me like a map," Bat said, leaning closer to squint at the markings in the flickering light.

"It is a map."

They turned to see Wei standing on the ladder in the hatchway. He had his revolver trained at them, the barrel steady on Lee. A second revolver was tight in his other fist and trained toward Byrus snoring on the deck. The Ranger moved on the bench to shield Bat. Wei clicked his tongue and shook his head.

"Please return the scroll to its place," Wei said in a flat voice.

English with no accent. Like he learned it from a machine. "Looks like Wei was playing his game close all this time, babe," Lee said.

"Return the scroll to its place. It is not yours," Wei said, stepping off the last rung to aim both revolvers at them.

"Sure, it belongs to your boss. We were just taking a peek. We'll be handing it to Mr. Taan when we get back," Lee said, judging the distance between them. More than ten feet over an uncertain surface. He'd get one shot at it. He'd take some slugs. That was sure. He could drop the smaller man in a rush. Bat would have to follow up, finish it. Lee let his breath out all the way. He didn't want Wei to see it in his eyes. He'd go in three.

"You will not be going back," Wei said, raising the barrels of the revolvers to center on his targets.

Lee flung himself forward.

An explosion of sound filled the hull.

Lee collided with Wei through a fog of black powder, slamming him to the deck.

He raised a hand to drive a fist into the face of the other man. He felt a warm stickiness running down his brow. Someone tugged at his arm.

Wei was under him, body limp. Half of the man's face was gone. Jagged bone shards gleamed white around the lip of a fist-sized hole where his right eye had been.

Lee looked up as Bat pulled him off, her shouts muted through the ringing in his ears. Shan stood midway down the ladder, a smoking rifle in his fists.

60

KILLER APP

Jason Taan insisted on being in the manifestation chamber when the team returned. He was joined by five of his guards. All five were armed with handguns they made no effort to conceal under the jackets. They viewed the swirling fog with barely concealed suspicion. These were not curious men. They only knew to distrust what they could not understand. And they neither trusted nor understood this large space refrigerated to freezing with the weirdly humming tubular structure dominating the center of the room.

The first to emerge up the steel platform was the American Ranger Lee Hammond. He was followed by the woman, the Israeli. The pair stopped at the end of the ramp and looked about themselves to see weapons aimed at them.

"This how you keep a promise, Taan?" Lee said, spotting the billionaire huddled in an ill-fitting parka.

"Disarm them," Taan ordered in Cantonese.

As the others emerged down the ramp from the past, they were forced to drop what weapons they had left. Rifles, pistols, and blades dropped to the ramp. Jimbo seized Byrus' arm to keep the Macedonian in check. The little man maintained his grip on his gladius while his eyes bored into the eyes of the closest guard. After a few seconds, he cast the blade down to clatter to the deck, sending an arc of spittle that froze in the air to fall to the floor in tinkling crystals.

Shan was the last up the ramp. He held a rucksack in his arms. His expression was impassive as he shouldered through the others to reach Jason Taan.

"The other man? His name was Wei Li, right?" Taan said, accepting the filthy rucksack.

"A regrettable casualty," Shan said, eyes hard.

Taan turned away to undo the straps of the pack and toss it aside. He held the ivory reliquary in his hands, the surface of it still warm from a Shanghai summer one hundred and fifty years in the past.

"You got what you want. Time to let us go," Lee Hammond said, stepping forward. Two guards raised their weapons to train on the big Ranger. The rest stood ready to spray the others with bursts of point-blank fire.

"I am sorry. That won't be possible," Taan said, a smile curling his lip.

Morris Tauber's voice came out of speakers mounted on the glass observation wall. "Don't tell *us* what's possible, asshole."

Taan looked up to see Morris standing at the frosted glass tabbing keys on the wireless board cradled on his arm.

"Whatever you're doing, you will stop it right now!" Taan shouted.

"Too late," Morris said and brought a finger down onto the board with a smirk.

The deck below Taan's feet shuddered violently as if the ship had run aground. But the vibration continued along with a deafening shriek of tortured steel. The hull of the ship popped and screamed as the metal came under stresses it was never built to withstand. The temperature dropped further until the cold was stabbing into every joint on his body. Every patch of exposed skin seared in a blaze of freezing air.

But worse than the sights, sounds, and sensations was the disabling wave of vertigo that crushed Taan to his knees on the deck. His vision swam. His gorge rose. He pressed his eyes closed to shut it out, and the grip of disorientation only sharpened until he felt his consciousness slipping away.

He came around, seconds or hours later, his cheek stuck to the steel deck by a layer of frost. His face was caked with a skein of frozen vomit. The taste of rancid raisins filled his mouth. Taan screamed in pain as he was lifted to a seated position. He left a patch of skin from his cheek on the frozen deck. The sting served to bring the world back in focus.

The mist in the manifestation chamber was dropping away. Before him, his five bodyguards were down on their hands and knees. Their weapons were stripped from them and in the hands of the Americans. Most wore frozen vomit on their clothes. They looked pale as ghosts. Shan stood aside, the ivory tube capped with golden swan and frog in his arms. Taan raised a hand, fingers splayed, eyes anxious, to have the reliquary back in his arms.

"You changed the deal, Taan. Now we're changing the deal," Lee Hammond said, lifting Taan to his feet by the collar of the Italian suit worn under the borrowed parka.

"What have you done to me?" Taan croaked, gulping to keep from retching.

"Taken you for a little trip. Tauber style," Lee said. That brought a hoot from the red-bearded giant. Even Shan was smiling.

Taan blinked. He could not comprehend the American's words.

There was a second explosion of light in the night sky as the five Zodiac rafts approached. The flash was followed by a rumbling boom of thunder. Within seconds, the river foamed with chop. A sudden gust of wind turned the tops of the wavelets white with frost. The gale force wind was gone as swiftly as it came, and the river was quiet and dark once more.

With engines whining as they slowed, they drifted toward the towering wall of the sheltered anchorage.

Quan Ho stood at the bow of the lead boat and waved them ahead. The men behind raised weapons and steeled nerves for the jump-off. They had their orders and they understood the mission. Each team had an assigned section of the container ship, a kill zone they were responsible for. The directions were simple. Get on board, sweep the ship, and eliminate everyone they met.

The hardest part of this op was concentrating on the job at hand rather than the pay. They were each contracted for one million UK pounds apiece.

The outboards puttered to a stop. The inflatables continued on their courses silently toward the foot of the broad piers running down either side of the inner wall of the shelter. From the piers, it was a short charge up the gangways to the main deck, and from there the *Ocean Raj's* deck and cabins and holds would become a free-fire zone.

Except that the massive steel shelter contained nothing but empty water.

The huge container ship that had been housed there only seconds before was gone.

61

SLAVE SHIP

Dwayne guessed that he was in Chula Vista. The blue of San Diego Bay lay below with the Pacific vanishing in mist beyond. Where he was hiding was some of the most valuable real estate in the world. Multi-million dollar homes sat on these hills like books on a shelf. That was another time, another world. Now the canyons around the bay were chocked with aloe plants and populated only by pumas, coyotes, and wild pigs. Dwayne stayed out of the way of all of them.

He lay in the concealment of rocks along a ridgeline above the bay. Far below, a fat ship sat at anchor. It was a design he was unfamiliar with. A big wooden craft with a high deck fore and aft. It was tub shaped and ungainly. A single mast rose from amidships and from it hung a triangular sail that even at this distance showed signs of patching. It drooped unmoving in the still air. There was a symbol painted on the sail, but it was so sun-faded that Dwayne could make nothing of it.

The hulls were lined with openings that had to be gun ports. It was a warship of some kind or an armed merchantman. Still, it wasn't like any sailing ship Dwayne had ever seen in books or movies.

CHUCK DIXON

A pair of smaller craft were making their way from the larger vessel. Oars swept them along. The sail mounted on each was as limp as the cloth on the mother ship. The boats made it through the lazy surf, and men leaped out to help push the craft up onto the sand. The boats disgorged more men, an astonishing number from what looked to Dwayne, from his perspective, like toy boats.

Men splashed through the water in curious columns. Dwayne squinted to see that each man had loops of something connected one to the other.

Ropes or chains. Slaves.

This was confirmed by the rough treatment at the hands of those who swung whips over their heads, the cracks of the leather loud enough to carry up to Dwayne's position.

The men were too far away to see any indication of their race or nationality. But all appeared to be dark-skinned. Probably the same sort as the Asian Indians he found dead on the beach two hundred miles south. The slaves were set apart by their nakedness. Their masters wore loose-fitting clothing as faded by the sun as the sails of the big boat. The ones wielding the whips wore turbans or puggarees wound about their heads.

He never recalled reading about Arabs or Sikhs landing in the New World. Of course, he knew from his own experience that a lot of history was pure bullshit. Dwayne kept watching, wishing he had binoculars until the column of slaves was driven inland and out of his sight in trees that grew close to the beach. The rowing crews boarded their boats and rowed for the big ship.

There had to be a settlement of some kind farther inland, someplace they were taking the slaves to put them to work. Mines or farms or something like that. He'd work around east to avoid them. After dark, he'd be able to locate the settlement, if that's what it was, by the glow of the cook fires. Then he'd find a canyon that skirted the area and follow that north.

His plan was to get deeper into what would one day be California then activate the bracelet to see if it would return him to The Now, well out of spatial reach of the hunters who were after him and Caroline. His only question was where to make the jump. Caroline had explained over and over again why she and her brother initially chose the desert to locate the Tauber Tube. There was little chance of manifesting into the side of a mountain or a structure. The open ocean made an even more suitable base for jumping. He'd have to find a place that he could reasonably rely on being wide open and free of obstructions before taking the leap.

The two boats drew in oars as they neared the larger vessel. Each drifted out of sight around the hull. With nothing else to see, Dwayne started to move back from his hide to start his hike inland.

Something huffed behind him. A shift of sand.

Dwayne rolled to his back and into a crouch, the needle gun leveled in his hands.

On the crest of a slope behind him, a mounted figure sat watching, the rising morning sun at its back. It was a man with copper-colored skin, his chest bare. He wore a jaguar skin girdled at the waist. Atop his head was a wooden headdress fashioned like the snarling head of a snake with long, tattered feathers rising from it. The man's face was painted stark white with black circles drawn about his eyes, and he stared at Dwayne as though from the mouth of the fanged serpent. Across the pommel of his saddle rested a matchlock musket. In his clenched teeth, he held a smoking fuse. His mount stamped its feet and huffed through its nostrils once more.

An Aztec.

Sitting on a camel.

And, as Dwayne weighed his options, a score more of the mounted warriors topped the ridge behind the first.

A WISH GRANTED

The *Ocean Raj* cut across twenty-foot seas against a forty-knot wind. The sky and sea met in a purple convergence of angry clouds and angrier water. Rain was coming down in a mist but promising to build to a torrent any second.

Up on the bridge, Boats piloted them up each swell, and down into the troughs, the white caps stretched before them to the horizon. Geteye assisted him at the radar, watching for shoals in the unknown waters. From the glass-pane smooth seas of the Yangtze estuary, the *Raj* has materialized in the middle of monsoon weather.

Down in the forward hull, Jason Taan rocked sullenly on a mattress thrown on the deck for his comfort. Taan, and his bodyguards, as well as the security men tasked with watching over the crew of the ship, were confined together in a locked cargo container. He and his bodyguards had been easily overwhelmed by the returning Rangers in the moments of extreme physical discomfort created by their first experience with a mass manifestation field. The crew of the *Raj* had taken the rest of his men.

Lee stopped by one of the crew cabins where Shan sat on the

edge of a bunk in the dark. He was still in the filthy uniform of a barbarian mercenary.

"Yo. Take a shower, bro. We're having a pizza party in the chartroom," Lee said.

"I am not in the mood for a party," Shan said.

"You have to eat."

"I am not hungry."

"Bullshit. I could eat the ass out of raw possum," Lee said. Shan did not respond.

"You did the right thing. Though I don't know why."

"Repaying a debt. Is that enough explanation?"

"You mean me saving your life? You had a mission, Shan."

"Not a mission. A job. Not the same," Shan said.

"I get that. Debt paid, brother. Shower off that funk and come have some beers with us," Lee said and departed.

Shan sat quietly in the dark, listening to the laughter and music echoing down the corridor from somewhere forward.

In the chartroom, the team wolfed down pizza chased by beer and listened to Morris Tauber's update of their current situation. Parviz and Quebat joined them. The Iranians still looked stunned by the twin charges they pulled out of their mini-reactor. Enhancing their expressions of surprise was the fact that their hair still stood on end after the massive static field that had engulfed the entire ship. Even their eyebrows stood up rigid.

"I had Taan's contractors build the ship shelter to my specifications even down to the materials used. They carped and moaned, but I was ready with a whole lot of technobabble," Morris began once the boombox had been turned down.

"You mean bullshit," Chaz snorted around a mouthful of pepperoni and sausage.

"Yeah, a lot of that too," Morris continued, beaming. "Essentially, I had them construct an enormous Tauber Tube, one with the capacity to take the whole ship with it."

"And you knew that would work," Bat said.

"Theoretically," Morris said, face reddening.

The Rangers howled at that. Morris reddened further and went on, "I was desperate. I knew, as I'm sure you did, that Taan was never going to let us go after he got what he wanted. I had to make a move that he wasn't looking for. In any case, it worked."

"So, now we can just jump back to The Now when we get clear of the China coast, right?" Jimbo said.

"Not really. We need a manifestation field created at our destination to do that. One large enough to take the ship and us in it."

"But you can still send personnel down the Tube?" Lee said. "Sure. But that would mean abandoning the *Raj* and the reactor. It would be our last trip," Morris said.

"There has to be another way around this," Bat said.

"The man didn't have time to worry about Step Two. He was only thinking about getting us clear of Taan," Chaz said.

"Hey, everyone's forgetting the big question," Jimbo said. "When the hell *are* we?"

A speaker on the wall piped up with a voice shouting. It was Boats calling down from the bridge. He wasn't making any sense at all. What emerged from the speaker was more a series of whoops and laughter.

They made their way to the bridge where Geteye was alone at the wheel. He nodded forward. A shape in yellow, barely seen through the spray swept glass, was dancing in the downpour along the open deck. It was Boats in a slicker, clinging to the rail and howling like a Viking in heat.

"Shit yeah! Shit yeah!" the big SEAL said, pointing off the bow at the rising sea.

There, in a wall of a green swelling before them, dimly seen through the verdant translucence, a massive shape glided to starboard out of the path of the ship. The *Raj* climbed the roller to the top and began the descent to the trough. Lee and Jimbo joined Boats out on the heaving weather deck. They fought for footing and clutched the rail to remain upright.

"There! There! That's what I'm talking about!" Boats shouted, stabbing a finger at the water beyond the bow.

In the trough below them, a torpedo-shaped object splashed out of a wall of water with an explosion of white spray. A flash of teeth and a long body with a pebbled hide. A pronounced fence of triangular fins ran down its spine. It vanished into the next swell, its whipping tail creating an eruption of foam.

"Sixty feet if it's an inch! I saw it in one of Mo's books!" Boats shouted.

"What the fuck is it?" Lee called through the shrieking wind.

"Mosasaur! A fucking dinosaur, bro!" Boats said, turning with them, his face open with childlike delight.

AFTERWORD

The bloodiest civil war in human history, a conflict second only to the Second World War for total fatalities, began when Hong Xiuquan failed the exams to become a civil servant in the Qing Dynasty. His poor marks resulted in what could only be a total mental breakdown, during which he lay in a catatonic state for weeks. During this period, he had vivid hallucinations in which he visited the afterlife and was informed by God Himself that Hong was the second son of God and little brother to Jesus Christ.

With the help of a brother and other family members, Hong traveled the northern provinces of China, spreading a gospel that was a twisted mix of the Christian gospel and his own mythology inspired by his imagined journeys to Heaven. As hard as it is to believe, Hong was able to create a large following of acolytes and finally an army to help spread his ideology from city to city. The Heavenly King was able to swiftly engulf large areas and turned his evangelism to open rebellion against the emperor as well as the Confucian philosophy that provided the reigning school of thought informing everything from the law to manners and education.

The Qing emperor and his mandarins were slow to act against the rising tide of rebellion. Partly because of sheer disbelief and denial that anyone could successfully defy their centuries-long hold on China. Another factor was the off-again-on-again wars with foreign interlopers, chiefly Britain and France. China was a huge market for a new commodity called opium. European exporters found China to be a consumer base too lucrative to resist and lobbied their respective governments to provide protection for their merchants to keep trade routes open. This led to years of warfare along the Yellow and Yangtze rivers that would flare up and die away on an almost seasonal basis until the British army and navy under Generals Hope Grant and Lord Elgin took Peking and forced an infant emperor and his regents to flee.

The mandarins were forced to agree to trade deals that would allow the addictive substance to be sold freely throughout China. These struggles with foreign devils proved to be a near-lethal distraction that allowed the cancer of the Taiping ideology to metastasize.

For fifteen years, war raged over China. The Imperial army met its match in the fanatical Taipings who learned the art of war quickly. The Taiping armies were well trained, armed and led by capable generals who could lay successful sieges of Qing cities as well as beating the emperor's troops in the field.

I make mention of the Ever Victorious Army. This was one of many mercenary forces employed by the Manchus to blunt the threat of the rebels. The most successful of these was the EVA, founded by the American adventurer Frederic Ward. Ward's army was composed of a foreign legion of Europeans and Asians. He was a creative and reckless leader who had tremendous success against the armies of the Heavenly King despite being often outnumbered by as many as ten to one. He was paid a generous monthly stipend by the mandarins with bonuses for each city that he retook from the rebels. Dubbed the "White

Devil" by the Chinese, Ward's bold and fearless style inspired his men to incredible feats of daring and not a few military miracles. But it was his insistence on leading from the front that ended his life at the foot of the walls about Cixi at the age of thirty-one.

As referred to in my story, command of the Ever Victorious Army was taken over by Charles Gordon, later famous as "Chinese" Gordon, a legendary adventurer of the Victorian Age. He would meet his end at the siege of Khartoum in 1885. Gordon was a highly religious man who did not seek monetary gain or fame for his actions. At the close of hostilities in 1865 he refused a fortune in gold offered by the Manchu court as a bonus for his part in defeating the Taiping rebels. It was a staggering amount that would have made him one of the richest men in Britain. He did condemn the use of alcohol and is, in other ways, as I portray him here. If he seems casually racist or cruel, well, those were the accepted mindsets of the day for gentlemen at war with heathens. It's not for me to pass judgment on the man. I only present him in as honest a way as I can without regard to the mores of our culture.

I wrote here that the EVA and Gordon were in the midst of disbanding and departing. The final fighting around Nanking, the ultimate blow to the followers of the Heavenly King and his followers, was left up to the emperor's generals. In truth, at the time I portray here, Gordon would have been well on his way back to England but, bowing to my toy-soldier fascination with history, I couldn't resist including him.

Prince Kung, regent to the boy emperor, was also a real person and as nasty a piece of work (or worse) as I've presented here, though he was probably not on familiar terms with Charles Gordon as I present here. Manchu royalty were virtually unapproachable by anyone but their closest court members and certainly not by barbaric occidentals. Still, a villain is a villain, and Kung is one of history's most bloody-minded bad guys. I couldn't resist including him as a personification of the kind of leader who would spend the lives of his thralls with no more thought to their suffering than you or I might spare for the fowl winding up in a bucket of fried chicken.

As to the siege of Nanking, the weapons and methods (mining, countermining, siege artillery, rockets, and the rest) are based on my research of the period. There's little written about the fall of the city other than that a section of the outer wall was collapsed by a massive explosion detonated in a mine at the time and on the day I denoted. It is also true that the imperial troops and their conscripts surged into Nanking bringing on an appalling massacre. The finer details of the battle as presented are fanciful, my imagination at work. General Sang is also a creation of mine made from whole cloth, a compilation of several Manchu military leaders.

But some of the most unbelievable aspects of my story are actually factual. Hong Xiuquan did indeed die of some kind of gastrointestinal condition brought on by eating weeds that he insisted were manna from Heaven. And I have, if anything, downplayed the amount of sheer carnage that was commonplace during the Taiping civil war. The rivers would often become choked with the dead. Mountains of severed heads and miles-long heaps of the dead were an everyday sight. And there are many witnesses to the fighting who have mentioned walking across battlefields literally carpeted with the dead so that it was impossible to make progress without stepping upon corpses.

The weapons that the team uses for this operation also only exist in my imagination. But the Henry repeating rifle had been around more than a decade at this point. Adding a second magazine tube to increase the round capacity would have been well within the technology of the period had anyone thought of it. But a capacity of ten rounds was pretty astonishing at the time. Hence Henry's oft-repeated slogan, "Load on Sunday. Shoot all week."

And cartridge-loading revolvers would have been rare but not unheard of in 1865. The army of the Manchus was armed with bolt-action rifles of the type that would not be standard issue to any army for another twenty years. Losing either of their made-up brand of weapons would not cause the kind of chronal pollution that regularly costs Morris Tauber a night's sleep. The 1800s were awash in wild, experimental firearms produced in small numbers. The rifles and revolvers mentioned here would not be among the craziest weapons under patent in 1865.

The treasure vault of the East King is also something I dreamed up, but jaw-dropping collections of valuables were not unheard of in the China of the day. All of the lower kings of the Taiping court lived in sumptuous palaces packed with plunder from all over China, and they would certainly have put the artisans of their captured cities to work on more. There is no inventory of the East King's hoard, but the descriptions I provided are within reason. The raiding of the emperor's treasure houses by British soldiers, sailors and sepoys in 1860 are well documented by witnesses. The looting of the Forbidden City created a staggering transfer of wealth that would be hard to calculate by today's rate of exchange. Even more shocking than the extent of the hoard was the destruction of irreplaceable artifacts destroyed by soldiers who had no idea of their value.

Genghis Khan's autobiography is not an invention of mine either. The first khan did indeed dictate his amazing life story to a Chinese scholar so that his tale was recorded. It is not known if any existing copies of the biography are the original or the definitive version. And none of them included a map of any sort. We'll learn more about the significance of that when the Rangers return.

Chuck Dixon April 4, 2016 AD

BIBLIOGRAPHY

Just a few of the books that helped me recreate the world of the Taipings and Manchus.

God's Chinese Son, by Jonathan D. Spencer. First edition. 1996, Norton.

A beautifully written and exhaustive history of the Taiping rebellion.

Gordon of Khartoum, by John H. Waller. First edition. 1988, Atheneum.

A marvelous biography of the legendary Victorian adventurer.

The Ever-Victorious Army, by Andrew Wilson Elibron. Classics series, 2005.

An eye-witness account, for the good portion, of the events of the Taiping uprising and its suppression. First published in 1868.

Flashman and the Dragon, by George MacDonald Fraser. First edition. Knopf, 1986.

Flashy provides a vivid account of the Opium Wars that occurred concurrently with the start of the Taipings' rise to power. A ripping yarn filled with period-accurate nomenclature and dialogue that helped inform the style of my own work.

The story continues with Pirates of the Cretaceous, book six in the Bad Times story from Chuck Dixon.

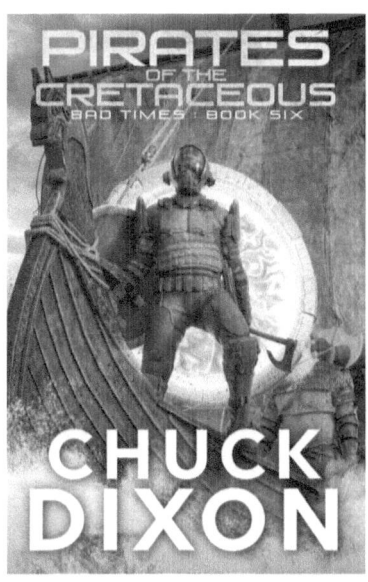

Trapped in a prehistoric hell, the men (and woman) of the Ocean Raj will need all their courage and all their intelligence to escape back to the present.

The latest volume in Chuck Dixon's epic Bad Times series finds the Rangers separated from each other and the ones they love by thousands of miles and millions of years.

While Lee, Jimbo, Chaz and Boats battle to survive on a world of monsters, Dwayne finds himself a captive of Aztecs and drafted by Vikings to fight a murderous naval battle.

And Caroline Tauber remains in the present where she is hunted across the globe by killers from another time.

Loaded with the kind of bloody action, lightning pace and high intrigue that readers all over the world have come to expect from this wild read of a series.

Order now at Amazon and through Kindle Unlimited.

ABOUT THE AUTHOR

Chuck Dixon is the prolific author of thousands of comic book scripts for *Batman and Robin, the Punisher, Nightwing, Conan the Barbarian, Airboy, the Simpsons, Alien Legion,* and countless other titles.

Together with Graham Nolan, Chuck created the now iconic Batman villain Bane. He also wrote the international bestselling graphic novel adaptation of J.R.R Tolkien's *The Hobbit.*

His first foray into prose, the *SEAL Team 6* novels from Dynamite Entertainment, have become an ebook sensation. He currently scripts *GI Joe Special Missions* for IDW publishing as well as the *Pellucidar* weekly comic strip for ERB Inc.

He calls Florida home these days.

You can connect with Chuck here:

Facebook:
https://www.facebook.com/chuck.dixon.779

Website
http://dixonverse.blogspot.com/

Amazon
https://www.amazon.com/Chuck-Dixon/e/B001HOL26O

www.ingramcontent.com/pod-product-compliance
Lightning Source LLC
Chambersburg PA
CBHW031616100726
47898CB00006B/1808